HOT TARGET

ALSO BY MARLISS MELTON

The Echo Platoon Series

Danger Close

Hard Landing

Friendly Fire

Hot Target

Insider Threat

The Taskforce Series

The Protector

The Guardian

The Enforcer

HOT TARGET

THE ECHO PLATOON SERIES, BOOK FOUR

MARLISS MELTON

ePublishingWorks!
love what you read.

Book and cover design by eBook Prep
www.ebookprep.com

April 2022
ISBN: 978-1-947833-03-6

ePublishing Works!
644 Shrewsbury Commons Ave
Ste 249
Shrewsbury PA 17361
United States of America
www.epublishingworks.com
Phone: 866-846-5123

This story is dedicated to Senior Chief Kyle Milliken, U.S. Navy SEAL, who lost his life while assisting Somali forces in their fight against al-Shabaab. Kyle's heroism attests to the bravery of all special warfare operators. His sacrifice is a poignant reminder of the risks they take to keep terror at bay and not only for Americans. Rest in peace, true and faithful son of freedom.

ACKNOWLEDGMENTS

I wrote HOT TARGET during one of the greatest transitions of my life. It's not easy to focus on fiction when your reality is disintegrating. But that's when you turn to your readers for encouragement and inspiration. My heartfelt thanks go to Suzanne Gochenouer for her thorough and professional editing. Thank you to all the members of my Special Reconnaissance Team, especially Penny, Deborah, Mellena, Lori, Jan, Regina, and Amy for your helpful comments and proofreading. And, as always, thank you to my best friend, Sydney Jane Baily, for being the one constant I can always, ultimately count on in the end.

PROLOGUE

S tay calm, Juliet. This isn't really happening.

Two loud explosions echoed in her ears. It felt real. The family Oldsmobile fishtailed on the rain-slick road. Clutching the armrest of the seat behind the driver, Juliet Rhodes screamed as the car slid into the ditch.

She threw her hands against the driver's seat to brace herself.

"Oh, God!" her father cried as the car's front end started up the ditch's opposite side only to slam into the trunks of trees lining it. At impact, the hood of the car rose up like a dark wave. Her mother flew face-first into the dashboard, and the windshield exploded inward. Shards of glass burst into the car's interior, spangling her mother's slumped body. The car tipped onto its left side as its rear end settled into the trough. Metal crumpled inward, trapping Juliet's hand between her father's seat and her door.

This isn't really happening.

The teenager, her arm pinned tightly, didn't believe the words in her head. It felt real. It looked real.

"Mom!" Anne Rhodes lay slumped across her husband, Gerald, whose inhalations sawed like fingernails on a chalkboard. Juliet had to get her mother off him, but regardless of how hard the girl pulled, she couldn't free herself.

"Mom! Dad!"

Anne's head lolled at an impossible angle. With the engine pushed into the body of the car, Gerald Rhodes sat pinned by the steering wheel. Given his labored breathing, his ribs were broken, possibly perforating his lungs.

It's just a dream, Juliet. Wake up.

But she couldn't wake up any more than she could move. Rain fell through the shattered windows, each cold droplet splatting against her cheek and holding her captive in this nightmare.

Her father's agonizing breaths played quartet to the ticking, steaming vehicle, the patter of raindrops, the peeping of tree frogs.

"Help!" The distraught teen was already aware no one would hear her feeble cries. Somehow, she knew her mother was already dead.

Just wake up.

She blinked furiously, hoping to rouse herself, but all she saw was a face looming at her mother's window. The dimly lit dash illumined a man's large head, broad cheekbones, and pale eyes.

His dispassionate watchfulness warned her to remain silent. For a long time, he studied the front-seat occupants, never once taking his eyes off the man and woman to notice the girl trapped in the dark behind them. Rattling emanated from her father's throat, followed by an exhalation, and then silence.

As suddenly as he'd appeared, the silent observer was gone.

Who the hell was that man?

The memory, long buried and bubbling up from some deep well in Juliet's mind, jolted her awake. She lurched straight up in bed, her heart pounding, mouth dry. The accident was as fresh in her mind as when it happened eleven years ago.

Gooseflesh rippled over her body, raising the hair at her nape and assuring her she hadn't invented the new detail in her recurring dream. If anything, she'd repressed the memory until now—one so crisp and clear she could still picture the man's face. And it changed everything.

Juliet was twenty-seven now, a private investigator living alone in a high-rise apartment in Fairfax, Virginia. And the adult Juliet had the power to do something with this unearthed information.

Kicking off the covers, she vaulted out of bed and plucked up her cell phone. On her way to the bathroom, she glanced at the time and winced. It wasn't yet four in the morning, but she couldn't keep this to herself. She needed to make a composite drawing of the stranger's face and to record every new detail she'd just recalled.

The man in her nightmare had looked into the car, seen her parents dead, and disappeared, making no attempt to call 911. That made him Juliet's primary suspect in a tragedy the authorities had deemed an accident.

Snapping on the bathroom light, Juliet averted her gaze from the mirror. With trembling fingers, she speed-dialed her assistant. No need to disturb Emma, her sister, until Juliet had confirmed her suspicions, or at least clarified them in some way.

The impulse to call Tristan, her one-time Navy SEAL lover, caught her unawares. Since when did she rely on a man for reassurance? So what if he'd held her together the last time her world had imploded? That was six months ago in a different country. This situation was unique. It didn't involve one of Tristan's friends. She could handle it alone.

Forget about him.

Hilary Alcorn, her assistant, answered after three rings.

"What?"

"I need you to meet me at the office in thirty minutes. Please," Juliet added to soften what must sound like an early morning dose of crazy.

Two beats of silence. "Are you OK?" Disgruntlement gave way to concern.

"I don't know. I just remembered something about my

parents' accident—a man was there, long before help came. I don't want to forget the details."

"OK." Hilary sounded intrigued. "I'll get there as soon as I can."

"Thanks. Bye." Thumbing the call closed, Juliet released a shaky breath then slowly raised her gaze to her reflection.

Golden hair, tousled from sleep, hung in long layers to her breasts. Wide gray eyes set in a chalk-white face looked back at her. Her nose was straight. Her lips, lush and full, betrayed the tough image she attempted to project. She looked like she'd seen a ghost.

"Who are you?" she demanded, picturing the man's distinct features. A chill skittered up her spine.

Whoever he was, the Mystery Man had neither assisted the crash victims nor called for help. The accident had remained undiscovered until the driver of an eighteen-wheeler glimpsed their Oldsmobile lying in the ditch. Juliet had spent four hours trapped in the dark with her parents' bodies. Little wonder she was claustrophobic.

If Mystery Man hadn't gone for help, that could only mean one thing.

He'd caused the accident.

She had *known* it. All these years, she'd considered the series of events with skepticism—first the explosion of two tires that caused them to fishtail, her mother's seatbelt giving way, and the airbags failing to deploy. Deep ditches and trees lined both sides of the road right where the crash happened.

The sheer number of unfortunate circumstances was suspicious in itself. Juliet had only been sixteen at the time but, backed by her big sister, she had demanded the authorities investigate the possibility of homicide. She was certain someone had sabotaged her father's car.

Unfortunately, a lengthy investigation had ruled out her suppositions. The tires had been old, in need of replacing. For some unknown reason, her father had turned off the airbag feature, and her mother's seatbelt simply hadn't worked correctly. The police concluded that school teachers Gerald and

Anne Rhodes hadn't had the money to keep their vehicle maintained. Officials chalked the accident up to misfortune.

All lies. Juliet's spine quaked with the force of her trembling.

Anne and Gerald *were* murdered, and Mystery Man was behind it. Too bad for him, she had been there to see him. Worse for him, Juliet had grown up to become a private investigator. She'd worked two years for an established firm before taking over when her mentor retired. In three short years, she'd established a reputation for finding answers.

Her personal life was no exception. She would find the monster who'd killed her parents and make him pay.

1

For a man who once hurtled a fifty-foot canyon in a desert patrol vehicle, a simple outing to a restaurant should not be wreaking havoc on his adrenaline system.

Tristan Halliday seated himself across from his companions at a table in a popular restaurant in Fairfax, Virginia, with his heart pounding. His mouth hadn't been this dry since he'd stopped a fourteen-year-old Afghan boy from blowing up a mosque in Aleppo. And all he was doing was waiting for the only woman in the world who'd ever rejected his advances to join him and his friends for lunch.

Well, she hadn't rejected him unequivocally. She'd given him a challenge—no dating for six months and in return, he would earn a date with the delectable Juliet Rhodes. Well, he'd risen to the challenge. He'd managed to resist all of them; no easy feat considering women literally threw themselves at him. The prize, in his opinion, was worth any amount of deprivation. Having reached the six-month milestone just yesterday, he was here to claim his reward.

The last time Tristan had seen her, he still had eight weeks to go. The occasion had been his teammate Jeremiah's wedding in August to Juliet's older sister, Emma. Juliet had danced and flirted with him. He'd been certain, at one point, she was going back to his hotel room with him, putting an end to his miserable stint of celibacy and picking up where they'd left off in Mexico. He'd been wrong. She'd untangled herself from his arms, reminded him that he still had two dateless months left, and banished him to his room. Alone.

Tristan hadn't so much as called her in the meantime. Let her think he'd forgotten all about her. Hell, if he was going to be lonely, then so was she.

Today, however, his purgatory would be over. He'd done what Juliet had asked of him, so she had better live up to her end of the arrangement.

And just in case she tried wriggling out of it, he'd brought along reinforcements. Actually, they had brought him along, and Juliet didn't even know he was coming. Emma, having moved from Fairfax to Virginia Beach after her wedding, was back to visit her sibling. She'd brought along her new husband, Jeremiah, and Tristan had tagged along.

He had no idea how Juliet would react to his unexpected presence, but the images in his head weren't all pretty. Hence the churning stomach and the cold sweats.

"And what would you like to drink?" the waitress asked as Tristan stretched his legs under the table. He tugged his shirttail out of his pants in an attempt to get comfortable.

"I'll have a beer—Foster's," he decided. One beer to calm his nerves, but only one.

"You can bring my sister a Dr. Pepper," Emma said to the waitress. "She'll be here any minute."

Tristan made a mental note of Juliet's soda preference while imagining knowing Juliet as well as Emma did.

"She just pulled up," Jeremiah stated while perusing the menu.

Tristan didn't ask how his teammate knew without even looking up. Bullfrog, as the Team called him, laid claim to a sixth sense that had never proved wrong. Tristan's heart pounded while his expectant gaze swung toward the restaurant's double doors.

Three seconds later, one of the doors opened and Juliet

walked in. Tristan's stomach went into free fall simply looking at her.

Was there ever a more striking woman?

Her pale gray slacks paired with a persimmon-colored blouse suited the season. Long, honey-blonde hair slipped over her shoulders as she inclined her head to speak to the shorter hostess. The woman turned and pointed out their table. Juliet's gaze followed the woman's finger, and surprise widened her eyes for an instant. Immediately she recovered her default expression of cool inscrutability. As she headed in their direction, every male in the restaurant took note.

Galvanized by hormones and adrenaline, Tristan pushed to his feet, which prompted Jeremiah to do likewise.

Hello, gorgeous.

Six months ago, Tristan would have greeted Juliet with those words. But his confidence had taken a hit at Jeremiah's wedding. Fear that she would renege on her promise made her the scariest opponent he'd ever faced. If she tried brushing him off this time, he might do something he regretted.

Her lips quirked at the men's show of gallantry. "At ease, gentlemen." She sounded amused. "Hey, sis," she added more warmly. "Hello, Bullfrog."

Ignoring the chair Tristan pulled out for her, she bent over Emma's auburn head to kiss her sister's cheek. "How was your drive up? Did you run into traffic?"

Barely acknowledging Tristan, she then slipped into the proffered chair. He promptly pushed it in.

"The traffic wasn't bad," Emma answered, "aside from a little construction."

"Where's Sammy? I thought *she* was coming with you." Emma rarely went anywhere without her pre-teen daughter.

"She's staying at her friend Gracie's."

"Oh, too bad." With a visible breath, she finally deigned to address Tristan, her gaze as friendly as a honed blade pressed against his jugular. "No one said you were coming."

His temper ignited. "I'm sorry. Did I need your permission?"

Her eyebrows rose at his sarcastic tone, but that was her only reaction. She went back to ignoring him, giving the waitress her order, and chatting with her sister and new brother-in-law.

With rising frustration, Tristan listened while they discussed Emma's new teaching position in Virginia Beach. They talked about the renovations underway in the house the newlyweds had bought. Emma regaled her sister with news of Sammy's foray into the seventh-grade. All the while, Tristan pondered how to get and keep Juliet's attention.

They had met in April on a cruise ship bound for the Western Caribbean. Freshly dumped by the girl he'd planned to marry, Tristan had been nursing a bruised ego. Juliet's prickly demeanor and feisty intelligence had intrigued him. She was the first woman he'd ever run into who regarded him with apparent indifference. Except that turned out to be a ruse. When tragedy struck, and she was overwrought by her sister and niece's kidnapping, she'd seemed to like him plenty.

What's more, she hadn't been as impervious to their chemistry as she pretended to be. She might have used the word "distraction" to describe the red-hot sex they'd had, but she'd loved every minute of it. In the harrowing days that followed, Tristan had glimpsed a side of Juliet that made him want to be her superhero.

Deep down, Juliet Rhodes needed him. She simply didn't see it the way he did. Given the chance, he would prove to her he was indispensable to her happiness. Whatever obstacles she encountered in life, he wanted to face them with her, the way they had down in Mexico.

With their meals in front of them, the conversation turned to politics and the new president's position on foreign policy. Tristan offered up his opinion, but only Jeremiah challenged it. Juliet kept her mouth shut, which wasn't like her. The Juliet he knew would have voiced a thoughtful but opposing view.

Watching her from the corner of his eye, Tristan realized she was picking at her salad, scarcely eating. As Jeremiah chimed in with cautious enthusiasm for the President's anti-terrorism policies, Tristan studied Juliet more carefully.

She wore more makeup than usual—perhaps to disguise the dark circles rimming her eyes. Fine lines of strain bracketed her lovely lips. Something was bothering her.

Suddenly she laid her fork down and dug into her purse. Pulling out a square of folded paper, she handed it to her sister.

"Do you recognize this man?" she inquired, changing the topic of conversation out of the blue.

Curious, Tristan watched Emma take the paper and study it with her soft blue eyes. A frown creased her forehead. "No. I've never seen him that I know of."

With a look of disappointment, Juliet took the paper back.

"Who is he?" Emma prompted.

Tristan saw that the drawing was a computer composite of a mature man's face—prominent cheekbones, high forehead, light eyes. Juliet's lips pursed with disappointment as she retrieved it. Watching her refold the paper slowly, he was struck with a sense of relief. Juliet needed his help finding her suspect. She just needed to be reminded how well they worked together.

Where to start? Juliet wondered. Her awareness of the demi-god next to her—the one who smelled so good she wished she could bottle him—made it hard to think straight. Of all the days Tristan could have chosen to pop up again, why this one? Of course, she knew the answer.

She should have guessed he would materialize precisely six months to the day after she'd given him that ridiculous challenge. After all, he'd given her a heads-up, at her sister's wedding two months earlier, that he hadn't dated anyone in the previous four months, thus abiding by her wishes. He must have made it to six months. Given his reputation for always being in a relationship, that had to be the longest he'd ever been single.

Now, somehow, some way, she had to get out of her end of the bargain. Not only did she abhor becoming a link in Tristan's chain of girlfriends, whether he'd broken the chain or not, but she didn't *do* relationships any better now than she did six months ago. She had made up her mind years ago to stay single. That way, apart from her sister and niece, she would never have to grieve the loss of someone close to her. Tristan, with his endearing grin and can-do attitude, tempted her to change her mind. Given his highly dangerous career, how stupid would that be?

His timing, however, undermined her determination. She could use his help the way she had down in Mexico.

You're not in Mexico, she reminded herself. She was on her own turf in Northern Virginia, and she already had a competent assistant in the form of Hilary Alcorn, working at her office.

Ignoring Tristan, Juliet leaned across the table to tell Emma about her dream. "Ever since what happened to you and Sammy in the Yucatan, I've been dreaming about Mom and Dad's accident. Something came back to me the other night—something I must have repressed."

Emma's eyes widened. "What?"

"There was a man at the scene after the crash happened." Juliet waved the folded composite. "This guy. I remember opening my eyes and seeing him next to Mom's window. Dad saw him, too. I could tell because his breathing changed. Something told me not to move because the man hadn't seen me. He just watched until Dad stopped breathing, and then he walked away. And, no, he didn't call for help," she added seeing her sister's mouth open. "No one came until much later."

Morose silence fell over the table. Jeremiah slid a protective hand over Emma's, rousing Juliet's gratitude that Emma had found a man worthy of her.

"Are you sure it wasn't a dream?" Emma asked.

"I'm sure. You know we've always suspected foul play," Juliet reminded her sister. "I need to find out who that man was. Then maybe I'll discover why he killed our parents."

Emma nodded and pushed her plate away.

Juliet looked down at her sister's half-eaten sandwich. "Sorry to ruin your lunch."

"It's OK."

The feel of Tristan's hand settling on her forearm incited a mix of resentment and self-pity. She wasn't fragile like her sister. She didn't want or need a reminder of how comforting it felt to lean into his powerful body and let him hold her.

"Please don't touch me," she said under her breath.

In her peripheral vision, she saw him straighten. He removed his hand, taking his heat with it.

Shame prompted her to add, "I'm sorry. I just…I need to focus."

Wrong words. Damn it. The instant they left Juliet's mouth, she wanted to retract them. Because the implication was if she couldn't focus, she clearly wasn't immune to him.

"What can we do to help?" Jeremiah's steady offer pulled her back into the conversation.

Juliet sighed. "Honestly, I don't know. Dad's car was crushed and melted down years ago. I've requested the original police reports which are on microfiche in Burlington Township's archives, but I already know there wasn't any mention of a stranger. I simply don't understand why I didn't remember him before."

Jeremiah sat forward. His hazel eyes conveyed both intelligence and sympathy.

"You were sixteen years old," he reminded her. "You'd just survived the worst experience a child could have. Assuming you saw this man the way you now remember, you might have realized you were looking at your parents' killer, and your conscious mind refused to accept it."

His words brought unexpected tears to her eyes. She turned her head, pretending to regard the other restaurant patrons until the moisture evaporated.

Tristan, despite her earlier warning, put an arm on the back of her chair as if to erect an invisible wall around her. To her discomfort, she felt immediately protected.

Juliet looked back at Jeremiah. "I'll go with that theory, but why now? Why would I suddenly remember after eleven years?"

"Because you're stronger now than you were at sixteen," Emma suggested.

"That's right." Jeremiah nodded with approval at his wife. "Because you beat the odds in Mexico. Maybe your subconscious mind figures you can handle the truth now."

Juliet did feel stronger for her victory over the ruthless *capos* this past spring. But wasn't eleven years a little too long to repress a memory as important as this one? The trail leading to her parents' murderer was bound to have grown cold, especially since Emma didn't recognize the man in the sketch. And that was Juliet's only lead.

Emma held out her hand. "Let me see the picture again."

Juliet handed it back, and Emma unfolded it, studying the man's shadowed features for several moments. As her sister's tawny eyebrows knit with concentration, Juliet's desperation rose. It was clear Emma had no idea who he could be.

"No idea," she confirmed, handing the drawing back. "But here's a thought," she added.

"What?"

"Why don't we both go through our childhood albums? I left half of them at your place when I moved. You go through those, and I'll look through the ones I have. If this man killed Mom and Dad, he might have known them. Maybe they considered him a friend. Who knows? We could recognize him in a photo."

Juliet pictured the two of them sifting through old albums, looking for a man who resembled the shadowy figure in her dreams. Talk about finding a needle in a haystack. "I'll try that tonight."

Producing her cell phone, Emma snapped a photo of the drawing before handing it back.

Juliet stuffed it into her oversized purse.

"I'll look, too, as soon as I get home," Emma promised.

A suffocating feeling ambushed Juliet. Desperate for more

space, she pushed her chair back, causing Tristan to drop his arm. "If you'll excuse me, I need to use the restroom."

Emma eyed her with concern.

Sending everyone a tight smile, Juliet picked up her purse and, conscious of Tristan's brooding gaze, walked rapidly away.

Given Tristan's persistence in the past, she guessed at once that he would follow her and seek to waylay her the instant she emerged from the ladies' room.

Call her a coward, but she was feeling a tad too vulnerable right then to have the kind of discussion he most certainly had in mind. Seeing their waitress ringing up a bill, Juliet detoured on her trek to the bathroom. Tristan couldn't see her from his present vantage.

"Hi, I need to leave early," she said, gaining the girl's attention as she pulled her wallet from her purse. "Can I pay for our bill?"

The waitress looked at her and blinked. "Oh, sure. I just rang you up," she said, handing her the black folder from the pocket of her apron.

Juliet stuck several bills inside it. "Keep the change."

"Thank you."

With a smile and a nod, Juliet pretended to proceed toward the restrooms. Emma would forgive her for leaving. Tristan not so much.

Regret latched onto her ankles, slowing her retreat. Truth was, she wished they could have one more adventure with Tristan before she ditched him, but considering how much she'd cramped his style these past six months, it would be awfully unkind to use him like that. Leaving now was honestly the nicest thing to do.

Dodging behind a wave of people entering the restaurant, Juliet skirted the restroom and slipped out the front door, certain no one at her table had observed her departure.

Marching swiftly toward her silver SUV, she thanked herself for having the forethought to back into her parking space. By luck, this space was on the side of the lot Tristan couldn't see from the table. He would never notice her departure, though he'd find out soon enough.

And he'd be justifiably outraged. That was why Juliet had thought of a way to make amends. As soon as her consolation package was ready, she would send it to him and hopefully ease the sting of her rejection. Would it really appease him, though?

A sliver of doubt slid through her mind as she shut herself in her driver's seat and reached for the ignition.

She'd never seen Tristan get angry, except briefly when she'd driven off in a Belize jungle looking for a short cut so she could beat him in a race. He'd scolded her for eschewing the buddy system. Other than that, the SEAL tended to laugh off irritants. He didn't sweat the small stuff—though she doubted he would view her disappearing act as minor.

Jamming her seatbelt into place, she sped out of the parking spot and left the restaurant, heading for home.

Tristan had no idea where she lived, but he wasn't above extracting that bit of information from her sister. Juliet had better warn Emma not to tell him.

Ding! The chime reminded her about her empty gas tank, the one she hadn't filled that morning because she'd been running late. Crap, she'd better have enough gas to get home. But first things first.

"Call Emma." She floored the accelerator while accessing her Bluetooth with a voice command. The call went through, but Emma's phone rang and rang.

"Oh, come on."

She knew her sister had her phone with her because she'd taken a photo of the suspect, but it was probably set to silent mode.

"End call," Juliet snapped, glancing at the display on her dashboard.

She would run out of gas in three miles, and her apartment was nearly four miles away.

"Call Bullfrog." She decided to call her brother-in-law,

who'd earned his moniker for being the fastest frogman in the water.

He answered after only one ring. "You OK?"

"Um, yeah. I just tried to call Emma, but she didn't answer."

"She's looking for you in the restroom, but you're not here, are you?"

"Um, no. I'm sorry. I needed to leave. I paid the bill, though," she added, hoping the gesture made up for some of her rudeness.

"That wasn't necessary."

Jeremiah's reply was uncharacteristically terse.

"Is Tristan mad?" she guessed.

"That's not the word I would use."

"What do you mean?"

"Nothing." His tone was suspiciously neutral. "It was good to see you again. Keep us posted on the situation. Bye."

The call ended abruptly.

She frowned and gripped the steering wheel harder. Why had Bullfrog's comment sounded like a warning?

Sudden suspicion had her checking her rearview mirror. Was Tristan coming after her? How could he? He'd caught a ride with Jeremiah and her sister.

Besides, he didn't know where Juliet lived unless Emma had already told him.

She licked her dry lips. At that exact moment, her favorite gas station came into view. Seeing the street light ahead turn red, she swerved into the station, figuring she could fill her tank in the time that it took the light to turn green again.

Leaping out of her vehicle, she studied the cars on the road while pumping her gas. Her heart beat unevenly.

It took a card key to get into her building, and Tristan didn't have one.

With her tank half-full, Juliet jumped back into her SUV and shot out of the station just as the green light turned yellow.

I've seen the last of Tristan Halliday, she assured herself.

Weird how the thought of never seeing him again failed to cheer her.

By the time her apartment building loomed in the distance, her heart was beating at a normal rate again. She'd seen nothing in her mirrors to suggest anyone was tailing her.

She turned into the underground parking garage, practically deserted on this weekday afternoon. Her footfalls echoed in the concrete enclosure as she crossed to the elevator, swiping her card key to summon it.

Any other day, she'd have taken the stairs. Today her knees felt too wobbly to handle the five-story climb. As the elevator rose steadily, Juliet drew a deep breath and exhaled. The scent of Tristan's sports soap still clung to her.

Stepping out on her level, Juliet proceeded to her door, secured with a deadbolt requiring a four-number combination. As she entered her code, she gave a thought to how long it had been since she'd changed it. The light flashed green. She depressed the latch and thrust the door open.

The silhouette of a man standing in her darkened living room startled a gasp from her. The door thumped shut behind her. With the blinds closed and her lights out, the shadowy figure brought to mind her parents' killer.

Juliet's hand reached automatically into the depths of her purse where she stowed her 9mm pistol when she wasn't working. But then the intruder swiveled her blinds, flooding the room with light and revealing his identity.

"Tristan!" Astonishment rooted her in place. "How the hell did you get in here?"

He shook his head, tsking in disapproval as he walked toward her. His dark blue eyes gleamed predatorily. Every hair on her body rose in wariness as he closed the distance between them.

"You don't get to ask the questions, honey."

She ordered herself to pull out her gun, but she'd frozen. Jeremiah's earlier comment made sudden sense. *That's not the word I would use.* He'd known Tristan was beyond angry. He was, in fact, so upset he had left the restaurant to pursue her.

Jeremiah and Emma hadn't managed to stop him. If anything, they had helped him find his way in.

Damn it, she wasn't going to get away with disappearing and apologizing later. Her resolve to stay single was suddenly under siege. If she didn't hold the line, she would surely suffer for it down the road. God help her because she wasn't sure she had the strength to resist what Tristan had to offer.

2

"Ah-ah." Spotting Juliet's hand sliding into her purse, Tristan wagged a warning finger at her. "No you don't. Give me the bag."

The outrage that had goaded him to ride his motorcycle like a demon through a suburban neighborhood still flowed through him like lava. The relentless and inexorable heat of anger staved off the insecure voice in his head insisting Juliet didn't want him. Like his birth mother, she'd rather walk away than get to know him.

"Give it to me." He thrust out his hand.

Her full upper lip curled into a sneer. Tristan had to give her credit for looking unafraid. Yet the flutter at the base of her slender neck revealed that he'd succeeded in freaking her out. Good. It was about time he got her attention.

"Or what?" she taunted.

He snatched the purse so fast she only had time to blink. Digging into it, he found her Ruger and tossed the handbag down. He made a show of checking the magazine and shaking his head when he found it full of bullets.

"If there's going to be a crime of passion here," he grated in his best Dirty Harry impersonation, "it's not going to involve bullets." Slapping the magazine closed, he laid the pistol on the narrow table in the entryway and gave her a "what now?" look.

Juliet lunged for the purse, most likely going for her cellphone. He grabbed her, catching her up in his arms and eliciting a growl as he carried her, fighting him vigorously, toward the couch. She landed a few good blows, but her physicality didn't surprise him. He'd found out down in Mexico she handled herself like a cage fighter. That was something he liked about her, actually. However, their wrestling wasn't so much a fight as it was a prelude to lovemaking.

Her heeled pumps struck his shins before they mercifully fell off. He tossed her onto the sofa, but she'd sunk her hands into his hair, so he went down with her. As they descended, she kicked his upper thigh—three inches from the nuts she was targeting.

He had to admit her training was thorough, but his was more extensive in scope. Plus, he was twice her size.

Exerting pressure on her wrists, Tristan freed his hair from Juliet's grasp. Straightening, he picked her up again and flipped her belly-side down onto the cushions, promptly sitting on her bottom to keep her from going anywhere.

"Get off me, you son of a bitch."

"No name calling," he warned. Catching Juliet's flailing arms, he pinned them behind her back. "You don't want to go there. I'm not the one reneging on a promise or running away from an honest conversation. If we start slinging names, I'm bound to call you a manipulative bitch or a low-life coward. See what I mean? Doesn't get us anywhere."

She squirmed beneath him, fighting ineffectually to free herself.

"You really should hold still," Tristan warned, pinning her with a fraction of his weight. "I haven't been with a woman in six months. Every time you raise your ass, I think about how much you like getting it from behind."

Juliet stilled instantly, though her chest still heaved with fervor. He knew she worked out daily. That heavy breathing wasn't just due to exertion.

"Maybe you need me to remind you how much you like it," he suggested.

"Don't you dare!"

"I can still picture it—that cute motel room in Playa del Carmen. You practically forced me to have sex with you."

"What? You bastard, I didn't force you."

"I remember you throwing yourself at me. I remember you sliding out of my arms onto your knees to pull my zipper down."

"Stop it."

Tristan held both Juliet's wrists with just one hand, freeing his other hand to stroke the backs of her legs through her lightweight slacks. He skimmed the curve of her bottom and felt her shudder.

"God, you were hot that night," he reminisced. "I've never known a woman as hot as you. I could just touch you like this," he moved his caress into the warm groove between her thighs, stroking it once, twice, three times, "and make you come."

She made a sound between a moan and a shriek. "Don't!"

"What are you afraid of?" He was happy to realize that his blood no longer pulsed with righteous anger. High emotion tended to get a SEAL into trouble. He was having fun sparring with her. He hoped she was, too. Repeating his caress, he was pleased to feel her female flesh swell and firm under the pad of his finger. "You're a hot-blooded woman. I'm a hot-blooded man. Why shouldn't we enjoy each other?"

"You can't force me," she insisted, her breath still coming in pants.

That remark had him springing off her instantly, moving out of range of her long legs should she think to retaliate. He'd never forced himself on a woman, never would do such a thing, and he wasn't about to start now.

"No one's making you do anything," he insisted as she whipped onto her side, putting one arm on the back of the couch and eying him suspiciously.

Crossing his arms over his chest, Tristan gazed at her and waited.

"What do you want?" Her husky voice betrayed both anger and arousal. Her gaze dropped briefly to the bulge at the front of his jeans before she jerked it away.

"I think I've made that pretty clear. I went six months without sex so I could be with you."

Her eyes widened with surprise. "I never asked you to be celibate. I asked you not to *date* anyone. Your pathological need for female companionship worried me, that's all."

Her psychoanalyzing thoroughly annoyed him. She was the one with relationship issues, not him. "Well, clearly I surpassed your expectations. If you're done toying with me, I'm here for my date."

She kept mutinously quiet.

"Or are you planning to renege on your promise?"

"I never promised you anything," she insisted. "I said I *might* date you in six months."

"With the stakes as high as you made them, honey, 'might' doesn't qualify. You owe me a date." He held his breath wondering what he'd do if she still refused him. She was all he'd thought about for six months straight.

Her lower lip disappeared between her teeth as she gnawed on it. Finally, she asked in a small voice, "What if we just have sex again and call it a truce?"

Frustration exploded inside of him. "Shut up," he warned.

His vehemence must have scared her. She rolled suddenly to her feet and lunged at him, grabbing his hands. "Listen to me," she implored. "I'm sorry. I am. I *do* like you."

A portion of his anger subsided.

"But I don't date. I can't date." Her gray eyes pleaded for his understanding. "I have a business to run that requires all of my time. I can't be there for anyone."

He shrugged. "My job's not any different."

"True, but I'm also moody. And I have appalling habits—"

He was dying to know all of them. "Like what?"

"Like eating junk food and drinking too much coffee and forgetting to fill the gas tank in my car."

"Ah. I wondered what took you so long."

She tossed his hands away and propped her own hands on her hips. "Emma and Bullfrog are in on this, aren't they? How did you even get here? I thought you caught a ride with them."

"I trailered my bike behind their Jeep. Figured you might give me the slip, so I mapped out a short cut to your place just in case."

Her eyes glinted with interest. "You have a motorcycle?"

Score one for him. "Sure do."

"You need to show me that shortcut later," she demanded. "Listen." Stepping away from him, she began orbiting her couch. As she walked, she wrung her hands betraying just how much he unsettled her. "I'm not about to change who I am just to please a man. Girlfriends are supposed to be pliable. They shape their lives to suit their lovers. Look at Emma." She gestured. "Emma quit her job so she could be with her new husband. That's not me. I like what I have here. I like what I do. And I don't need a man in my life." She came around the couch and looked at him with an almost-desperate expression.

Was she trying to convince herself or him? He let his gaze drift from her flushed face to her rumpled jacket to her stockinged feet, and back up again. "You sure about that? I thought you just asked for sex."

"Well, yeah, but…"

"But you can get that anywhere," he finished for her. The thought of her having sex with anyone made him faintly nauseated. "How many men have you slept with since Mexico?"

A nervous laugh escaped her lips.

"Answer the question. While I was going to bed with a hard-on for six months, how often were you getting laid?"

"That's none of your business." Color stained her cheeks, and her eyes flashed. "We're not together. I don't owe you my fidelity."

"How many?" he repeated.

"None!" She threw her hands in the air. "There, you feel better?"

She had to be lying. A woman like her could get a guy in five seconds flat.

"Wait." She seemed to reconsider. "Maybe I should tell you that I've slept with half the guys in this building. Maybe then you'd realize that I'm not the best girlfriend material and leave me alone."

He could tell by her expression that wasn't true. "Is that really what you want? You want me to leave you alone?" he pressed.

Her mouth worked hard to form the word "yes," but honesty warred with her stubbornness, and she ended up saying nothing.

Sensing her capitulation, he hid a smile and suggested a compromise. "How about this? How about we spend time together and see how it goes?"

Wariness melted into skepticism, which heated into sexual consideration, as her gaze drifted appreciatively over his chest and thighs. "You mean, enjoy the moment," she interpreted.

He had her now. "Sort of," he qualified. She wasn't going to like his stipulation, but then he wasn't going to tell her about it.

Her eyebrows snapped together. "What does 'sort of' mean?"

"It means we do stuff together," he explained. "Like find this asshole who might have killed your parents. We make a good team. Remember?"

She clapped a hand to her forehead, closing her eyes as she rubbed it. "But I work alone," she protested.

"You need me," he insisted. "I have relevant skills."

She heaved a sigh. "I'm not hunting anyone specific just yet. I need to look through family albums, first, like Emma suggested. Hopefully, I'll find something."

"Great, let's do that."

She searched his expression. "Are you serious? You want to help me look through old photographs?"

"Sure. As long as we're working as a team, I'm happy."

Tristan grinned to show her just how happy he was. He caught Juliet staring at his mouth, like she'd forgotten the shape and feel of it, and he could tell what she was thinking.

The girl still wanted him—in a bad way. However, it had occurred to him in the last ten minutes that he stood a better chance if he *didn't* give her what she wanted. As long as he kept her hungering for more, she would keep him around. And the longer he stuck around, the better his odds of making their relationship permanent.

He dropped his hands on her shoulders, jarring her from her trance. "So, what are we waiting for?" he demanded. He gave her a squeeze. "Let's do this." Letting her go before he was tempted to kiss her, he swatted her bottom and stepped away.

With a dazed shake of her head, she turned toward one of the two doors off her living room and threw it open.

"This is my spare bedroom," she explained, flicking on the light.

The bookcase, desk, file cabinet, and futon made the room a perfect place for guests, but it was cluttered with boxes and a large, metal trunk.

"When Emma moved, she dropped off a bunch of stuff she didn't want to take with her," Juliet said explaining the mess.

Tristan counted the number of boxes in front of them. "All of these are full of photo albums?"

"Oh, no. The albums are in the footlocker. These boxes are just stuff Emma couldn't bring herself to part with, like my mother's sketches."

"Your mother was an artist?"

"Art teacher. She tried to help me find my creative side. But I didn't take after Mom, Emma did."

"Who made the composite of the guy you're looking for?"

"Hilary, my assistant, using a specialized software program."

Flipping the latches on the locker, Juliet lifted the lid releasing a wave of the lavender scent that always reminded her of her mother. A wave of pointless longing clutched at her heart. Hiding her reaction, Juliet leaned over to pick up one of the six albums inside. She carried it to the futon, presently situated to serve as a couch, plopped down, and snapped on the nearby lamp.

Tristan picked his way across the room to join her. As he settled into the spot immediately next to her, their thighs brushed. Her body prickled with awareness. Her pulse quickened.

How long were they going to sit in here looking at old albums? Much as she appreciated his help, now that he was actually here, beside her, her body wanted him as it had from the first time they'd met. Distractedly, she opened the cover and forced herself to examine the pictures. Tristan looked over her shoulder.

"Aww, is that you?" He touched a long, tan index finger to her first baby picture. All six pounds, seven ounces of wrinkled pink flesh and a squished nose.

"Afraid so." None of the pictures featured anyone besides her and her parents, so she turned the page quickly, scanning photos at a fast clip.

"Wait, wait. I want to see," Tristan protested.

"This is not a trip down memory lane. I'm looking for the man who killed my parents," she reminded him.

"Yeah, but look at your mother. Wow. Now I see where you get your good looks."

"Stop flirting. I'm working here."

"She was a blonde, too, huh? And your dad had red hair like Emma. Interesting."

Juliet rolled her eyes. Was he really going to pretend fascination with her family's genetics? He probably could not care less. No doubt Tristan was biding his time, waiting for the perfect moment to snatch the album out of her hands and kiss her. Her body thrummed with anticipation.

Focus! Focus on the picture.

There were people on this page she didn't recognize. She studied each face with suspicion, searching for a large man with an oddly rectangular-shaped head.

"Oh, sweet Jesus, look at Emma," Tristan exclaimed, bumping her shoulder so he could get a closer look at the four-year-old with auburn pigtails and two fingers in her mouth. "Jeremiah needs to see this. That is adorable."

"I'm sure she's shown him. Are SEALs even allowed to say that word?"

"What word—adorable? Of course. Why wouldn't they be?"

"Never mind. You're distracting me." She elbowed him in the ribs. "Stop talking."

He moved away so she could study the pictures without interference. But only half of her attention was on the photos now. She skimmed through several pages, all the while aware of Tristan's sudden silence. And it hit her. She'd used the hateful *distraction* excuse.

A sidelong glance at his set features confirmed her suspicion. She'd annoyed him by using that word, the same one she'd used in Mexico to explain why she'd had sex with him—to distract her from the kidnapping of her sister and niece.

"I'm sorry." Great, she was up to three apologies in half an hour. "I have to do this. I have to find this person if I'm ever going to get a good night's sleep."

The hard look in his eyes softened. Tristan studied Juliet's face a moment. "No worries. You're entirely right. We're working here." He stood up and walked out of the room.

Juliet gaped after him. Where was he going? Had she driven him away?

She heard him cross her living room, headed for the door. The urge to call Tristan back stuck in her throat like a chicken bone. They hadn't even had sex yet, and she would probably explode if he walked out of her life at this point. But his footfalls grew louder, and he walked back into the room carrying her purse.

"Is the drawing still in here?" He held it out to her.

"Oh." She nodded sarcastically. "Now all of a sudden you

respect my personal property." She waved it away. "Go on, help yourself like you did the last time."

"To keep you from shooting me." A hint of a smile hovered around his mobile lips. "This is different."

"Fine." She snatched the bag from his hands and withdrew the folded paper. Tristan, in the meantime, swiped a second album out of the chest. He sat down next to her, took the composite, and spread it open.

For the next twenty minutes, they worked in relative silence, with Tristan making noises now and then that ranged from a tongue click, to "Hmm," to outright laughter.

Juliet glanced over, distracted by his commentary but not deigning to ask what amused him.

"How about this guy?" he finally asked, angling his album so she could see.

She leaned toward him, brushing his forearm with her breast. "No." Her nipple tingled and pearled from the contact. "That's Uncle Joe."

"Your father's brother or your mother's?" he asked.

"Neither. My parents had no relatives."

"Really?"

"Dad was an orphan and Mom was an only child," she explained. "Her father died in the Vietnam War, and her mother drank herself to death."

"Lovely." He fell thoughtfully quiet. "So, no family whatsoever."

"Right, for the reasons I just explained."

"What about second cousins or great aunts and uncles?"

Juliet considered and shrugged. "I never heard of any."

"Huh." He scratched his cheek and looked back at the pictures. "Then who are all these people if not family members?"

"Colleagues, mostly. My parents were both school teachers, with lots of friends. Everybody loved them." Hearing the wistfulness in her voice, Juliet pretended to look back at the album on her lap.

Several seconds elapsed.

"I bet you miss them, don't you?"

Tristan's gruff question made her eyes sting. She stared down at a photo of her five-month-old self. Such a happy, roly-poly baby with flaxen curls. Poor thing had no idea she only had sixteen years in which to soak up her parents' love. "Of course," she said shortly.

The large hand smoothing the hair on the back of her head drew her gaze to his. She'd seen him look at her with humor, frustration, desire, and most recently anger, but she'd never seen his eyes go bottomless. His tender look unsettled her.

"You can cry in front of me, you know," he told her gently. "I know these pictures bring up a lot of emotions. Hell, I want to cry and I didn't even know your parents."

Tears sprang into her eyes, unbidden. "Stop it," she ordered, blinking them back. "You're doing it again. I'm trying to work here. Please, stop—"

"Being a distraction," he supplied.

"I didn't say it this time, you did."

"True." He removed his hand from her hair, cleared his throat, and made a show of concentrating on the drawing, then turned to the photos in front of him.

Juliet worked her way through the last two albums while Tristan went through one.

With nothing left to peruse, Juliet felt her spirits sinking. It wasn't like she'd expected to find anything when she followed Emma's suggestion. But with no other leads, she might never identify the monster who'd returned so unexpectedly to her memory.

Dropping to the floor, she shuffled on her knees to the trunk and laid the books back inside. The hollow sound they made hitting the paper-lined plywood had her pulling them out again. Taking closer stock of the chest's construction, it appeared there ought to be more depth to the trunk than was immediately apparent. Could the plywood be a false bottom? Sliding her fingers along the edge of it, she teased it up and exposed another inch of storage underneath.

"Check it out!" She removed the false floor.

Tristan thrust aside the album on his lap and dropped to his knees beside her. Together they stared at the single white envelope lying in the hiding place.

Juliet's heart pumped with excitement. She shared a look with Tristan who urged her to open it.

Picking up the envelope, Juliet cautiously turned it over. The front and back were blank. She broke the seal and slowly withdrew a few sheets of paper, carefully unfolding them.

"What is it?" Tristan asked, leaning into her to peruse the top page.

"A marriage certificate." Juliet scanned it with rising puzzlement. Aged to a rich cream color, old typewriter marks on the paper identified the document's genesis. "September 3rd, 1983," she read. "They were married in West Berlin, Federal Republic of Germany."

"Who are 'they'?" Tristan pressed. "Your parents?"

"No," she said, gaze glued to the paper. "Gerard Brause and Anya Ausfeld. I've never heard of them."

"Why would anybody hide a marriage certificate?" Tristan queried.

Juliet turned to the next page. "There's a letter."

Wanting to read it in comfort, she moved back to the couch. As Tristan resumed his seat beside her, she set the certificate aside and skimmed the letter. "It's from my mother," she realized, her pulse quickening.

With rising excitement, Juliet read aloud, while Tristan leaned over her shoulder, following along.

"My Dearest Daughters, One day, when you are old enough to understand, I hope to show you this letter along with this marriage certificate, and you will know the truth about me. I want to believe your love for me will prevail over your judgment of the events of which you are about to read. My real name is Anya Ausfeld—" Juliet paused as the reality she had known fragmented, and the bride's name on the certificate of marriage became her mother's. *"I was born in West Berlin, the only daughter of well-to-do parents, who sent me to Freie University to study languages and literature. Brought up with undeserved privileges, I felt guilty for my advantages over those born*

with less. Moreover, I was ashamed of my country's history and its blind acceptance of a dictator who had murdered millions while my parents and grandparents turned a blind eye."

Reading her mother's words, Juliet fancied she could hear Anya's voice layered over her own.

"While at university, I became intrigued by the ideals espoused by the older brother of one of my friends. He spoke of Marx's and Lenin's visions of social and economic harmony and shared my antipathy for fascism. One day, he revealed that he was an agent for East Germany and talked both his sister and me into visiting that country. He took us through the Wall to meet their leader, Dieter Goebel, an elegant, articulate man who loved art as much as I did. My friend fancied herself in love with this man. Goebel entranced us. He made us feel we were part of something truly significant. By the end of our visit, we had both been recruited to be his eyes and ears.

"Upon graduating, I got a job in Westend, Berlin. It was there I met your father at a soccer match—neither one of us was interested in the game. Gerard was a U.S. citizen, employed by the National Security Agency and working at the American electronic surveillance installation in Teufelsberg. When I disclosed your father's job to Goebel, he encouraged me to get to know the American better. I was expected to relay any and all information Gerard might reveal regarding intercepted radio and telephone messages. The East wished to know what information was being passed on to NATO. When your father proposed, I was devastated, for East German agents were forbidden to marry. However, with the expectation that I would be privy to more secrets if I married your father, Goebel allowed me to wed.

"As you can see by the certificate enclosed with this letter, your father and I married in West Berlin, not far from the stadium where we met. Our parents attended, and to the world, our marriage was an average, blessed union. Throughout the first year, I endeavored to pass secrets to my handlers. But your father neither spoke of his work nor brought any papers home for me to peruse. Goebel ordered me to secure a secretarial position within my husband's office or else divorce him. By this time, I had begun to abhor the lies I told Gerard and dreaded the deceptions I was forced to enact to rendezvous with my contacts in the East. I begged Goebel to release me from my obligation. He informed me in no uncertain terms that I would be terminated if I backed away. I knew I had to make a choice, but couldn't bring myself to divorce your father. Therefore, I confessed the truth to him and cast myself on his mercy. Bless his kind heart, he forgave me and vowed to protect me. However, due to the nature of his job, he could not keep the information to himself.

"The only way we could remain together was to confess the situation to his superiors. Gerard and I were confined by his government for three months while federal agents interrogated and debriefed us. When they were finally satisfied that I was giving up all my ties to East Germany, they granted me permission to accompany your father back to the States. The NSA stripped Gerard of his security clearances and his job. The U.S. Marshals service placed us in Witness Protection. We received new identities as Anne and Gerald Rhodes. Emma was born shortly after we settled in New Jersey, where we led peaceful, ordinary lives."

Drawing a shaky breath, Juliet paused to collect herself before plowing on.

"Darlings, I have lived with the guilt of costing your father his career. Being the man he is, he will tell you he would have it no other way. But I have seen his restlessness and remorse, and know it is my fault. I also accept the blame for embracing the ideology of Marx and Lenin without considering the reality of human nature.

"If you are reading this, you are old enough to understand that we must keep the truth about my history and your father's a secret. The agents I betrayed, including my best friend and her brother, were recalled to East Germany and barely escaped imprisonment — although I warned them. But Dieter Goebel, head of the Directorate, would gladly murder me for disclosing information about my associates and the inner workings of the Stasi. Therefore, you must keep our family secret safe while finding it in your hearts to forgive me for my naiveté. Your loving mother, Anya."

Juliet swallowed hard. "Anya," she repeated the name, thinking it suited her German-speaking mother more than the name Anne.

"Holy hell."

In her peripheral vision, Juliet could see Tristan gaping at her. "You had no idea about this?"

"None." She shook her head. She had thought herself the product of an ordinary family growing up in a small house outside of Moorestown, New Jersey. "It makes so much sense, though," she added. "I always wondered why my parents, who were brilliant, hadn't done something more with their lives than teach school. Not that there's anything wrong with that. They just had an energy about them that made it seem like they ought to be doing more."

"Your mother was a *spy*," Tristan exclaimed, imbuing the word with all the mystery and romance it implied. "No wonder you became a private detective. It's in your blood!"

And here she thought she'd taken after her father. Then again, since her father had worked for the NSA, he'd been a spy, too. To think that her parents had been working for opposite sides until they fell in love and put their union first. The truth obliterated every presupposition she'd ever had about her parents except one. They had always adored each other, clearly more than she even realized.

"I have to tell Emma," she declared, snatching up the certificate and pushing to her feet. "This information changes everything. Now I know why someone would kill them. I have a motive. I even have suspects."

"Who?" Tristan asked. "That Goebel guy? You think he tracked her down, all those years later? What for? East Germany collapsed. What would be the point of seeking revenge against her?"

Tristan's input stumped her. Both Goebel and the man who'd recruited her mother in the first place had good reason for wanting to kill her, but would they really harbor a grudge for twenty years?

"I don't know," she admitted. "I need more information. I need Hilary." Pulling her phone from her purse, she speed-dialed her assistant. "Don't leave the office," she requested. "I'm coming back in." Ignoring Hilary's groan, she hung up and placed the letter and certificate back into the envelope, sliding it into her purse.

"I'm coming with you," Tristan stated.

His temerity amazed her. "I have a lot of work to do. You'll be bored out of your mind." More likely, she would be entirely unable to concentrate.

"Nah. We'll take my motorcycle. That way I can tool around the area if I get in the way. I'll pick you up when you finish your work and bring you back here."

The implication that they would then spend time alone together caused her traitorous body to respond and for her to accede. "Fine," she heard herself say. "How long are you in the area?"

Tristan shrugged. "Couple of weeks. I'm on leave."

The answer disconcerted Juliet. Two weeks? Was he planning to hang around her that entire time? What happened if she got used him? It would be that much harder to push him away. Without comment, she brushed past him to return the albums to the footlocker. As Tristan moved to help her, she deliberated asking what his intentions were. What was he looking for—a short affair? A long-term relationship? Marriage?

She was afraid to ask. No way in hell was she going to let someone who could die in the line of duty get anywhere close to her.

Sex was one thing, but if Tristan wanted more, she couldn't give it to him—hence the consolation package she had thought up weeks before. She'd asked her assistant to work on it, and Hilary was waiting for confirmation that her research was accurate. She would know for certain any day now, hopefully soon. Because one thing was certain, whatever this was between her and Tristan, it wasn't going to last long.

"You ready?" she asked, closing the full chest. "I'm calling my sister on the way out."

3

Tristan looked around Juliet's office with interest. For some reason, he'd expected Precision Investigating, her P.I. firm, to take up more square feet. Then again, rental space came at a premium in Northern Virginia. Her office consisted of a single room of moderate size on the third floor of a newly constructed office building. A wall of windows overlooked George Mason University's main campus.

Two striped armchairs, an artificial fichus tree, and a side table smothered in gossip magazines occupied one corner of the room. The rest of the space had been split down the middle by an invisible line demarked by the level of clutter on each side. Juliet's half was as pristine and spartan as her apartment. The other half, belonging to her assistant, was crammed with computer equipment, framed pictures of a cat, a collection of coffee mugs, and at least a hundred science fiction novels.

Juliet introduced him to her assistant with a wave of her hand. "Hilary, this is Tristan. Tristan Halliday, Hilary Alcorn."

The ruby-haired pixie spun in her chair to gape at him. Thick-lensed, teal-framed glasses made her turquoise eyes look enormous. Roughly thirty, with voluptuous breasts that drew attention to her wildly colorful attire and costume jewelry, he saw at once that the only type of ring she *wasn't* wearing was a wedding band.

44

"Holy crap," she breathed. Crystal earrings tinkled as Hilary looked him up and down.

"Nice to meet you." He stuck out a hand to give her something to do besides gape at him.

"Better for me, I'm sure," she drawled, tearing her gaze off him to look at Juliet. "How's your sister? Did she recognize the composite?"

"She's good. And no, she didn't," Juliet said, briskly. "Before you ask any more questions, read this." Juliet handed Hilary the letter they'd found, then stood over her assistant, reading along and worrying her lower lip as Hilary absorbed the letter's meaning.

"Jesus, Joseph, and Mary," she finally breathed, every bit as astonished as Emma had been when Juliet called her. "Your mother was an East German spy?" Hilary's voice held a note of disbelief.

Juliet retrieved the letter. "Apparently so. But that helps me narrow down possible suspects. In her letter, my mother said Goebel would gladly kill her. Then there's the older brother of her friend, the one who recruited her. Either one of them would have a motive. Have you gotten any hits on the facial recognition software?"

"Jeez, I'm working on it!" Hilary gestured at her hardware —three monitors and a couple of laptops. "It's not like I can scan the composite and hit a single button. I have to access literally a hundred separate databases. This isn't television where they can pin down the suspect in thirty seconds flat."

"No, I understand," Juliet assured her. "Just asking."

Tristan realized he might as well have been invisible—not that he blamed either woman. At the moment, Juliet's life was way more interesting than he was.

"Actually, I did get two possible matches." Hilary faced her monitors and jiggled her mouse, rousing the computer under her desk. As it hummed, several windows popped open on her screens, making Tristan think of Hack, a techie in his platoon who would totally appreciate Hilary's setup.

Opening an onscreen folder, Hilary cast several documents

including a state driver's license and a mug shot onto separate monitors. "This guy's an ex-convict living in Wisconsin. He drives a truck for a living."

Juliet took one look at the man's photo and shook her head. "No, that's not him. The mouth isn't right."

"No worries." Hilary closed the folders and opened another file. "How about this guy? He's a math teacher at a private school in Charlotte, North Carolina."

Juliet stared hard at the image. "Too young," she finally decided. "Can't you filter the search using an age range?"

"Sure. What range do you want?"

Juliet frowned. "Well, to me he looked maybe in his fifties. That was eleven years ago, so let's say fifty-five to seventy, just to be on the safe side."

As Hilary made the adjustment, Juliet placed the marriage certificate next to her. Hilary looked it over. "What's this?"

"My parents' certificate of marriage with their real names. Their parents' names, too. My mother's folks would be German, but my father's parents were American. And they might still be alive. Can you find them?"

Hilary gawked at her boss for a moment. "You doing OKOK with all this?" she asked gently.

Ah, so he wasn't the only one who realized Juliet tried to look tough, but that was mostly veneer. Tristan watched her stand a little taller. "I'm great," she said breezily.

She probably wasn't. That was OK, though, because Tristan would be there to hold her if she needed him as she had in Mexico.

"All right." Hilary gave a skeptical shake of her head. "I'm on it." As she dove with alacrity into her search, Tristan thought again of Hack who could find just about anything using his laptop.

Juliet caught his eye and gestured to the armchairs behind them. "This could take a while," she said.

Heeding the cue to back off, Tristan ignored the chairs to prowl the perimeter of her office. The framed certificates hanging over her desk captured his notice. He stepped closer to read them. Juliet had graduated with honors from the University of Maryland—College Park with a degree in Criminology. She held a license from the state of Virginia and a certificate from the National Association of Legal Investigators.

"Nice," Tristan said, giving her a respect-filled look.

"Thanks." She looked like she might ask about his background but, instead, she locked her hands behind her back.

"Me, I only finished community college," he volunteered with a self-deprecating shrug. "Thought I was a real hotshot, too busy racing cars to think about going to a four-year school."

Hilary shot him an owl-like glance over her shoulder.

"Tristan was a NASCAR driver," Juliet explained, her tone just the tiniest bit derisive. "He spent several years on the circuit, but that got too boring for him."

"Yeah, that *does* sound tedious," Hilary drawled.

He felt the need to defend himself. "It was, actually. The only obstacle in racing is physics—speed, mass, and inertia. Trust me. It gets dull after a while."

"Unh-huh," Hilary agreed.

The lone knickknack sitting atop Juliet's file cabinet captured Tristan's attention. Picking it up, he turned the jade figurine over in his hand, trying to decide what it was.

"What is this?" he asked, holding it up.

Juliet and Hilary exchanged an amused look.

"What do you think it is?" Juliet challenged him.

"Uh, I don't know. A fertility goddess?"

Hilary snorted, snatched up the nearest coffee cup, and took a swig. Juliet colored and looked away.

Puzzled, Tristan waited for an explanation. "What?"

"It's called a wishing stone," she said tersely. "Supposedly it takes the shape of your innermost desires."

"Like the Mirror of Erised in Harry Potter," Hilary chimed in, while madly clicking her mouse.

"Hilz gave it to me for my birthday," Juliet tacked on.

The allusion to the mirror went over Tristan's head, but Juliet's explanation didn't. He shot her a lascivious grin while stroking the figurine's smooth edges. "I guess it's pretty accurate, then."

The color rising into her cheeks betrayed her naughty thoughts. *Hooyah.* Tristan's plan was totally going to work. As long as she persisted in wanting him, she was going to let him stick around, and the more he stuck around, the more she'd get used to him.

Hilary murmured to herself as she deepened her search.

Juliet stood over her, eyes fixed on the middle monitor.

Putting down the wishing stone, Tristan walked over to the coffee table covered in magazines. He picked up one and turned it over. Hilary Alcorn enjoyed a subscription to *People*. She'd apparently read this issue before bringing it in. Since it featured an article on his older look-alike, Matthew McConaughey, he dropped into one of the chairs to read it.

The actor was enjoying fatherhood. Good for him. Tristan intended to be a father, too, one day. First, he had to marry the perfect woman.

Juliet walked past as she paced the length of the room and back.

Pretending to read, Tristan watched her feet go by. The pacing was obviously a habit. She'd already worn a path in the carpet.

"Oh, dear," Hilary exclaimed, causing Juliet to hurry back to her assistant's side.

"What?"

Tristan gave up pretending interest in the magazine and peered toward Hilary's computer.

"I found your grandfather's obituary." Hilary relayed the news apologetically. "Sorry, but he just passed two years ago. It says he married your grandmother, Faith Rose Carter in 1955 in Arlington, Virginia."

"Is *she* still alive?" Juliet asked with cautious hope.

"Um, hold on a sec." Hilary's fingers played hopscotch on her keyboard.

Sensing a breakthrough, Tristan set the magazine aside and stood up.

"There's a Faith Carter Brause still in Arlington. Assuming she took Paul's name in 1955, this has got to be the same woman."

"Arlington," Juliet repeated, swinging an astonished look at Tristan as he stepped up next to her. "That's just up the road."

"I have an address," Hilary added, narrowing her search. "It matches up to the Golden Pond Retirement Community."

Juliet consulted her watch. "What time do visiting hours end?"

"Checking that...8 p.m."

Juliet turned to Tristan. "I need to go to Arlington."

"I'll take you on my bike," he offered, pleased to play a part.

"OK. One second." She made a duplicate of both the certificate and the letter using the copier in the corner. "File the originals for me, will you, Hilz?" She handed them to her assistant and slid the copies into the envelope, which she stuck inside her purse alongside the composite of the killer.

"Ready." Juliet looped the purse strap onto her shoulder and strode to the door.

"Bye, Tristan," Hilary sang out as Tristan turned to follow Juliet.

"Later." He sent the redhead a parting grin.

To his amusement, she sank back onto her seat clasping a hand to her heart in a mock swoon. Women like Hilary were good for the ego, he reflected, chasing Juliet down the stairs.

So why did he desire the one woman who wanted him only for sex and transportation?

Smoothing her wind-blown hair, Juliet approached the Golden Pond Retirement Community's information desk. The rambling facility, just a stone's throw from the nation's capital, had evidently been converted from an apartment complex to a senior care facility. It boasted a well-maintained lawn, fifty-year-old shade trees, and a bright yellow awning over the entry.

Fresh-cut flowers filled vases in the lobby and cheerful watercolors adorned the walls. The aroma of food under preparation for the adjoining dining area reminded Juliet that it was nearly suppertime. She hoped they wouldn't interrupt her grandmother's meal.

The receptionist, overly made-up and wearing a practiced smile, greeted them, her gaze sliding predictably to Tristan who hung back several paces.

With difficulty, she turned her gaze to Juliet. "What can I do for you?"

"I'm here to see Faith Carter Brause," Juliet informed her. "Does she still live here and can she have visitors?"

"Are you family?" Penciled eyebrows rose at the question.

"No," Juliet said, deciding that this stranger needn't know the truth before her own grandmother did. Producing a business card, she laid it on the counter between them. "I'm Juliet Rhodes, a private investigator. A client claims to be one of Mrs. Brause's heirs. I'd like to check his story with her, if possible."

Mascaraed eyes widened with interest. "Let me see if Mrs. Brause is up to receiving guests." The receptionist plucked up the phone beside her and punched in three numbers that Juliet memorized.

"Hello, Mrs. Brause. There's someone here to see you. She says she's a private investigator."

Juliet's intestines coiled with nervousness. It wasn't every day that one encountered a long-lost family member, especially when said person had never before been mentioned.

The woman hung up. "She says you're to go right up. Room 216," she relayed. "The elevator is behind you." Her gaze strayed toward Tristan again. "Is he going with you?"

The woman looked like she might devour him for supper if Juliet didn't whisk him away.

"Yes," she said, grabbing Tristan's arm and pulling him along.

As the elevator closed behind them and rose to the next floor, Tristan studied her with a sidelong look. "Are you nervous?"

Her heart skipped at the reminder that she was about to meet a grandmother she hadn't even known existed. "Do I look nervous?"

"No one could tell but me," he said.

In that case, she needed to work on her poker face.

Room 216's door stood open. Juliet gave it a tentative knock.

"Come in," warbled a sweet voice.

A strange emotion blew through Juliet as she walked into a space gilded with evening sunlight. A twin four-poster bed occupied the wall by the window. A cozy seating area took up the rest of the room. Juliet's gaze locked on the white-haired woman seated in the embroidered easy chair knitting something peach-colored. In her eighth decade, Faith Brause's figure still appeared lithe beneath her green blouse and navy slacks. Her polite smile froze as Juliet approached her.

"Anya?" she inquired, snatching off her reading glasses to blink up at the younger woman.

One look at Faith's blue eyes stripped the last remnants of doubt from Juliet's mind.

She faltered to a halt. Those were her father's eyes. *My God.* She bit back the exclamation with difficulty. "No, I'm...I'm Juliet," she said, uncertain how to continue.

Faith Brause pushed the knitting off her lap and came unsteadily to her feet. "I'm sorry," she apologized, still looking stunned. "You look so much like..."

"Like Anya Ausfeld?" Juliet suggested.

Startled silence filled the tidy chamber. The old woman covered her mouth with a blue-veined hand, betraying both shock and wonder.

"Anya was my mother," Juliet explained in a voice hoarse with emotion. "That makes me your granddaughter."

The old woman swayed on her feet, and Juliet and Tristan both leaped forward to steady her. "You should sit," Juliet said with concern.

"I'm OK," Faith assured her, though she sank back into her chair all the same.

Juliet found herself kneeling in front of her grandmother. "I'm sorry." She felt an urge to hug the older woman. "I'm as shocked as you are. I never heard of you before today. But this is how I found you."

Reaching into her purse, she produced the copied paperwork and handed her grandmother the certificate. Faith glanced down at it and put her glasses back on. As she studied the single page, her hands began to tremble.

Juliet glanced up at Tristan, secretly grateful for his company. It felt as if the earth's very core was shifting beneath her.

At last, Faith lifted tear-filled eyes.

"We flew to West Berlin for the wedding," she volunteered. A faraway look entered her eyes. "My son had never looked more handsome, or happier." Her gaze shifted to meet Juliet's. "WITSEC told me, eleven years ago this past October, my son was dead. An accident, they said."

"Yes," Juliet concurred, withholding the whole truth for just a moment longer. One shock at a time.

"When I asked what would happen to the children, I was told you were old enough to fend for yourselves. That you were safer staying away from us."

Juliet blinked. "You knew about us?" Why hadn't her mother ever mentioned any relatives?

"Oh, I wasn't supposed to know," Faith replied. "But every year on my birthday, I received a large envelope with no postmark, filled with pictures and writings made by little girls. Their names were blacked out, but I knew your parents had sent them to me."

Juliet swallowed the lump in her throat. "I was sixteen

when the accident happened," she confessed. "My sister was almost twenty-one. She looked after me." In point of fact, Juliet had looked after Emma as much as the other way around, but Faith didn't need to know the details.

"My poor child." Stretching out a trembling hand, Faith stroked Juliet's hair. "Your grandfather and I would have welcomed you both."

Juliet nodded. "It worked out well enough." She and Emma had learned to grow up quickly, relying on each other. "Did WITSEC tell you how the accident happened?" she added, wanting to prepare Faith for the blow she was bound to experience.

The old woman lowered her hand and visibly braced herself. "No," she said.

Juliet queried the need to cause her grandmother added grief, but how else would she learn whether Faith recognized the man Juliet had so recently remembered? "The tires on our car blew out for no reason," she said, seeing no way around telling the truth. "We fishtailed, crashed into a ditch, and struck a tree. Dad's airbag didn't deploy. Mom's seatbelt failed." Watching her grandmother's reaction, Juliet saw the color drain from Faith's face.

"Then it wasn't an accident," Faith whispered. Instead of being shocked, as Juliet expected, she appeared heartbroken.

"You're not surprised," Juliet realized.

Faith shook her head, and Juliet handed her the letter. "I found this today, hidden under a false bottom in my parents' trunk."

Taking it, Faith shot a cautious glance at Tristan.

"I'm sorry," Juliet apologized, realizing she had yet to introduce him. "This is my friend, Tristan. He's a Navy SEAL."

Faith visibly relaxed. "A patriot," she concluded. "Would you shut the door please, young man?" she asked.

"Yes, ma'am." He strode to the door, closed and locked it.

"Draw up a seat, child," Faith advised Juliet. "It will take me a while to read this."

As Tristan whisked a chair from the desk, Juliet got off the floor to sit in it. She shot him a grateful smile then watched Faith's reaction as she read through her daughter-in-law's words.

Reaching the letter's end, her grandmother looked up and grimaced.

"You already knew?" Juliet guessed.

"Most of it, yes," Faith confessed. "Your parents explained the situation so that Paul and I would understand why they had to disappear. Anya told us there was a price on her head, but she never mentioned her associates as specifically as she did here." She held the letter up and gazed earnestly into Juliet's eyes. "Your mother essentially betrayed the Stasi. She had to go into hiding. She had no other choice, and neither did my son if he wanted to stay with her."

"I understand," Juliet assured her.

"From what you told me of the accident," Faith added, looking suddenly every one of her eighty-some years, "it sounds as though the Stasi must have found her anyway."

Juliet swallowed against a dry mouth. "I was with them when it happened," she admitted, looking down at her hands.

"Dear God." Faith covered her hands and squeezed them.

Juliet plowed on. "I saw a man, right after it happened, looking into my mother's window. He didn't see me behind the driver's seat." She neglected to mention she'd been trapped there.

Her grandmother's grip tightened. "I don't know who he was but—this is what he looked like."

Freeing a hand, Juliet drew the composite sketch from her purse and gave it to her grandmother. She hoped for recognition to flare in Faith's blue gaze, but it didn't. Her grandmother's face reflected her rising repugnance and loathing as she realized she was looking at her son's killer.

"I've never seen him before," she stated with certainty. "You think he killed them?"

Juliet questioned her intuition one last time. Armed with the evidence she'd happened upon earlier that day, her certainty had only increased. "Yes. I saw his expression as he

54

peered into the car. He saw my father gasping for breath. He saw my mother was already gone, which seemed to please him. Something told me to keep quiet. It was hours after he walked away that a passing truck driver happened to see our Oldsmobile in the ditch. He was the one who called the police."

"Dear child," Faith exclaimed. Scooting to the edge of her seat, she leaned forward and caught Juliet in an embrace.

Tears sprang to Juliet's eyes as she submitted to her grandmother's comfort. After a moment, Faith released her and sat back.

"And you're sure he looks like this?" Faith asked, looking again at the sketch.

"Yes, but it was eleven years ago," Juliet replied. "He would be older now."

The wrinkles on her grandmother's forehead deepened. "But Gerard and Anya went into witness protection in December of 1984. Communism collapsed in '89, and the two Germanys were promptly reunited. What year was the accident, dear?"

"Two thousand and six," Juliet replied.

"That would have been"—Faith tallied on her fingers— "twenty-two years after she defied the Stasi. Would anyone hold a grudge all that time?"

It was the same question Tristan had brought up hours earlier. Would the Stasi, which no longer existed, still be seeking vengeance after twenty-two years? "Maybe it just took that long to find Mom and Dad. The killer would have had to get insider information from the U.S. Marshals Service. That could have taken decades."

"Your mother did say Goebel would gladly kill her," Faith pointed out.

"Right. Plus, he apparently loved art as much as she did. What if they'd hit it off? If they were close, like student and mentor, he might have considered her actions a personal betrayal as much as a political betrayal."

"Was Goebel even alive in 2006?" her grandmother asked.

Juliet sighed. "I don't know. I need to get back to my office and do more research." At Faith's curious glance, she added, "It's true what I told the receptionist. I am a private investigator by occupation. Finding people is what I do."

Faith smiled with approval. "Oh, Juliet. Why doesn't that surprise me? Your parents would be so proud of you. But tell me about your sister before you go."

"Of course." Taking her cell from her purse, Juliet accessed her photos so she could share them. "Here's Emma. As you can see, she looks like Dad with his red hair and your blue eyes."

"Hah! She looks like me," Faith corrected her proudly. "And who's that?" she asked, pointing to Sammy.

"Well, Emma got married out of college to a man named Gary. It didn't work out, but this is their daughter Sammy, who's twelve now."

Faith threw her hands up in delight. "I'm a great-grandmother!"

"Emma just got married again, to Jeremiah, a Navy SEAL who works with Tristan."

"They look so happy together." Faith studied the photo with approval.

"They are," Juliet assured her. "They live in Virginia Beach, but Emma is visiting the area this week. I told her about you, and she said she could bring Sammy by in the morning if you'd like them to visit."

"I would love that," Faith declared. "What a day," she exclaimed, shaking her head incredulously as Juliet put her phone away.

"You can say that again," Juliet agreed. Collecting the paperwork she'd brought, she deliberated leaving a copy for Faith but decided it best not to scatter around her mother's secrets. "I'll be back to visit," she promised, putting everything back into her purse.

"Don't worry about me, dear. You have a mystery to solve."

"Yes, I do," Juliet agreed, standing up.

Tristan, who'd remained on his feet the whole time, put her chair back next to the desk. Bending over Faith, Juliet gave her a heartfelt hug.

"Thank you," she said.

"Whatever for, dear?" Faith asked as her granddaughter straightened.

As she gazed down at her newfound family member, Juliet's throat tightened. "For not blaming my mother."

Sorrow darkened Faith's blue eyes. "What good would that serve?" she asked. "Gerard loved his Anya more than anything, and vice versa."

Not trusting herself to speak, Juliet gave a jerky nod and turned away. "Take care," she said, heading for the door.

"Pleasure meeting you, ma'am," Tristan called as he led the way and unlocked the door.

"You, too, dear," her grandmother called. "Please shut the door behind you."

As they headed down the hall, Juliet noted Tristan's sidelong glances.

"You OK?" he asked, pushing the button for the elevator.

The mystery of her parents' death gnawed at her. "Of course," she said automatically.

When he looped his arm around her and hugged her all the same, she didn't resist. It came as a relief to lean on someone in the wake of so much change.

"Where to?" Tristan asked once they were outside and crossing the dark parking lot.

Juliet had anticipated an evening in bed with Tristan, but finding her parents' killer took precedence to getting him out of her system.

"Back to my office," she said with an apologetic grimace.

"You got it, partner." With sanguinity she was beginning to appreciate, he threw a leg over the seat of his Harley. "Hop on board."

Clasping her purse firmly under one arm and settling onto the seat behind Tristan, Juliet swallowed the impulse to correct his choice of words. First, she wasn't his partner. Second, did he have to sound like he could not care less where they went so long as they went together?

Their relationship was temporary and superficial. The

sooner they exorcised their desire, the sooner Juliet could stop feeling like she wanted Tristan to hang around. Unfortunately, she was too pressed for time to look out for her heart.

She had a killer to catch and only the scantiest of clues as to who he could be.

4

"Have a seat, hon." Tristan pushed Juliet down on one of the stools that lined her breakfast bar. It was ten minutes past midnight. He'd already dug into the fast food they'd bought on their way back from her office, but she'd yet to eat her sandwich. Considering how little he'd seen her consume at the restaurant more than twelve hours ago, she had to be famished.

"I'm not hungry," she protested as he unwrapped her chicken sandwich and placed it in front of her on the counter.

"Just give it a try," he insisted. Tristan crossed to the refrigerator and opened it to consider the contents. "Jesus." The scarcity of food dismayed him. She had stocked up on Dr. Pepper. There was a half-empty bottle of white wine and a nearly empty box of donuts, and that was it. "Don't you ever cook for yourself?"

"Not really," she admitted.

He grabbed two cans of soda and let the refrigerator door swing shut as he set them next to the food. Juliet had picked up her sandwich and was eyeing it with rising interest.

"Let me guess. You spend all your time either working or working out," Tristan said.

"Yeah, that pretty much sums it up." She took a small bite and slowly chewed.

He couldn't blame her for feeling dispirited. Her afternoon had been one big rollercoaster ride of emotions and had ended on a flat note.

They'd left Golden Pond hopeful of finding evidence suggesting Dieter Goebel was her parents' killer. But after five straight hours of sifting through the internet—*without* Hilary's help because her assistant had gone home to feed her cat— Juliet had found nothing to corroborate her suspicion.

Dieter Goebel might have been head of the Main Directorate for Reconnaissance and number two in power behind General Secretary Erich Honecker himself, but there wasn't a single photo of him online. Considered one of the greatest spymasters of all time, Goebel had always taken great care to avoid publicity. As a result, he'd been dubbed "The Man Without a Face."

After the Cold War was over, and with Germany reunifying, Goebel had made a vain attempt to seek asylum in Russia. He'd returned to Germany, where he'd been convicted of treason and sentenced to six years imprisonment—a sentence Goebel never completed because he mysteriously disappeared from the prison in 1992, never to resurface.

Refusing to call Hilary back to the office, Juliet had hammered away at the mystery of Goebel's vanishing act, to no avail.

She'd been wilting in front of her computer when Tristan had taken matters into his own hands. He'd hauled her to her feet and dragged her home—with Juliet too tired to protest.

The bloodshot look she sent him as he stood beside her stool made him hide a grin behind a swig of soda. Even given her exhaustion, he could read sexual interest in her heavy-lidded gaze. If the events of the last six hours hadn't occupied her life so exclusively, she would probably have torn his clothes off by now.

At the moment, she could barely sit up by herself let alone seduce him, and that was a good thing. Honestly, if she'd truly put a move on him earlier, he'd have had a hard time holding out. Resist her he must, however, because the only way to raise his odds of becoming her boyfriend was to keep her wanting him.

"Finish it," he cajoled when she put her half-eaten sandwich down.

She glared at him and shoved a huge bite into her mouth.

"You got a bathtub?" he asked, figuring she probably did.

Her bleary eyes cleared. Feeble flames of lust flickered in them.

"Just off my bedroom," she said around her mouthful of food.

Still hiding his grin, he walked toward the master bedroom.

"Oh, sure, help yourself," he heard her mutter. But her tone lacked acerbity. If he didn't hurry and draw a bath, she'd fall asleep waiting for him.

Her oversized Jacuzzi tub incited his envy. *Now, this is a tub.* He'd give both his eyeteeth to get in there with Juliet, but that wasn't going to happen.

In good time, he assured himself. Twisting the faucets, he set about filling the tub with warm water. To his surprise, Juliet had amassed a collection of girlie bath stuff in a basket—proof she had a softer side even if she rarely showed it.

He sprinkled bath salts under the gushing water. They started to foam, releasing the scent of lavender. Turning to fetch Juliet, he found her standing at the door. She leaned against the doorframe, her eyes half closed.

"What're you doing?" Her words slurred.

"Gettin' you ready for bed." Before she could protest, he marched up and started to undress her, unbuttoning her persimmon-colored blouse. She wore a pink lace bra beneath it.

With uncharacteristic docility, she submitted to his ministrations.

When his hands dropped to the button at the front of her trousers, he thought for sure she would stop him, but she didn't. He released the button, lowered the zipper, and peeled her gray slacks over her hips and down her long, toned legs. Tristan crouched to pull them off her bare feet. At eye level with her pink panties, he forced himself to avert his gaze.

Standing up swiftly, he ordered her to turn around.

With the appearance of holding her breath, Juliet did so, and he efficiently unhooked her bra. Before he caved to temptation, he pushed the straps off her shoulders, divesting her of both her undergarments, all with a practiced swipe of his hands.

"In you go." He palmed her elbow and turned her toward the tub. His gaze went straight to her pink nipples, both flushed and taut with arousal.

She thought he was going to make his move on her—no question. If that kept her cooperative, he wouldn't bother to correct her assumption.

"You look amazing," he said, unable to withhold a comment. "Just like I remember."

"Thanks." She stepped into the tub, shaking off his assistance and groaning with unabashed enjoyment as she collapsed rather ungracefully into the fragrant bubbles.

"Not too hot?" he asked, reaching for a washcloth and a bar of soap.

"Un-unh." Sliding lower into the water, she eyed him from beneath half-closed eyes as he wet the cloth and rubbed soap into it.

"Aren't you coming in?" Her question betrayed confusion.

"Nope. This is all about you. Hold your arms out."

"I can bathe myself," she said, but she offered him an arm, all the same, while dropping her head against the end of the tub. "Mmmm." She moaned her appreciation as he ran the washcloth from her hand to her shoulder then reached across the tub to do the same to her other arm.

"Sit forward," he instructed. "Better get your back before you fall asleep."

"I am tired," she admitted, adjusting her position. Her head nodded, and her hair concealed her face.

By the time he pressed her back into a reclining pose, her eyes were closed, making it easier for him to apply the washcloth to her full, pert breasts without bending toward them to flick them with his tongue. They puckered at his ministrations, a treat that turned him as hard as a rock under the confines of his zipper.

This ain't about you, hotshot, he reminded himself.

Still, he had to confess to a teensy bit of self-interest as he slid the washcloth to her waist then underwater to sluice it over her hips. To his immense gratification, she parted her legs wordlessly. He drew the washcloth lower, wiping it slowly and sensually along the insides of her thighs. Her knees emerged from the water as she bent her legs. Her pelvis tipped subtly to give him better access.

Abandoning the washcloth, he skimmed his palm lightly over the petals of her sex, watching her response before repeating his caress. Her breasts rose as she gave a light gasp, but she didn't attempt to stop him. He stroked her again.

In spite of her exhaustion, she lay as open and inviting as a flower in bloom. He traced the silky soft folds with his fingertips and felt them swell. Her clitoris made itself apparent, firming beneath the pad of his thumb as he teased it.

Juliet whimpered, but her eyes remained shut. Her lips parted as though she were suddenly short of breath. He took that as his cue to continue, thumbing the sensitive nubbin with a skill he had learned the good old-fashioned way. When her thighs began to tremble, he teased her slick opening with his middle finger.

Her breathing grew faster, shallower. A shimmer of sweat appeared on her upper lip. Beckoned by the slippery moisture at her opening, Tristan slid his middle finger inside her and was rewarded with a lift of Juliet's hips. Hidden muscles squeezed him. He added a second digit, pushing them both into her snugness to caress her G-spot. As he drew them out, she gave a whimper of deprivation.

He thrust again, and she rose to meet him.

When she covered her own breasts with her hands, squeezing and rolling her nipples right in front of him, he thought he might disgrace himself.

God Almighty. He took a mental snapshot of how sexy she looked with her head thrown back, tongue riding the curve of her lush lips. Lost in the throes of ecstasy, too tired to care what she revealed to him, she gave herself to him unabashedly.

Did she even realize it was he who was doing this to her? Or would she have let any old Joe have his way?

"Tristan." Her ragged cry reassured him. "Please!"

He'd have given anything to drive his aching flesh into her responsive body, but that was not his plan. For the moment, he let his fingers do the talking.

Her muscles clamped down on him and her face contorted with rapture. She issued a keening cry that was almost a scream.

His testicles responded helplessly. A small spurt of semen wet the insides of his boxer briefs in what had to be the world's most unsatisfying climax. But triumph took the edge off his frustration as Juliet slowly relaxed, heaving a gratified sigh.

She'd think about this night every time she took a bath. Mission accomplished.

"That was wonderful," she whispered, her words running together as he gently withdrew his hand and reached for the washcloth like nothing had happened. Her eyes remained shut. Her breathing slowed. He finished rubbing down her calves and feet.

Not a word more was spoken. Suspecting Juliet was fully asleep, Tristan opened the drain on the tub, wrung out the washcloth, and set it aside. He stood and reached for the fluffy blue towel hanging on the towel rack.

Getting Juliet dried off and into bed would take more than a feat of strength. At five foot seven and made of lean muscle, she wasn't exactly a featherweight. It would also be a real test of restraint. But what the hell, he'd been celibate for six long months. A couple more days wasn't going to kill him. He'd fulfilled his objective. Come morning, when Juliet awoke refreshed and hankering for more than he'd given her last night, she was going to reconsider her hang-up with relationships.

Juliet squinted at the alarm clock by her bed. Reading 10 a.m., she jerked up onto her elbow to find her room awash with morning sunlight and her apartment smelling of coffee and bacon.

What the hell? She hadn't slept this late on a weekday in her life!

Kicking off the covers, she sat up to realize two things at once. First, she was completely naked. And secondly, someone had slept next to her, given the imprint in the other pillow. She bet she knew who that someone was.

Tristan had shared her bed. No, wait. Pleasant memories flowed through her. First, he'd fondled her in her tub, giving her the most fantastic orgasm in recorded history. And then what? Had they had sex after that?

She put a hand to her forehead. No. Recalling the physicality of their sex in Mexico, she was positive she would remember if Tristan had ravished her as he'd done last spring. Besides, she would surely be tender down there, if they'd done the deed, considering how long it had been.

So...he'd only slept beside her. And he'd apparently switched off her alarm clock because it hadn't gone off at six as it should have.

Bastard! He couldn't just show up in the middle of an investigation and take over her life. She had work to do!

Stalking across her bedroom in search of her robe, she was still tying it around her waist when she stormed into the kitchen. Tristan stood at the stove, cooking breakfast.

"Mornin'." His grin made her stomach cartwheel. The memory of his fingers stroking her G-spot derailed her thoughts for several seconds. "Hope you slept as good as I did. Hilary called," he added, nodding toward her phone which was now sitting next to her purse. "She says she got your note last night, and she's got stuff about Goebel that you can look at when you make it in. Also, she found another match for the composite of your suspect."

Juliet processed several things at once. Tristan had violated her privacy yet again by digging into her purse and answering her phone. Moreover, he'd forced her to sleep in when she had work to do. What's more, he intended for them to share a hearty breakfast. It took another second to find her voice.

"Get out," she said. Her ears started to burn, and her hands curled into fists when Tristan sent her an unruffled glance and picked up two eggs.

"How do you like your eggs?" he asked. "Over-easy or sunny side up?"

"Scrambled." Juliet forced the words between her teeth. "Because that's what I'm going to do to your brains if you don't stop trying to run my life!"

He glanced at the eggs in his hands, shrugged, and reached for a bowl to break them into. "Suit yourself." A strange light twinkled in his eyes as he glanced at her again.

The gall of the man! Juliet took closer stock of him, wondering why he looked so at home in her galley kitchen. Watching him break open the eggs, two at a time, and dump them into a bowl, it occurred to her that some time while she'd been fast asleep, he'd gone shopping for groceries. While she resented his nerve, she had to admit she was ravenous. Her stomach rumbled noisily. Scrambled eggs and bacon sounded really, really good right then.

"Did you get any bread?" she asked, venturing closer.

"Yep." He glanced at her toaster, and she saw two slices peeking out of it. "Toast is on the way."

His cheerful tone annoyed her. And so did the fact that he hadn't taken her threat seriously. Surely, he realized he had overstepped his bounds. If any other man tried to pull the stunts Tristan was pulling, she'd have given him the boot hours ago. Juliet was only letting Tristan slide because she was hungry—and that was the only reason.

Besides, he looked incredibly sexy in the navy crewneck sweater he had paired with cargo pants.

"Hey, where'd you get those clothes?" she demanded. They weren't the same ones Tristan had worn yesterday.

He shot her an innocent look. "From my suitcase."

She cast an eye around but didn't see it. "You didn't have a suitcase yesterday."

"Sure, I did. In Bullfrog's Jeep. I picked it up this morning while I was out getting groceries."

Although they were staying with friends of Emma's, her sister and brother-in-law were obviously aiding and abetting Tristan's cause. "You brought your suitcase here on your motorcycle?"

"Uh—" Tristan cast her a wary glance. "No, actually, I had to borrow your SUV to carry groceries anyway. Hope that's OK."

A pulse began to tap at her temples. She felt herself sizzling in tandem with the milk-and-egg mixture Tristan poured into the hot pan.

"Sure," she bit out tartly. "Is there anything *else* of mine you'd like to help yourself to while you're here?" She gestured sarcastically at the interior of her apartment.

His gaze slid with unmistakable appreciation over her silk-clad figure. Given her question, she expected him to say, *How about I help myself to you?* Instead, he turned his attention to stirring the hardening egg mixture.

"No thanks. I'm good," Tristan said lightly.

Juliet realized both her hands were buried in her hair. "I'm going to get dressed," she muttered, turning away before she killed him.

"Don't take too long," he sang out as she marched back to her bedroom. "Breakfast is just about ready."

Closing the door firmly behind her, she leaned against it a moment feeling her heart thumping in her chest.

Damn it! What was this game Tristan was playing? He'd babied her last night in a way most women would find endearing, if not downright seductive. But Tristan had also invited himself to *stay* in her apartment. He'd even helped himself to her vehicle without her permission.

The man had some gall. He must think that simply because he'd pleasured her last night without asking for anything in return, she owed him her hospitality.

Bullshit. Juliet owed him nothing. And as soon as she could comfortably extricate herself from his unwanted company, she would do so.

But given the stubborn twinkle she'd glimpsed in his eyes earlier, he had more plans up his sleeves. Getting rid of him wouldn't be all that easy. Good thing she had Hilary working on his consolation package. If anything could tear Tristan away from her, it would be the promise of a reunion with his long-lost birth mother.

"Goebel was a huge patron of the arts," Hilary announced swiveling her chair to face them as Tristan and Juliet blew into the office.

Tristan blinked at the woman's outfit. Today, Hilary wore a hot pink jacket over a lemon-yellow, figure-hugging dress. A beaded necklace that contained every hue of the rainbow drew his gaze straight to the dress's plunging neckline and her voluptuous bosom. Surprisingly shapely legs sheathed in sheer, cream-colored stockings emerged from beneath the dress's high hem, held up by a garter belt, if the eyelet and satin strap he glimpsed were any indication.

Holy hell. He averted his gaze with difficulty to take in her five-inch, hot pink high heels.

"Show me," Juliet demanded, unaware of her assistant's effect on Tristan's ocular nerves.

Tugging primly at her skirt, Hilary swung her chair back around to display her findings.

Juliet tossed her purse aside and went to stand over her right shoulder. As Hilary brought up an image of a whitewashed brick building, Tristan flanked Hilary's other side.

"Goebel collected artwork, specifically works of Art Nouveau and Art Deco."

"I have no idea what that means," Juliet admitted, though her mother most certainly would have.

"I'll show you some," Hilary promised. "He displayed his collection in this building just blocks from the Stasi's headquarters in Lichtenberg. The pictures would have looked something like this," she continued, directing their attention to a different monitor. "Though these aren't actual pieces in his collection because that was seized by West German officials when the Wall came down."

Hilary clicked through a series of oil paintings that displayed gritty images of downtrodden factory workers, farmers in the field, and small, grubby children.

"You see, Goebel was a Marxist," she continued, warming to her history lesson. "He was born into a Jewish family, and when Hitler gained power, Goebel's family moved to Russia where he attended school and got involved in politics. When Russia gained control of East Germany, he was appointed as head of the Main Directorate of Reconnaissance.

"You've heard of how the Stasi spied on Germany's citizens to weed out potential dissidents? Well, Goebel was behind that, detaining, torturing, and coercing his own people. He was also in charge of espionage against the West, and he sent hundreds of moles, whom he called his Romeos and Juliets, to seduce unsuspecting government workers, NATO employees, and scientists, all with the objective of squeezing intelligence out of them and reporting back to the East."

"Moles like my mother," Juliet murmured, thinking it ironic that her mother had named her Juliet, considering its Cold War meaning.

"Right. Anyway, Goebel's efforts ultimately failed. The Cold War ended, and East and West Germany united. Goebel was thrown out of office, sentenced, and imprisoned. Only, he disappeared from prison, and no one ever saw him again."

"Right, I read about that last night." Juliet shifted impatiently.

"Anyway, back to the art, which I found interesting. Goebel was a painter and an art collector. He saw art as a means of propagating Marxist ideals, and he proudly exhibited his own original paintings in a building close to where he worked each day."

She clicked her mouse, and the picture of a white brick building reappeared. "It's now an elementary school."

"What happened to his art when he went to prison?" Juliet asked.

"It was seized and sold," Hilary replied. "But that got me thinking. If Goebel was that proud of his collection, he might have tried to get it back in the last few decades. Maybe if we track down the art, we can track *him* down."

Juliet expelled a long breath. "Then we don't yet know if he was alive in 2006."

"Not yet," Hilary admitted. She glanced over her shoulder at her boss and added, "But he would be eighty-one by now, so there's a good chance he's dead."

"I need to know for sure."

Hearing the stubborn note in Juliet's voice, Tristan realized she wouldn't give up until she had an answer.

"You know," he said, "I've got a friend on the team who could help. You want me to ask him to look for Goebel, too?"

Juliet and Hilary shot him identical looks of affront.

"If Hilary can't find what I'm looking for, I doubt your friend can," Juliet retorted.

Hilary cast her boss a grateful smile even as she lifted her chin higher. "Well, thanks, Jules. Nonetheless, I'd like to see what this friend of yours has got," she challenged. "Go ahead, Tristan. Ask him to find Goebel for us." Multicolored bracelets jingled on her wrist as she plucked a business card from a holder on her desk and handed it to Tristan. "Tell him to give me a call if he finds anything."

Glancing at the card, Tristan wasn't surprised to find Hilary's full name written in lime-green cursive next to the silhouette of a black cat. Her cell number and email appeared in bold font under that. He wondered if she wasn't angling for some internet romance.

"Sure," he said, pocketing the card.

Juliet eyed him severely, her hands on her hips.

"What?" he asked innocently. Hack could use a little romance, internet or otherwise. Tristan couldn't remember the last time he'd seen his friend talk to a woman.

"Nothing." Juliet focused her attention back on Hilary. "You said you found another match to the composite," she reminded her.

"Oh, yeah." Hilary swiveled to face a different screen. "This guy came up in a more recent search. He's a retired police officer living in San Francisco, sixty-six years old. While he was on the job, he received some award for getting gang members off the streets and got his picture in the paper. That's how I found him."

She brought up a picture of a policeman shaking the hand of a long-ago Mayor of San Francisco. Next, she tossed up two more images—the man's LinkedIn photo and California driver's license.

Tristan watched Juliet's reaction. Seeing the blood drain from her face, he took a closer look at the pictures.

"My God, that's him!" Juliet whispered, her voice conveying a depth of fear he'd never before heard from her.

"Wait," Tristan protested, thinking she had to be wrong. It was true the man resembled the composite drawing, but.... "What are the odds that a mole for East Germany is living in California doing police work?"

Juliet just looked at him. "It's possible," she insisted. "We don't know what his job was back in Germany."

Hilary glanced back at him. "Facial recognition pegs this hit at eighty-three percent accurate," she informed them. "That leaves only a seventeen percent chance of error."

"What's his name?" Juliet asked, leaning closer to the monitor. "Hans Coenen. Isn't that German?"

"I think it's Dutch," Hilary replied.

"Dutch. German. What's the difference?" Juliet leaned toward the monitors to skim the news article and peruse the LinkedIn page. "Nothing here connects him to Goebel, though," she said straightening. "We need to keep digging."

"You got it, boss." Hilary looked at Juliet. "You want to tell Tristan what we found for him?" she asked.

Tristan's antenna went up. "What?"

Both women fell quiet, and Juliet's expression became unreadable. "Hilary found your birth mother," she announced. "She got confirmation just this morning."

Tristan felt like the walls were slowly spinning around him. "My what?"

"Your real mother, Tristan."

His heart started to thump. "Why'd you do that?" he asked.

Juliet visibly hesitated. "I don't know. It just seems like something you should know. Maybe it explains—" She cut herself off and crossed to her side of the office to busy herself with the coffeemaker. "If you don't want to know who your mother is, that's your prerogative."

He eyed her stiff back, conscious of Hilary's owl-like gaze as she watched their tense exchange.

"Finish what you were going to say," he demanded. "Maybe it explains what—why I'm always in a relationship? I've been single for the last six months. You really think Bullfrog knows everything about my life?"

Juliet swung around with a K-Cup in her hand. "That's not what I was going to say."

"What were you going to say?" He refused to back down.

"I was going to say maybe it explains why you sing so well," she said, taking the wind out of his sails.

"What?" He didn't understand what singing had to do with anything.

Juliet gestured to her assistant. "Go ahead and show him, Hilz," she said, turning back to brew herself a cup of coffee.

Tristan pivoted toward Hilary, who leaned back in her chair to look at him. "Here's how I found your mother," she explained. "I started by contacting the detective division in Wilmington—"

"Where I was born," he finished.

"Right. In October of '88, they investigated the case of an

72

infant left in the lobby of the emergency room at New Hanover Regional Medical Center."

"That was me. The authorities never found out where I came from." Behind him, the coffee maker gave a whine and a hiss.

Hilary snorted derisively. "True, they didn't. But they still had the security footage from the hospital, on VHS tape, and they let me look at it."

"The security footage never showed anything."

She shot him an arch look. "It did, actually. The police were looking for women coming into the ER. That led them to overlook the *man* who came in carrying a backpack. He loitered for a few minutes, pulled a baby out of his pack, and left it wrapped in a blanket under a chair."

Tristan nodded. According to his adoptive parents who'd both worked as doctors in the ER, that was where he'd been found, sound asleep under a chair in the hospital lobby.

"Lucky for me," Hilary continued, "this man wasn't just some random unidentifiable person. Facial recognition software found a match immediately—Mike Fontana. He's been active in the music industry for decades as the manager of several country music stars."

Tristan's imagination caught fire. "So who's my mother?"

"Well, this is just an educated guess, but at the time Fontana was acting manager for the country music phenom, Cassidy King." Hilary shared a look with Juliet, who'd finally turned around.

Tristan glanced her way and found Juliet watching his reaction through the steam rising from her coffee mug. He had recognized the name, Cassidy King, but only a vague image of a cute, blonde singer came to mind. "How long have you been looking into this?" he asked.

"Since Emma's wedding," she admitted.

A buzzing filled his ears. That Juliet had gone to the trouble to find his mother might have been touching under certain circumstances. However, Tristan had a feeling her motives weren't that altruistic.

"Are you OK?" she asked when he didn't say anything.

He wasn't sure. Hearing that his mother might have been a famous country music star didn't bother him. Finding himself the object of Juliet's investigating did. "When were you going to tell me?" he demanded.

She shrugged uncomfortably. "When the time was right," she said vaguely. "Anyway, Hilary only recently found out where she lives. Where does she live, Hilz?" she asked, managing to dodge his question.

"California," Hilary said, glancing back to observe Tristan's reaction. "You've heard of Carmel-by-the-Sea, haven't you? Clint Eastwood used to be the mayor."

"I like Clint Eastwood," he said irrelevantly.

"If you see her picture, you'll know she's the one." Juliet nodded at Hilary. "Go ahead and show him, Hilz."

As Hilary brought up photos of Cassidy King, Tristan edged closer to the monitors. Images of a blonde beauty populated three screens at once, driving the breath out of his lungs. Hilary enlarged one photo in particular. The young woman with a mane of golden curls and devil-may-care blue eyes reminded him of his middle school class picture.

"Holy shit," he breathed. There was no question he was looking at his biological mother.

"Here, have a seat." Juliet wheeled the chair from her desk over and shoved it behind his knees. He sank wordlessly into it, his emotions too tangled to sort out. The excitement of finding the mother he had never known vied with the realization that Juliet, despite her assertion to the contrary, thought he had abandonment issues. Why else would she have gone to the trouble to locate his birth mother?

"I looked through tabloids that dated from around the time she would have been pregnant with you," Juliet volunteered from her spot directly behind him. "Cassidy disappeared from show biz for about six months, right around the time you were born."

"Why'd she leave me in Wilmington?" Tristan's voice was hoarse.

"That's where she's from, originally," she explained. "She must have gone home to have her baby."

He struggled to process all the information at once. "So, my birth mother's manager left me in the hospital." He wondered if Cassidy had instructed Fontana to do that or if the man had just whisked her baby away, hoping she'd get back to work.

"It would seem he did," Juliet agreed. "There's no way to know if Cassidy told him to leave you there, or whether she was left out of that decision since she was only sixteen. The only way to find out would be to talk to her in person."

And there it was again—the suggestion that Juliet wanted him to leave, just like when she'd ordered him out of her apartment earlier that morning. The confidence he'd felt last night was leaking from him like air out of an old balloon.

Hilary turned her head to look at him. "Mike Fontana's been dead for years. Your mother changed her name, which made it really hard for me to track her down. She goes by Casey Edwards, now. This is the most recent photo I could find online."

Facing forward, she brought up and enlarged a photo of a middle-aged, bleached-blonde in dark sunglasses who only vaguely resembled her younger self.

"Her stardom tapered off in the early nineties when she went to jail," Hilary explained.

"She went to jail?" Dismay added itself to the mélange of emotions swirling inside him.

"For stabbing a boyfriend," Juliet clarified, her tone suggesting that the guy might have deserved it. "She served a four-year sentence. After Cassidy got out, she changed her name and all but disappeared. I don't know how Hilary managed to find her."

"Through her veterinarians." The assistant smiled smugly as she leaned back in her chair. "She's either had the same dog for twenty-five years, or she names them all Dolly." Her magnified gaze conveyed sympathy as she looked at Tristan. "It's up to you if you want to meet her again. I have her address but she doesn't seem to own a phone. You could write to her and see if she responds."

"I think he should fly out and meet her in person," Juliet suggested.

Tristan tensed. Yep, she was trying to get rid of him. He swiped a hand over his face. The queasy feeling that had ambushed him earlier hadn't subsided. The need to escape the confines of Juliet's office had him rising from the chair and patting down his pockets for the key to his motorcycle. Then he remembered it was parked back at Juliet's apartment. They'd driven her SUV to work.

"I'm going to get some air," he announced, heading for the door.

The uncertain look on Juliet's face heartened him only slightly.

"Do you want company?" she asked.

"No, I'm good. I just need some time to think."

"OK, well…Keep in touch."

He regarded her more closely. Wearing slender black slacks and a pale pink cardigan that clung to her curves, it almost hurt to look at her. Especially with his memory of how she'd looked naked in her bathtub, climaxing.

What did "Keep in touch" mean? Send her a postcard from the road? Or catch up with her later that evening? He wanted to ask, but Hilary was all eyes and ears waiting for him to say something. Too proud to ask for clarification, he stalked out of the office.

Fresh air and a long walk would help him sort out his thoughts.

Concern tugged at Juliet as the door closed in Tristan's wake.

"I thought he'd be more excited," Hilary confessed.

"Well, it's a lot for him to take in." Juliet crossed her arms and hugged herself. She realized she'd never asked for nor received Tristan's cell phone number. She deliberated chasing after him to get it, but what would that accomplish? The whole point of finding his birth mother was to toss him a bone so he wouldn't resent her when she pushed him away.

She *did* want to push him away, didn't she?

Yes, but maybe not just yet. If Tristan took off to California right away, he might not get around to putting out the fire he'd stoked in her the night before.

"Maybe I should go after him," she mused aloud.

"Oh, no, you can't."

Hilary's assertion wrested Juliet's gaze from the door. "Why not?"

"You're working the Royer case today, remember?"

Juliet rolled her eyes and groaned. "Seriously?" Rolf Royer, a wealthy investor, had hired her to gather evidence that his wife was cheating on him. If not, she would take him to the cleaners when he filed for divorce. "I hate these adultery cases," Juliet declared.

"Yeah, but they pay the bills." Hilary pushed her wheeled chair toward the printer to pluck up a printout. "Here's Mrs. Royer's itinerary." She glanced at it before holding it out to Juliet. "She's probably still at the nail salon on Main Street. If you hurry, you'll get there before she leaves."

5

Tristan eyed the George Mason University campus across the street from Juliet's office with reservation. The substantial buildings, expansive lawns, and tree-lined sidewalks all screamed higher education—an experience he had personally avoided, though his adoptive siblings had both pursued postgraduate degrees.

Students taking advantage of the mild weather lounged on grassy areas flecked with crimson and gold leaves. Making up his mind to tackle the unknown, Tristan crossed the street to cruise a walkway that appeared to lead to the heart of the campus. A hum of intellectual curiosity sharpened the air. Looking at the bright faces of the young adults around him, he realized he was seeing the next generation of doctors and lawyers, teachers and scientists. Suddenly, the future didn't look so bleak.

Would he have become a different man if he'd taken the academic route? As a kid, he'd been too restless to sit in a classroom using only his brain. He'd wanted to challenge his body at the same time. That's what made Special Operations the perfect fit for him. Yes, he'd been the oddball in his family, but his parents had celebrated his uniqueness, and he'd never felt any less worthy. Until now.

He wondered if the young woman coming up the sidewalk

toward him could tell he was the by-product of a sexual liaison between a teenage entertainment star and what had most likely been some groupie?

The pretty redhead blushed at his greeting, smiled, and looked away.

Apparently not.

He didn't need to feel like a worthless, unwanted bastard just because Juliet was rebuffing him. His valiant efforts to woo her were evidently failing, even though he'd endured six months of abstinence for her sake. Apparently, that wasn't enough for her. Now she wanted him to meet his birth mother. What next, jump off a bridge?

Arriving at a plaza boasting a life-sized statue of the university's namesake, Tristan followed the stream of students swarming into a building designated as the Johnson Center. He found himself in an atrium-style food court looking up at the second, third, and fourth levels. The building looked more like a luxury mall or a high-end office complex than a college. His gaze snagged on a door labeled Gateway Library, and he wondered if there might be information not readily available on the internet in a brick and mortar library.

Only one way to find out, he supposed. Climbing the stairs, he pushed into the hushed, multi-level library only to come face-to-face with endless shelves of books. He almost turned and fled. But Tristan reasoned if he could ferret out insurgents hiding in the ruins of a bombed city, he could sure as hell find books about the Main Intelligence Directorate for the Stasi and its mysterious leader.

An elderly lady smiled at him from behind the checkout desk. Aha, an informant! He headed straight for her, determined to make an ally.

Ten minutes later, he sat at a window-side table, about to wade through five books on Dieter Goebel. While he'd never been much of a reader, SEAL training had taught Tristan to be observant. Cracking open the first book, he began his quest for information.

The books proved engrossing—various accounts of moles

like Juliet's mother, people whose ideals had led them to risk their lives sneaking information through the Wall and into Dieter Goebel's hands.

Setting the first book aside, Tristan realized he'd been reading for an hour.

The second, third, and fourth books contained much of the same information, making them redundant. He pushed them aside. In the fifth, he stumbled upon a chapter devoted to Goebel's artwork.

"Hooyah," he muttered, thumbing through the pages and skimming the passages that caught his eye.

The author had included photos of several paintings from Goebel's private collection, which went to auction shortly after his arrest. On each work of art, Goebel had marked his ownership using the Stasi emblem in lieu of a signature. The author provided a close up of that symbol, along with an explanation.

Goebel inked the emblem of the Main Directorate for Intelligence on the back of every painting in his collection. It consists of a hammer signifying the workers of the Democratic Republic, a compass representing the community's thinking men, and a ring of rye representing farmers, all surrounded by a twelve-point star, for the People's Police, as he was its leader.

With rising excitement, Tristan teased his cell phone out of his pocket and took a photo.

Call him naïve, but his instincts told him this emblem was significant. If, in fact, Goebel had identified all the pieces of his collection in this manner, that might make them traceable.

Tristan sat a minute wondering what to do with his discovery. Hilary would want to know, of course. He pulled out her business card while recalling her comment about Hack. Making up his mind to connect the two techno-nerds, Tristan dialed Hack's number instead of Hilary's. He glanced at his watch while waiting for Hack to pick up.

It was just after four. Tristan had become so caught up in research he hadn't realized the sun was already setting on the campus below him. Juliet hadn't sent him so much as a text. Since she'd never asked for his number, how could she?

"What's up?"

Hack's Vermont dialect always tickled Tristan's funny bone.

"Hey, I'm calling from a library," he whispered, gaining several sharp looks from students close enough to overhear him.

"I can't even picture that," Hack stated after a brief pause.

"It's true. Listen, I'm sending you an image via text. It's the Stasi emblem that Dieter Goebel painted on his artwork to identify it as his. Look him up, and you'll see who I mean."

"I know who he was—head of Intelligence for the Stasi."

There wasn't much Hack didn't know. Tristan shook his head, marveling at the genius's range of knowledge.

"I need you to run a search on the picture I'm sending you. See if it shows up anywhere after 1990. I'll call you later. I'm getting dirty looks."

"OK, but—"

Tristan hung up with a grimace of apology for both Hack and the students glaring at him.

Feeling his stomach rumble, he wondered if Juliet had finished her work yet. He'd hoped they might rent a thriller on DVD that evening and hang out at her place. But after her suggestion that he fly out to confront his birth mother, he had reason to doubt she wanted him around.

Maybe he should fly to California like she wanted.

He sat still a moment recalling Cassidy King's hauntingly familiar features. There wasn't any question she had given birth to him.

He had two weeks of leave, and Juliet didn't want him hanging around her place, so why not go west to meet this woman? If he couldn't find a military standby seat, he could purchase eleventh-hour airfare relatively cheap. On the West Coast, he could try to meet Cassidy King, explore the area, and still have leave time left over on the off-chance Juliet changed her mind.

Making a decision as suddenly as he did most things, he pushed back his chair and scooped up the books to return them to the information desk.

Apparently, you didn't have to be a student to get something useful out of a college library.

Juliet pushed the door to her dark apartment open and drew up short.

"Tristan?"

It was nearly ten o'clock at night. She reached out and snapped on the lights. Her astonished gaze searched the empty kitchen. Given the silence of her apartment, Tristan wasn't there. Her fluttering pulse subsided while her thoughts went into overdrive.

Where could he be? His motorcycle was still in the parking garage downstairs. She'd expected to find Tristan kicked back on her couch, waiting for her.

All the way home, Juliet had imagined what he'd been up to while left to his own devices. In her mind's eye, he had cooked her something delicious for dinner, waiting with a glass of wine for her and stories about his day. She had plenty to tell him, in turn, about the shenanigans of Rolf Royer's irresponsible and soon-to-be-ex-wife. The woman had spent two hours getting painted and waxed at her favorite boutique. After that, she'd driven her Lexus to a mansion in McLean that happened to belong to a professional football player.

Juliet had sat outside the ostentatious house in her SUV with her bladder about to burst from sucking down two cups of coffee. The woman had finally emerged with her lover still pawing at her under the lights above his doorstep. Juliet had raised her long-range camera just in time to snap off some highly incriminating photos before putting her car in gear and burning rubber in search of the nearest restroom.

She hadn't heard from Tristan in all that time—not that

she'd ever given him her number. But he'd probably gotten it from Emma or Jeremiah ages ago. Since he wasn't waiting at her office, which Hilary had locked up tight when she'd left work for the day, Juliet had decided Tristan must have found his way back to her apartment.

Except, he wasn't there.

Maybe she should have texted Jeremiah to find out Tristan's number. Why should she have to keep tabs on him, though? *He* was the one who'd swept into her life demanding to be her boyfriend.

She paused to consider his behavior. In all fairness, he hadn't ever used that word. Nor had he demanded much of anything from her. He'd driven her to Arlington to meet her grandmother. He'd bathed her and put her to bed. *Don't think about that!* Her girl parts tingled at the memory. He'd shopped for groceries and cooked breakfast that morning.

And now he wasn't there, which felt very odd because she hadn't expected him to give up so easily.

"Tristan?"

She headed toward her bedroom, hoping to find him passed out on her bed. She knew he'd hardly slept a wink in the past two days. The light blinked on, revealing her empty bed, still unmade from when she'd awakened late that morning.

Juliet wheeled away, marching to her study where Tristan had stowed his duffle bag that morning. Snapping on the light, she stared at the spot on the futon where it had been earlier. The bag wasn't there now, which meant he'd broken back into her apartment to get it, and now he was gone.

Stripped of anticipation, it took her a second to realize Tristan had left a note in place of his belongings. She plucked up the folded piece of paper and warily opened it.

Hey, beautiful. I'm taking the first flight from Dulles to Monterey Regional tomorrow, so I opted to stay at a hotel by the airport. Please look after my bike for me. When I come back, we can finish this. Tristan

She swallowed at the last sentence, her stomach twisting with a mix of relief and consternation.

He'd scribbled his cell phone number at the end of his message, providing her a modicum of comfort. Now she could reach out to him. She'd managed to get rid of him, if only for a while. He'd said he was coming back. And what did *finish this* mean, exactly?

Balling up his note with inexplicable frustration, she hurled it at the trash bin and stalked out of her study to find some supper.

The contents of her refrigerator offered no inspiration. Fortunately, Tristan had put away their leftovers from breakfast, so she had two pieces of bacon and some toast to grind between her teeth.

As she warmed her makeshift meal in the microwave, she stood with her arms crossed, feeling like a cat with its fur rubbed the wrong way.

Juliet had wanted Tristan out of her life; now he was gone. Why was she feeling so put out?

Because he hadn't given her what her body wanted, that was why. He had primed her for sex with his selfless foreplay the night before, and tonight, he wasn't there to follow through. Damn it!

Her bacon popped in the microwave, and she snatched open the appliance, burning her fingers on the hot plate as she pulled it out.

Ouch! Shit! Hot. Hot. The plate clattered onto the counter where she dropped it.

Oh, wait, she had Tristan's phone number. Should she call him? Text him? What would she say to him—that he hadn't needed to leave so suddenly? He'd already ensconced himself in some hotel so he could take the first flight out in the morning. What was his hurry when he had almost two weeks of leave left?

Was it selfish of Juliet to want to stop him at this juncture? Yes. Obviously. She was the reason he had taken off. Guilt bit into her for making Tristan feel unwanted.

"Way to go, Juliet," she muttered, turning to the fridge to get butter for her toast.

She'd just popped the lid off the container when her cell phone rang. Dropping the knife, she pounced on her purse, pulling out the phone with the irrational hope that Tristan was calling.

Seeing Emma's name on her caller ID, she expelled a ragged breath and answered the call. "Hey," she said. "How'd it go?"

Emma had met their newfound grandmother that afternoon, taking Jeremiah and Sammy with her.

"Oh, my gosh," Emma exclaimed. "It was...so bizarre and yet so gratifying."

"Do you like her?"

"I love her! I can see Dad in her when she talks."

"The eyes," Juliet agreed, picking up the knife again and carving out butter to spread on her toast.

"Exactly. Dad got her eyes, and her intelligence, too. And guess what? She used to teach English at the college level, just like me."

"No way."

"And she's giving me her classic book collection, which she keeps in storage."

"Awesome."

"And she told me so many stories about Dad when he was growing up. He sounded just like you, really into information-hunting. Once, when he was ten, he cracked the case of a neighbor's dog that went missing."

Juliet took a bite out of her toast. The crunch of crisp bread between her teeth drowned out the rest of Emma's story.

"That's interesting," she said, realizing Emma was done talking and waiting for Juliet's reaction.

"Oh." Emma hesitated. "Sorry, I wasn't thinking. You've got company right now."

Juliet stopped chewing. "Tristan's not here," she stated tersely.

"Why not?" Emma sounded puzzled. "Where is he?"

"Some hotel near the airport, about to fly out to California to meet his biological mother."

Emma's muffled voice made Juliet realize she'd covered her speaker so she could relay the news to Jeremiah.

"Emma." Juliet tried to recapture her sister's attention.

"You just let him go?" The shrill voice had Juliet pulling the phone from her ear.

"I didn't *let* him do anything. I told him where I found his birth mother, and he took off."

"By himself?"

"Of course, by himself. Tristan is a SEAL. He doesn't need anyone holding his hand."

"But—"

"Listen, I'm eating supper right now. Gotta go." Severing their call with a jab of her finger, Juliet laid the phone on the counter and reached for her bacon. Using her teeth to tear it viciously in half, she lifted a brooding gaze to the dark window overlooking her neighborhood.

Tristan was out there, not too far away, lying alone in some hotel room, wondering how his birth mother was going to receive him.

"I don't need to feel guilty for that," Juliet muttered, pulverizing her meager dinner with her molars. But she did. She felt guilty. And cheated. And oddly alone.

Tristan lurched out of a deep sleep to the sound of his phone ringing. He found himself sprawled face down on the bed in the hotel room, having collapsed there in a fit of despondency over an hour earlier, according to the bedside clock.

"S'up?" he asked, recognizing Hack's number with a pang of disappointment. It wasn't Juliet calling to wish him bon voyage. She was probably glad to see the last of him.

"Oh, were you sleeping?" Hack asked.

Tristan cleared his throat and rolled over, rubbing the grit from his eyes. "Yeah, well, some people do that, you know."

But not Hack, who seemed to be up at all hours of the night keeping tabs on terrorists lurking on the internet.

"You said you'd call me back and you never did," Hack reminded him.

"Oh, yeah. Sorry." Tristan had been a bit preoccupied with thoughts of landing on Cassidy King's doorstep unannounced. Plus, he'd been feeling sorry for himself. If Juliet had been so relieved to see him gone, Tristan had to doubt his ability to win her over, even if he was able to track down Goebel through his scattered art collection.

Unwilling to throw in the towel just yet, he swung his feet to the floor and started at the beginning, explaining to Hack why Juliet was looking for Goebel. Right up to the part where her mother had been a mole.

"No shit," Hack exclaimed.

Tristan gave his buddy a condensed version of the facts uncovered over the previous two days, adding that Goebel might have tracked Anya down, exacting revenge for her betrayal.

"I suppose it's possible," Hack commented. "When East Germany crumbled in '89, Goebel got tossed into prison only to disappear right out of it two years later. How he managed his escape remains a mystery. There are lots of conspiracy theories about that."

"Well, fast toward twenty-two years." Tristan interrupted before Hack could dive into a history lesson. "The night Anya and her husband were killed, Juliet saw a stranger peering in one of the windows of the wrecked car, making sure her parents were dead. So the million-dollar question is, could it have been Goebel? Or did he send someone to kill her on his behalf?"

"That's two questions," Hack pointed out.

"Right. But we start with Goebel. Maybe we can locate him by tracking down his art. If he was that passionate about it, he might have tried to reassemble his collection."

"That's not a bad tactic," Hack agreed. "Since he identified these pieces with his mark, there might be some record of them showing up in a transaction somewhere. I'll see what I can find in online art auctions."

Tristan could almost hear the gears turning in Hack's head. "Thanks," he said. "Uh, listen, I'll be on a plane for most of the day tomorrow. If you find anything interesting, you'll need to contact Juliet's assistant. She's a geek like you," he added, "only smoking hot and conveniently available." Unlike someone else who was smoking hot but wanted nothing to do with a relationship.

Hack went warily quiet.

"I'll send you a picture of her business card. She wants to see if you're any better at finding information than she is. I guess she's got a competitive streak. Please call her tomorrow if you find anything. Here's your chance to impress a woman. Go ahead and knock her socks off," he encouraged, picturing Hilary's garter and stockings.

"Come on," Hack mumbled. "You know I can't talk to women."

Hack had been raised by a single mother. He ought to know how to talk to women. "Dude, if I haven't seen you staring at hot chicks, I would think you were gay. Not that I'd care if you were. I'd find you a hot guy instead."

"I'm not gay," Hack insisted.

"OK. Prove it. You still have Oscar, right?" Tristan was familiar with Hack's leopard-sized cat.

"Yeah," Hack said with a question in his voice.

"Send her a picture of him. She's crazy about cats."

Hack heaved a sigh. "Fine," he finally agreed. "Let me have her number."

"I'll send you her contact info now. Get some sleep," Tristan added, ending the call. Taking a picture of Hilary's business card, he forwarded it to his teammate.

Pleased with his matchmaking efforts, Tristan put his phone down, snapped off the light, and laid down only to stare at the hotel-room ceiling. His hopes had been so high yesterday. He'd been sure that after meeting Juliet's challenge to forgo dating for six months she would welcome him with open arms.

Instead, she'd deflected his efforts to win her over, then tossed him a bone in an obvious ploy to distract him.

Hell, Hack had more chance of finding happily ever after with Hilary than Tristan had with Juliet.

Heaving a long, despondent sigh, he closed his eyes and fell asleep.

6

Juliet rubbed her aching temple while fighting not to close her burning eyes. The client seated in her office continued to rant. She'd come bursting through the door about an hour earlier, red in the face and hot under the collar. For twenty minutes, the plump brunette had complained about her lying, conniving, philandering asshole of a husband who'd been cheating for over a year.

This, Juliet reminded herself, *is why I am single.*

Then she thought of Tristan who would be landing in California in a couple of hours. The sense of loss that flooded her made her want to pick up one of the magazines next to her and lob it at her newest client's head.

She had hardly slept the previous night. Not like the one before that, when she'd slept so deeply she hadn't even been aware of Tristan sharing her bed. Unlike most males, the man didn't snore. She'd learned that much about him back in Mexico. He had put her to bed, made her breakfast, and been so helpful in regard to her personal crisis that Juliet now felt ill-equipped without Tristan at her side.

Sure, she still had Hilary, who was hammering at her keyboard in her corner of the office, following every loose thread Goebel might have left behind. But Hilary didn't make her feel the way Tristan did.

Good thing he's gone, then, Juliet's logic insisted. *If he got under your skin in less than a day, imagine what could have happened if he'd stuck around.*

"How much do you charge?" the new client asked, breaking into Juliet's private thoughts.

Seizing the chance to wrap up their initial interview, Juliet popped out of her chair and crossed to her file cabinet to pull out some paperwork. "My fees are laid out in this agreement. It'll depend, of course, on how long it takes to prove your husband's infidelity. From everything you've said, he doesn't go to great lengths to hide his indiscretions. It shouldn't take long."

"Good, because I only have five hundred dollars."

"That should cover it," Juliet replied. Like Hilary had said the other day, adultery cases were their bread and butter. She would much rather track down an arsonist or find a missing teenager, but those other jobs didn't come along as often as the former. "Why don't you fill this out and give it to my assistant when you've finished?"

Hilary's ruby head tipped in their direction.

"I need to head out for a while," Juliet said to her. "Let me know if you make any progress on that Goebel case, will you?"

"Sure." Hilary's flat tone intimated she wasn't getting anywhere with her research.

Grabbing her purse, Juliet bid goodbye to her newest client —she'd forgotten the woman's name already—and left the building.

A bright sun stabbed her eyes as she pushed through the door onto the bustling sidewalk. Well-heeled yuppies on their lunch breaks were hotfooting it to the nearest eateries for lunch.

Any other day, Juliet might have joined them. Today, she needed to work out—hard—before she hurt somebody.

Her foul mood, she assured herself, had nothing to do with Tristan taking off. But she imagined him in Carmel, California, mingling with tanned and voluptuous movie stars. Golden Boy —that was the nickname Tristan's teammates had given him.

With his movie-star looks, he was one SEAL who would fit right in on the West Coast. She couldn't help but wonder if he might enjoy himself there getting to know the local women. She sure hadn't gone out of her way to show him a good time here.

Why are you jealous?

It made no sense not to want Tristan for herself while seething at the thought of him with someone else. She'd only spent a day with him. He could not have gotten to her in that short a time.

Could he?

Engrossed in a firsthand, online account of innocent civilians tortured by Dieter Goebel for various offenses against the Republic, Hilary ignored her cell phone as its chime signaled the arrival of a text message. The German citizen's description of how Goebel had chained his victim to the wall in a sewer where rats and vermin had crawled all over him made her shudder. His wasn't the only story of torture at the hands of Dieter Goebel. Hilary's loathing for the former spymaster had risen with every document she'd read.

It struck her as bizarre that this monster had patronized the arts to such a degree he'd kept starving artists from living on the streets.

Her phone chimed a second time, reminding her of the message. Plucking it off her desk, she frowned at the unfamiliar number texting her from the Virginia Beach area code. But the message let her know right away who it was.

Hey, I'm Stuart Rudolph, it said, *Tristan's teammate.* Right below those words was a picture of a Maine Coon cat, ear tufts and all. It looked big enough to eat a human.

Hilary admired the gorgeous creature, thought for a moment, then typed, *I'm Hilary,* and appended a picture of her orange and black calico with its big green eyes.

She waited for Stuart Rudolph to make his next move.

After several minutes, he replied. *I hear you're looking for Dieter Goebel. I found out something you might want to know.*

Right. Like this guy had found something she hadn't. *Like what?* Hilary texted.

Like the CIA offered him asylum in the U.S.

The ridiculous assertion made her laugh out loud. *That's BS,* she typed, her thumbs moving at the speed of light. *Why would they do that?*

He promptly answered. *U.S. agents in Russia were disappearing without a trace. CIA knew they had a leak and thought Goebel knew who it was, given he was friendly with Russia. Turned out to be Aldrich Ames. Ring a bell?*

Yes, she replied. Ames had been caught, suggesting Goebel might have admitted what he knew in exchange for a prison break and asylum. *What's your source?* she demanded.

Can't say, came the immediate response.

She frowned at Stuart's reply. *So you have access to sources you can't share with me?*

Roger that.

His military jargon disarmed her. Guys in the armed services—that was her weakness. For some women, it was chocolate; for others, wine. Not her. She'd been raised a military brat, living on bases all around the world while her father served in the U.S. Army. There was nothing sexier than a buff man in battle dress uniform who talked like G.I. Joe. Or texted like one, in this case.

Brilliant, she typed back. *Let's say you're right. Goebel was offered asylum in the U.S., presumably under a false name. He might have had his appearance altered, but why bother since no one knew what he looked like? I don't suppose your source tells us where he went.*

Nope. Can't penetrate the Justice Department...yet.

She smirked at his confident qualifier.

Tristan mentioned Goebel was a painter, Stuart tacked on.

She typed her reply. *Right, and he signed his original pieces with an emblem used by the Stasi.* Tristan had sent her the image the night before, along with an explanation of what it was.

Ding! Stuart sent her the identical image. Tristan must have sent it to him, too.

That's the one, she texted. *I'm looking all over the web for it. Managed to track down one of the paintings in Chile, but that's all I've found so far. It's up for sale at an auction house in Santiago.*

Need some help? Stuart asked.

Hilary's pride resisted. On the other hand, she was enjoying their text exchange, and the temptation of working with a Navy SEAL to solve a mystery was simply too good to pass up. She deliberated her next step.

Sure, she wrote, *but I don't trust anyone I can't see. Next time, Skype me.*

He took his sweet time answering. *I'll find something before you do.*

"Well, aren't you a confident SOB," she murmured. *Game on,* she texted back.

Putting her phone down, she jumped back online, determined to beat Stuart Rudolph to the prize. Her poor kitty would be starving by the time she got home, but Mitzie could survive for a week on the fat hanging around her midsection. What's more, Hilary would get to charge Juliet for the extra hours, which meant she could afford to indulge in another of her passions—shopping for new clothes.

Tristan considered the fleet of rental cars available at the airport and narrowed his choice to the small collection of sports cars enlivening the parking garage with their vivid colors—a red Mustang, yellow Camaro, or lime green GTO.

"Can I help you, sir?"

The roar of a plane taking off from the adjacent runway nearly drowned out the attendant's voice.

Under normal circumstances, Tristan would be salivating at the prospect of driving away in any one of the sports cars. However, he had to admit, he was still feeling the sting of Juliet's disinterest in him. It was now 6 p.m. on the east coast and she had yet to call or text, even though he'd left his number. She ought to have more interest in his undertaking since she was the one who'd suggested it.

Obviously, she could not care less where he went or what he did, so long as he left her the hell alone.

"Is the Camaro available?" Driving a vibrant yellow car ought to cheer him up. "I'm a gold cad member." Tristan whipped out his special membership card, one that identified him as a former sponsored driver and got him a sweet new ride wherever he went.

"Yes, of course, Mr.—" the agent glanced down at his card, "—Halliday." When he looked up again, his eyes had doubled in size. "Hey, didn't you used to race Number 33 for NASCAR?"

Pleased to be recognized five years after leaving the circuit, Tristan managed a smile. "That's me."

"It's a pleasure to meet you in person," the attendant avowed, sticking his hand out for Tristan to shake. "No need to fill out any paperwork with the elite member status. I just need to ask you a couple of questions, get your signature, and you'll be on your way."

Tristan's stomach clenched at the reminder. On his way to Carmel to meet his birth mother for the first time. He wasn't sure he was ready to do that—not tonight, anyway.

Ten minutes later, he had programmed his mother's address, supplied by Hilary, into the Camaro's navigation system and was pulling away from Monterey Regional, headed for Highway One. Lowering his windows, he invited the cool air to kiss his face and brighten his somber mood. With a deeply drawn breath, he tried to discern the briny scent of the Pacific Ocean, but he was too far inland to detect it.

California wasn't foreign to him. Like all SEALs, he'd spent the most grueling six months of his life training in Coronado, and he'd been back a time or two for more work-related activities. The terrain and climate this far north were nothing like Coronado, though. Here, low-lying hills undulated in all directions, topped by hardy trees, all cloaked in a thin mist.

He passed an organic fruit farm and the trellises of a vineyard. Prompted by his navigation system, he took a ramp at well over the speed limit and found himself on the coastal highway, still too far inland to glimpse the ocean.

It wasn't until he'd bypassed Monterey and was headed toward Carmel-by-the-Sea that the ocean, with the sun sinking like a fiery disc into its depths, came into view. He thought at once of Juliet and wished she were with him.

Glancing at his silenced cell phone, he noticed that he'd missed a call from her.

"Son of a bitch." He snatched up his cell phone to listen to her message, but there wasn't one.

To his great relief, she texted while his phone was still in his hand. *Safe travels. Let me know how it goes.*

The tension in his shoulders eased. The scowl on his face relaxed. Juliet had been thinking about him after all. Turning on his ringer, he ignored the impulse to respond and set his phone in the cup holder. Just knowing she'd been thinking of him beat back his despondency.

Up the road ahead of him, he glimpsed the town of Carmel through the trees. Backdropped by the glimmering ocean and the orange sunset, the picturesque view dazzled him. What better time than now to meet his long-lost mother? If they became friends, Juliet could hardly accuse him of still having abandonment issues, could she?

Prompted by the car's navigational system, he exited the highway then wound his way through a trendy neighborhood. Modest, well cared for homes surrounded him. Charmed by their appeal, he relaxed a little more. This meeting was meant to be. Everything would turn out right.

His mother, so young and possibly powerless when she'd given birth, would be thrilled to have him in her life again. Especially since he required nothing from her but acknowledgment.

An apology would be nice, too, but he wasn't expecting one.

"Your destination is on the left. 13 Palou Avenue," said his navigation system.

Tristan braked abruptly and stared at the tiny sage-green house behind the green fence. Fallen leaves were decomposing in the gutters. Blinds covered every window. The brick walk was cracked and filled with weeds. This house didn't look as loved as those surrounding it.

Parking at the curb behind an older-model Neon, Tristan killed the engine and sat a moment. Butterflies swarmed in his stomach. He'd busted down the doors of plenty of insurgents' houses, and, for some reason, this shuttered cottage reminded him of one. Maybe his mother didn't live here anymore. Maybe Hilary had given him the wrong address.

"Let's do this," he said, blowing out a breath and pushing his car door open.

Ten steps along a weed-choked walk convinced him that his mother wasn't home. Three old newspapers littered the front stoop. His mother might have gone to Bali on vacation, or something, and that was the reason she was letting her house go to pot.

Just to make sure she wasn't home, he applied his knuckles to the door and was startled to hear a dog bark. The sound reminded him of how Hilary had tracked down his mother. That must be Dolly barking her head off. Unexpected queasiness gripped his stomach as he strained his ears for the sound of a human occupant.

"Stop that." A female voice scolded the dog scratching at the inside of the door.

The blind at the nearest window crimped, and a woman peeked out.

His mother? Swallowing hard, Tristan wiped his sweating palms on the seat of his jeans and waited.

The door opened a scant three inches, caught by a safety chain. A poodle's snout poked through the opening at knee-height. "Yes?"

Was this his mother? Given the shadows behind her, all he could see were bloodshot eyes set in a haggard face. "Um. I'm looking for Casey Edwards."

Silence followed his announcement. "May I ask why?" the woman asked and, this time, he detected a familiar lilt of his native North Carolina dialect.

Tristan jammed his fingers into his pockets. "Well, I'm...I'm her son," he said, bracing himself for the woman's reaction.

After seconds of shocked silence, the chain scraped, and the door opened wide. The dog rushed out to greet Tristan. The porch light flicked on, spotlighting the woman as she stepped out to join him. "Casey never had a son," she said, but her keen examination of his face suggested she could see the resemblance.

"You're not Casey, are you?" Tristan asked. She looked too old to be his mother, who would still be in her forties.

"I'm her sister, Margot."

"Oh. I'm sorry. I thought Casey lived here."

Margot froze, and the lines on her face deepened. "She did live here. I came to...take her dog and pack up her stuff."

Tristan tried to read between the lines. "You mean, she moved?"

The woman—his aunt, he realized—shook her head and pressed her lips together in a bid to retain her composure. "No, hon. She passed, 'bout two weeks ago."

The word *passed* tore through Tristan like a bullet fired at close range. "As in died? From what?"

"Overdose," Margot said after a moment's hesitation. Her moist gaze registered his shock with compassion. "I'm sorry," she added.

The stoop under Tristan's feet seemed to tip. "I'm too late," he realized out loud. Now he'd never get to meet his birth mother, and she would never get to know him—a reunion that might have turned her life around. Apparently, she'd struggled with addiction. Maybe she'd turned to drugs after giving him away. Maybe...

Margot laid a tentative hand on his arm. "Why don't you come inside?" she offered kindly. "I found something of Casey's I think you should see."

Feeling numb all over, he followed his aunt inside.

7

Juliet groaned and rolled over in bed. The glowing numbers on the digital alarm clock signaled it was way too early to get up. Especially since it was Saturday and she could sleep in as late as she wanted. Her grueling workout the day before was supposed to help her sleep. Instead, she had tossed and turned the entire night wondering what Tristan was up to and why he hadn't returned her text asking if he'd met his mother yet.

Reaching for her cell phone, she took one look at the blank home screen and slammed it down again. "Ugh!"

Why had he bothered giving her his number if he didn't intend to text her back? Had he forgotten her already? Was he, even now, sleeping in the arms of some willing one-night stand he had picked up in downtown Carmel?

At that thought, Juliet jackknifed to a sitting position. Resentment burned in her empty stomach. Tristan had no right to leave her in the dark this way. She deserved to know whether he'd found his mother and what had ensued. If not for Juliet, Tristan never would have located the woman!

She would call and leave a voice mail since Tristan was probably sleeping. It was easier to convey her frustration that way than by text. Snatching up her phone again, Juliet accessed his number and thumbed the call button.

The ringer shrilled twice, then to her surprise, he answered in a slow, deep drawl, "Well, speak of the devil."

His southern accent was stronger than usual. "What are you doing up?" Juliet demanded.

"Well, technically, I ain't up. I'm lyin' flat on my back, and the ceiling is spinning."

"Why is the ceiling spinning?" She didn't really need to ask. She could tell by his slurred speech he was drunk as a skunk.

"Because I missed my mother by two weeks."

"You mean she wasn't there?"

"Nope. Not there, not here, not anywhere, anymore. She died two weeks ago. Overdose."

Holy shit! Tristan's words hit her like a punch in the stomach, rendering her speechless. "Oh, Tristan," she finally exclaimed.

He heaved a sigh. "Yeah."

"I'm so sorry." Guilt, remorse, and pity collided inside of her. Juliet wanted to reach out and hug him. Only, she'd shipped him to the other side of the country.

"Me, too."

"You said…she overdosed?"

"'Cording to her sister, Cassidy was addicted to pain pills. She took one too many, and her heart stopped."

"That's horrible." Tristan had to be thinking the same thing Juliet was—if he'd shown up just a few weeks earlier, Cassidy might have had more reason to overcome her addiction. "You know it's not your fault, right?" Juliet rushed to assure him.

"That's what Aunt Margot said."

"Aunt Margot?"

"My mother's sister. We talked for a long time. She showed me photos of my mom's life. And guess what?"

"What?" She smiled a bit, thinking he sounded like a little boy when he was drunk.

"I found out who my dad is."

Another surprise. Juliet swung her feet to the floor and stood up to pace the length of her bedroom. "You did? Aunt Margot knew?"

"She found pictures of him in my mom's album. Looks just like me—I mean, I look just like him, only he's got dark hair. His name's Gary Sigmund. I wanna find him."

"OK," Juliet assured him. "Sure, with a name like that he can't be too hard to find. Do you know anything about him?"

"Uh, yep. He was a Marine stationed at Camp Lejeune, an' my mother met him when she gave a concert there."

"Wow. That's great. If Sigmund's active duty or former military, that makes him even easier to find." She stopped pacing and tightened her grip on the phone. "Are you all right?"

He gave a bitter laugh. "You sound like you care."

His words stung. "Of course I care. I'm the one who sent you there." *Two weeks too late.* But she didn't say that out loud. "Where are you now?" she asked.

"'N a motel room," he said, turning four words into one, "in Carmel."

"You do realize it's two in the morning out there?"

"Why are *you* awake?" Tristan asked, showing more astuteness than she would have wagered, considering his condition.

"You didn't reply to my text," Juliet accused. "I was starting to worry."

"So I kept you awake," he deduced on a satisfied note.

"I don't sleep well generally," she countered.

He made a sexy sound in his throat. "You slept pretty well when I was there."

Touché, she thought, scrounging for a quick comeback and not finding one. "What's your plan now?" she asked instead. "Are you going to fly back or...?" Hearing the hopefulness in her voice, she snapped her mouth shut.

"Nah," he said, causing her hopes to plummet.

"Why not?" Juliet strove to hide her disappointment.

"I don't know. I was lookin' at some brochures here in the room. Since I came all the way out here, might as well make a vacation of it. There's plenty to see and do. I could go zip-lining through a redwood forest or whale watching off the coast."

Unexpected envy needled Juliet. Recalling the fun they'd had riding ATVs through the jungle in Beliz, she suddenly wished she were on vacation with Tristan.

"Suit yourself," she snapped.

"Made any progress on your end?" Tristan asked, shifting the focus onto Juliet. "Have you tracked down Goebel yet?"

She grimaced. "No, not yet. Hilary says she's following a lead, and your friend Hack is helping her."

"That's good. Hack'll help." His speech began to slur again.

"You sound exhausted," she said. "Why don't you get some sleep? I'll look for a Marine named Gary Sigmund later today and call you if I find anything."

"OK. Thanks for callin', honey."

Tristan's gentle tone made it impossible to reprimand him, so Juliet let him get away with the endearment. "Good night, then," she said, hanging up before she said something stupid—like, she missed him.

Three thousand miles away, Tristan dropped his cell phone over his heart and felt his heartache wane.

"Well, I'll be damned," he murmured. Absence really *did* make the heart grow fonder.

Yesterday Juliet had done her best to get rid of him. Yet today—or was it tomorrow already?—she was missing him, whether she wanted to admit it or not. Professional curiosity wasn't her only reason for calling in the middle of the night. He'd heard a faint trace of longing in her voice when she'd asked if he was coming home. Hell if it didn't make him want to fly straight back to her. But he couldn't do that. He had promised his aunt he would visit his mother's grave with her tomorrow.

It was going to kill him, but he had to spend at least one more day in California before heading back. His previous persistence had scared Juliet into pushing him away. He was better off playing it cool, giving distance the chance to make her heart grow fonder. By the time he did go back, perhaps she would have warmed to him a little.

He fell asleep hugging that hope to his heart.

Saturday mornings, Hilary left her laptop in her computer bag. On this particular Saturday, she slept in, rousing around ten. An hour of leisure passed while sipping coffee and poring over the newspaper. Finally, she dressed in figure-hugging Spandex and a neon-colored tank top. Drawing plenty of attention to herself, she took a brisk walk in the park not far from her apartment, all the while scoping out potential boyfriends while avoiding guys with dogs. Sure, they made easy targets. Unfortunately, Mitzie hated dogs, which eliminated a good sixty percent of all males under the age of thirty-five. If Hilary didn't love her cat so darn much, she'd get a lot more dates.

Having no success attractive love on this particular morning, Hilary returned from her walk to shower and eat lunch. At two, she stuck her new credit card into her purse and headed for the door, intent on purchasing the lingerie she'd been eyeing at Tyson's Corner Mall. Her hand was on the door when she heard the distinct tone that meant someone was asking to Skype with her.

Her pulse leaped. Stuart Rudolph? Snatching the phone from her pocket, Hilary took one look at the Maine Coon cat preening himself on the screen and decided her outing could wait. She tossed her purse on the nearest chair and hunted for Mitzie.

The black and white calico was nowhere to be found.

Hilary raced into her bedroom, dropped to her knees and peered beneath the bed. Not there.

"Mitzie!" she called. Stu was likely to give up if she didn't answer. With no cat to put on the screen, she would have to show her face.

Dear God.

She cast a quick glance toward the mirror to assess her appearance. Her charming yellow blouse flattered the glow achieved during her earlier walk. Her spiked hair stood up just right. She had recently applied her makeup and lipstick, so why not? Accepting the call with a press of her thumb, Hilary smiled brightly at the camera and said, "Hello, Stuart."

The Maine Coon looked up as if to answer her greeting, but only silence followed.

"Are you there?" Hilary asked, checking their connection.

"Yeah. Yeah, I'm here," a deep voice with a faint northern accent came through the phone speaker. "Is that really you?"

The view on her screen panned from the cat to a handsome young man wearing a bemused expression. With dark expressive eyes, a lean face and a cleft chin, he looked nothing like any techno-geek she had ever met. Hilary sank into the same armchair where she'd tossed her purse.

"Who else would it be?" she asked with a nervous giggle.

"I pictured an older lady," he said, sounding and looking dazed.

She touched the short red strands of her pixie cut. "My hair color must be blinding you."

"No, I like it. You're really pretty." He looked away as if appalled by the words that had come out of him.

The compliment, so artless and sincere, made Hilary's face heat. "Thank you," she replied. "So what's up? Did you find something?"

She'd be shocked if he had. She'd stayed late at the office the night before, searching the web *ad nauseam*, only to admit defeat around midnight.

"Yep. Let me show you." As she watched, he carried his phone across what appeared to be his bedroom. She caught sight of a Star Trek poster on the wall.

"Wait, you a Trekkie?" she asked, pouncing on the telltale clue.

"What?" The question seemed to startle Stuart. He glanced self-consciously toward the poster. "Yeah. No. Not really." And he repositioned the camera so that all she could see was his strong jaw and broad chest as he sat down in a computer chair.

Hilary's gaze locked on the swell of pectoral muscles clearly visible under the clingy fabric of his unfashionable sweater. The man clearly spent as much time working out as he did surfing the web.

"OK, check this out," he said.

She couldn't see his keyboard, but she could hear the keys clicking a mile a minute suggesting he typed even faster than she did.

"I've been searching for the emblem Goebel inked onto the back of his artwork. No luck finding any of his pieces. But look what I found painted on a mural in the Mission District of San Francisco."

He hit a final key, then turned his phone toward his computer monitor. Hilary squinted as his camera brought the new image into focus.

"There. Do you see it?" A long, finger appeared to point out an illustration integrated within an elaborate vignette. "That's Goebel's emblem, right there."

He moved his phone even closer, and suddenly she could see it for herself—exactly as it had looked in the illustration Tristan found.

"There's the hammer, the compass, and the circle of wheat, all surrounded by a twelve-point star."

A frisson of excitement shot through Hilary. She jumped up from the armchair and headed for her laptop, still stored in her computer bag.

"What's the Mission District?" she asked, setting the laptop on her dinette table and turning it on. With her phone propped against the screen, they could see each other as Stuart turned his camera back around.

"It's a neighborhood in San Francisco, primarily populated by Latinos but known for its art community."

"Art?" Hilary waited impatiently for the laptop to boot.

"This emblem is part of a huge mural started during the Chicano movement in the 1970s."

"Explain the movement," she requested as she logged in.

"Hispanic artists used their paintings to raise awareness of civil rights issues, police brutality, lack of social services, and so on."

"The same way Goebel used art to convey his Marxist philosophies. What's the URL?" she asked.

Following Stuart to the website, she browsed the photos of a long wall completely covered in bright vignettes of people acting out their daily struggles with police, powerful companies, and land owners.

"Wow, the murals are incredibly colorful." The bright yellows, reds, and blues appealed to Hilary. "I wonder how the Stasi emblem ended up painted there."

"Right. Who painted it and why?" he agreed. "Was it some random artist wanting to commemorate Marxist history or could Goebel have commissioned it? Maybe he painted it himself, claiming ownership of the entire mural, the way he owned his art collection."

"That's a little farfetched." Hilary brought him back to reality. "You just said the Chicano movement started in the 70s when Goebel was still in East Germany heading up the Stasi. He didn't disappear from prison until 1992."

"True, but since he was offered asylum in the States, he *could've* painted it after he came here. We need to find out, at least."

A memory niggled at Hilary. Didn't the man who matched Juliet's composite sketch also live in San Francisco? What were the odds of the same city popping up in two separate searches? Hilary crossed her arms beneath her breasts as she thought.

Stuart's gaze predictably went to the cleavage she'd created.

She hid a knowing smile. Keeping men off balance was her forte. Back in college, the other girls had called her a tease, but what was the point of having giant boobs if you couldn't put them to good use or have them admired? "You're staring," she commented.

He jerked his gaze up guiltily.

"It's OK." Hilary smiled at Stuart invitingly.

"Sorry," he mumbled, as a ruddy color crept across his cheekbones.

The temptation to rattle his cage rode Hilary hard. The panicked look in Stuart Rudolph's eyes warned her not to. She would move a little more slowly lest she scare the man away. She reconsidered the web page.

"Who owns the wall?" she asked.

"I checked. The city has ownership, but a nonprofit called The People's Eyes gained approval to paint whatever walls they wanted within eight city blocks."

"The People's Eyes," she repeated. The intriguing name had her typing it into a Google search bar to learn more. "Says here the director and founder is Renata Blumenthal, age fifty-nine. Isn't that a German name?"

"German and Jewish," Stuart confirmed, proving he'd already asked himself the same question.

"Goebel was Jewish, too." Hilary scratched her chin thoughtfully.

"There are lots of German Jews in the world," Stuart pointed out. "On the other hand, the fact that she's fifty-nine means she was in her twenties at the end of the Cold War."

"The same age as Anya Ausfeld," Hilary noted. "I think I need to call this Renata Blumenthal and ask about the emblem."

He inclined his head toward the camera. "Don't tell her what you're looking for. Make her share what she knows first."

His cautionary statement accompanied by the hardening of his expression betrayed the warrior in him. Hilary's pulse fluttered. "Right," she agreed. "Life is like a game of chess. You don't want to reveal your strategy too soon."

Stuart brightened. "Do you play chess?"

"I'm great at it," she avowed, leaning closer to her screen.

"Your eyes are an interesting color," he blurted.

Was he trying to flirt? He'd offered the words the same way he'd told her she was pretty, like he couldn't control what came out of his mouth.

Hilary leaned closer to her phone and blinked at him. "You think?"

"They're also really big." His gaze dipped toward her breasts again.

"Well, thank you. Your eyes are like dark chocolate. I like to melt it and drizzle it on—"

"You could call Blumenthal," he cut in, changing the subject on a nervous note. "Tell her you're an art student and ask about the emblem."

Hilary's lips twisted in momentary defeat. The poor man hadn't had much practice flirting, had he? "I could," she allowed, "but I don't know a damn thing about art."

"Me neither," he admitted.

"I'll put Juliet up to it," she decided. Unwilling to end their conversation just yet, Hilary added, "Watcha up to this weekend?" It was a shot in the dark, but maybe she could talk him into meeting her in person.

"Uh…," he cast around for an answer. "Not much. Just hanging around online."

"On a weekend?" Hilary scoffed at the mere idea. "Has anyone told you that you need to get a life?"

"My teammates have suggested it. They say I need to get a hobby."

"I can think of a hobby you'd like." Batting her eyelashes, Hilary gave him time to draw his own conclusions. "You know, if you're ever up in Northern Virginia, we could get together," she suggested, "and watch reruns of *Star Trek*."

His dark eyes glowed with interest. "You like *Star Trek*?"

"Love it. I've watched every episode of every Trek series, and now I'm a fan of the movies. The special effects just keep getting better. Did you notice in the last movie how a bubble formed around the *Enterprise* when it moved into warp speed?"

A smile lit up his face, turning him so handsome that Hilary's breath hitched. "I saw that," he exclaimed with boyish enthusiasm. "It was like space was bending around the ship which, if you've ever read Miguel Alcubierre's theory of faster-than-light warp drive, is exactly what happens. Are you into the special effects?"

"Ah, sort of." Having never heard of Alcubierre's theory, Hilary steered Stuart's focus elsewhere. "Mostly it's the characters that do it for me. Jim and Spock have a serious bromance going on in the movies."

The crease reappeared on the SEAL's high forehead.

He'd obviously never heard of a bromance. "You know, that deep, emotional bond between men. Being on a SEAL team, you have to know what I mean."

"Bromance," Stuart repeated the term on a dubious note.

"Oh, come on. It's not what it sounds like." Hilary tossed her head back with a laugh. "It's just intimate—and totally arousing from a woman's perspective. You know how we women feel about intimacy."

Her words rendered him mute. She watched his Adam's apple bob.

"Anyway," Hilary heaved a sigh of long-suffering, "I'd better call my boss and tell her what you found. Thanks for your help, Stuart. I'll let you know what comes of this."

"Yeah." He visibly roused himself. "No problem. Anytime."

"Talk to you later?" Hilary asked hopefully.

"Sure," he agreed.

As she went to end the call, Hilary saw Stuart's gaze slide one more time toward her breasts. Melting back into her chair, she fanned her hot face.

"Oh, my," she exclaimed. "One day, I am so going to ride that stallion."

The shrill ring of her cell phone startled her out of her fantasies. She glanced at her caller ID and read Juliet's name. "What's up, Jules?" she answered. "I was just about to call you."

"On a Saturday?" Juliet sounded highly skeptical.

"Yep. I've been talking to Tristan's friend, Stuart. We've discovered a lead. But tell me why you called first."

"I need your help finding someone."

"Wouldn't be the first time," Hilary muttered, thinking of Juliet's inability to find a date. "Who it is?"

"Tristan's birth mother is dead. She died two weeks ago of an overdose."

Hilary clutched her heart at the awful news "Get out. That's terrible!"

"Yeah, but Tristan met his aunt who gave him the name of his biological father. In '88, his father was a Marine lieutenant based at Camp Lejeune. I've found traces of his existence on the web, but there's nothing current. He doesn't have any social media accounts. Can you find him?"

"Pfff. Of course I can," Hilary asserted. And if she couldn't, she was fairly certain Stuart Rudolph could.

"What's the new lead you found with Tristan's teammate?" Juliet demanded.

"Stuart found Goebel's emblem on a mural in San Francisco." Saying Stuart's name like they were already a team made Hilary feel good.

"Seriously? San Francisco?"

"Yep."

"Isn't that where the match from my composite lives—Hans Coenen?"

"It is. And I'm finding that a bit of a coincidence."

"So am I," Juliet replied. "We need to dig more on him."

"The mural is located in the Mission District and owned by a nonprofit group called The People's Eyes, run by a woman named Renata Blumenthal."

"That's a German name," Juliet said, sounding more excited by the moment.

"*Jawohl*," Hilary replied.

"OK, I know it's the weekend, but I really need you to show me that mural. And I need your help finding Tristan's father. Please come to the office?" Juliet's tone became pursuasive.

"Ugh." Hilary threw herself back into her chair and sulked for a second. She'd have to wait another day to buy that bra and panty set. "Fine," she finally agreed. "But I want time and a half, and I still want Sunday and Monday off. It's a federal holiday," she tacked on stubbornly.

"Deal," said her boss, albeit reluctantly.

"See you in twenty."

Packing up her laptop, Hilary wondered if Stuart Rudolph had Columbus Day off. And what were the odds of convincing him to meet in person?

8

"What to look for first?" Juliet wondered out loud.

Hovering over Hilary's shoulder, she bit hard on her lower lip, impatient to uncover information buried by time. The office building echoed with Saturday morning silence. Every other professional was away enjoying his or her three-day weekend. While she'd never make money parking herself in her office today, Juliet had to find Tristan's father as much as she had to find her parents' killer. Enjoying a holiday break was not an option.

"Let's start with Tristan's father," she decided, eager to make amends for sending Tristan to California two weeks too late. "It's Gary Sigmund, spelled the normal way. He'd be around fifty or so. I already tried the white pages, PeopleFinder, and Intelius."

"And you think he's still in the military," Hilary recalled.

"Right. Because he has no social media sites. Armed services personnel are discouraged to post anything online about themselves and their loved ones. Not a good idea in today's social climate. So it's possible Sigmund's still active duty."

"In that case, he ought to be in the personnel directory on the Navy Marine Corps Intranet," her assistant deduced.

Juliet frowned. "I'm pretty sure NMCI is a classified site."

"Oh, it is. But I have a password," Hilary stated breezily.

Juliet cut her an appraising glance. "Let me guess. You slept with that bald guy in your building, the government contractor?"

Hilary rolled her eyes at Juliet's disgusted tone. "You are such a prude. That's why you're working in your office on a Saturday while the hunk who wants to be your boyfriend is zip-lining in Santa Cruz."

"Shut up." But it was true. Not five minutes earlier, Juliet had received a video clip of Tristan whooping with exhilaration as he soared through a misty forest of redwood trees. Envy seared her anew. He'd appended a message that whale watching was next on his list, an adventure Juliet had craved since she was five.

"Are you in yet?" Juliet consoled herself with the reminder of Tristan's loss. He was obviously trying to distract himself from the tragedy of his birth mother's death, not arouse her jealousy.

"Almost. OK, I'm in. Checking the personnel directory now for Gary Sigmund." Hilary typed the name into the search bar.

Juliet tapped a toe as she waited for the results.

"Oh, he's here all right." Contact information appeared on Hilary's screen.

They both leaned closer to read it.

"Looks like Gary Sigmund is a colonel now, and he teaches at the Naval Postgraduate School in Monterey," she added.

"In California," Juliet marveled. "That's close to where Tristan is now!" Talk about serendipity.

"Perfect," Hilary remarked. "He should go meet this man."

"He should," Juliet agreed, only Tristan would then have no reason to head back east right away. "Let's make sure this is the right guy, first. See if he's the right age."

As Hilary went back into search mode, Juliet prowled their limited office space, cursing the fact that Tristan's biological father apparently lived in California, of all places. Tristan might end up spending the rest of his two-week leave on the West Coast.

"Ho, boy," Hilary exclaimed, drawing Juliet back to her chair. "He's the one, all right. Just look."

Through wide eyes, Juliet studied the distinguished man in the photo. If Tristan were older and swarthier, he would look exactly like the image on the screen, from the handsome brow ridge to the broad shoulders. However, where Tristan was blond-haired and blue eyed, Gary was a brunet with hazel eyes.

Juliet's heart thumped. "We found him." She didn't know if she was elated or disappointed. Pulling out her cell phone she accessed Tristan's number.

Her call went straight to voicemail. With a frown of annoyance, she left a terse message. "Hey, it's Juliet. I've found your father. Call me."

"Oh, that was seductive," Hilary mocked, as Juliet put her phone away.

Juliet glared at her assistant. "Show me that emblem on the mural in San Francisco," she requested. "After that, I want to know everything you can find about Hans Coenen."

***

Six hours later, Juliet stepped aboard a Boeing 747 bound for San Francisco, only seconds before the attendant prepared to seal the cabin door. Panting as a result of her sprint from security to the last gate in the terminal, she searched for her seat, one of the few that remained empty. Considering the cost of her last-minute fare on the red-eye, she had to ask herself if she was crazy for making the impulsive decision to fly west.

Her instincts as a P.I. assured her she was not. The man whose features matched those of her parents' killer lived in San Francisco. A mural on a wall in that city featured Goebel's emblem. The only way to discover if the common setting of her two leads was pure coincidence was to fly out and ask some pointed questions.

Hans Coenen and Dieter Goebel couldn't be the same person. At sixty-six, Coenen was twenty years younger than

Goebel, who would be in his mid-eighties—assuming he was still alive. The CIA would have given Goebel a new identity, though maybe not a new face since no one alive today seemed to know what he looked like in the first place.

And Coenen, if he'd killed her parents, wasn't likely to admit it over the phone. Unless and until she quizzed him in person and saw his reaction, Juliet would never know for certain.

Her call to The People's Eyes Mural Center had sealed her decision. The woman who'd answered the phone informed Juliet that Renata Blumenthal was taking time off following a trip abroad. She would be back at the mural center for a planned community event the next day, to which Juliet had received a cordial invitation.

She'd made up her mind then and there to jump on a plane flying nonstop to San Francisco and arriving just past midnight.

"This has nothing to do with Tristan," she'd said in response to Hilary's arch expression.

Of course, it totally did. Dropping into a middle seat between two heavy-set strangers, Juliet considered how distraught Tristan had been over the unexpected death of his mother. He might be trying to distract himself with zip-lining and whale watching, but the truth was he must be heartbroken. If only Hilary had confirmed Casey Edward's identity a month ago, not just last week, Tristan might have gotten to his mother before she took her life.

With a sigh of regret, Juliet stowed her purse under the seat in front of her. She had barely fastened her seatbelt when the plane gave a lurch and backed from the jetway. Grabbing the arms of her seat, she remembered—too late—the anti-anxiety medication she was supposed to take before flying.

Oh, crap. In desperation, Juliet lunged for her purse and grubbed through it, hoping to find a stray pill. No such luck. The plane swung around and lumbered toward the runway.

"Ma'am, you need to stow that under your seat."

Yeah, yeah. Following the attendant's orders, Juliet sat back with her lap empty and concentrated on breathing.

Anxiety ambushed her. If only Tristan had assured her he'd be waiting at the other end she'd feel better. Yet the last time she'd checked her phone, there had been no message from him. She would arrive in San Francisco with no one to greet her.

Not that she had a right to expect him to drop everything in order to pick her up at the airport. That would be presumptuous, considering she'd practically kicked him out of her life less than thirty-six hours earlier. Still, recalling what a great team they'd made down in Mexico, she had to admit she didn't relish confronting Hans Coenen without Tristan at her side.

As she gripped the armrests and breathed deeply, she realized that she truly did desire his help, especially when she recalled his gift for winning the trust of strangers. Down in Mexico, that gift had been hugely handy. It would be handy to her now. Not to mention, Tristan also had a way of looking at the bright side whenever situations took a turn for the worse. She had to admit, she liked that about him.

What she didn't like was not having heard from him since his message stating he was going whale watching. What if the boat he'd boarded had capsized and he was presently lost at sea? That would explain why he hadn't called or even texted.

The plane turned sharply in order to line with the runway. Anxiety became panic, spurring Juliet's heart rate into a trot. The world without Tristan would be like Earth without the sun. OK, maybe that was taking it a bit too far. But she sure wished he'd texted her to say he knew she was coming.

See, this was why she didn't want to get involved with anyone. It would kill her to lose someone else after she let them get close, after they'd taken up residence in her heart.

The jet engines whined in preparation for takeoff. The plane surged forward, accelerating rapidly. As gravity pinned Juliet to her seat, the walls of the pressurized cabin seemed to shrink inward. *Oh, God,* came the silent cry inside her head.

It was going to be a very, very long flight to California.

Tristan studied the passengers descending the escalators on their way to baggage claim and ground transportation. He checked his watch—zero one hundred hours. Just knowing Juliet could appear at any moment kept his heart revving like the engine of a racecar at the starting line.

As with the other day at the restaurant, the element of surprise was in his favor—though not because he'd ignored her texts. Rather, his whale-watching expedition had taken him well out of range of any cell towers. By the time he'd received word that Juliet was on her way to California, she was likely flying over Colorado. Deciding he would pick her up at the airport, he'd hopped straight into his car and driven north. The urge to leave her a reassuring text had vied with the desire to witness her relief first hand. Call him callous, but seeing her face light up when she saw him would ease his lingering hurt over her cool reception of him the last time he'd surprised her.

A blond head bobbed into view, and his heart lurched, only to subside when he realized it wasn't Juliet. Suddenly, there she was, sidestepping an older gentleman to move briskly down the moving escalator, carrying nothing but her oversized purse. Blood pumped through Tristan's veins, heading generally south as he feasted his gaze on her.

It had been a mere thirty-six hours since he'd walked out of her office, so why did it feel like three weeks? She wore a pair of figure-hugging jeans, her hair in a ponytail, little or no make-up, and every man she passed took a second look.

Her indifferent expression suggested she hadn't noticed. Tristan wagered he was the only person in that terminal who could tell Juliet was actually tired, tense, and a teensy bit out of her element—like a woman wanting to be rescued.

With that private pep talk, he pushed off the wall and sauntered toward the point where their paths would intersect. She walked right past him, which proved how tired she really was. Tristan quickened his pace to overtake her. Reaching for her arm, he caught a sharp elbow in the ribs as she rounded on him.

"Ow," he exclaimed, flinching from her unexpected attack.

Her eyes widened as she recognized him. "Tristan, you're here!"

In the next instant, she was hugging him. Joy flooded his arteries.

"I'm so sorry for your loss," she murmured sincerely. Just as suddenly, she released him, stepped back, and socked him in the shoulder.

"Ow," he said again.

"Why didn't you answer my texts?" she demanded.

"I was out on the boat. Didn't get them until after you were already airborne."

"I thought your boat went down or something," she added, revealing a deep-down fear that touched him. "I had no idea you would be here waiting for me."

"Oh, come on, honey," he chided. "You know I'm big on the buddy system. I'd never let you wander into a strange city by yourself." To prove it, he put his arm around her.

She stiffened predictably, even as her weary body betrayed her by leaning into him. "Well, you're here now," she said in a prim voice. "Let's go get my luggage."

Of course she had checked her suitcase. How else would she have brought her firearm with her?

Minutes later, they hustled toward the short-term parking garage with her luggage in tow. Satisfaction fizzed in Tristan's belly, soothing the doubts that had plagued him since he'd left Virginia. Juliet had flown out west to be with him.

"So, we found your biological father," she stated, repeating what she'd already told him in her phone message.

Wariness rose in him. He didn't want to endure another disappointment. "What do you know about him?"

"You're not going to believe this. He's a colonel in the Marines, and he lives here in California. In Monterey, as a matter of fact." She had to shout to be heard over the traffic on the arrivals deck.

Surprise slowed Tristan's step.

"You want to meet him while I'm here?" she offered.

The prospect of meeting his father didn't sound so bad with Juliet beside him.

"First, we need to look at Goebel's emblem and have a chat with Hans Coenen," Juliet qualified.

"Of course." It would be just like it was in Mexico, with him and Juliet working side-by-side. "I'm parked over here." Tristan pointed toward the Camaro and popped the trunk using the key in his pocket.

"This is your ride?" Her approving tone raised his confidence another notch. By the time they left California and headed home, she would accept that they belonged together.

Showering with French milled soap in a hotel not far from the airport, Juliet marveled that she'd started her day clear across the country. Or maybe that was yesterday given that it was right around midnight, Pacific Time. The dull ache in her temples and the tightness in her lower back testified to how long she'd been awake. Her senses, however, remained alert and heightened as she anticipated the inevitable. She was sharing a hotel room with Tristan. Look what had happened the last time they'd shared a hotel room.

Aware of the passage of time, Juliet cut off the water, snatched up a towel, and briskly dried off. Apparently, Tristan hadn't picked up on her heavy hinting that he should join her in the shower.

Not a problem. She would rather have sex on a bed than against the cold tile anyway.

Enveloped in one of the plush robes left for guests, she exited the bathroom with her expectations brimming. The lights in the room still burned. Tristan lay face down across the king-sized bed, wearing only his boxer briefs. His indolent sprawl pulled her up short. She sidled around the bed to look at him. His eyes were closed and the steady rise and fall of his back suggested he was sleeping.

Wow. Talk about a disappointment.

Hoping he might yet stir, Juliet admired his physical appearance. From his broad, sculpted shoulders to the arch of his feet, his body would have made Adonis jealous. The screaming eagle tattooed across his upper back only heightened the visual appeal. Golden curls, now a tad too long for military duty, brushed the nape of his neck. It was his face, though, that she liked the most, his mobile lips, the way his eyes shone.

He'd managed to kiss her once at Emma's wedding. Before that, the last time they'd kissed was when she'd boarded a Navy helicopter with the rescued hostages and he'd run up at the last minute, planting one on her in front of God and everybody. The time had come for her to initiate.

Twisting her damp hair into a knot, Juliet put a knee on the bed and lowered her face toward his. Warmth radiated from his nearly naked form. With her heart pattering, she lightly pressed her lips to his sleep-softened mouth.

His eyes sprang open.

One second she was crouching next to him, the next she lay flat on her back with Tristan's weight crushing her into the mattress, arms pinned, the breath squeezed out of her.

"Oh." He blinked a wild, glazed look from his eyes. "It's you."

Juliet sucked in a grateful breath as he eased his weight off her.

"Sorry 'bout that, honey," he drawled, only to straddle her hips as he sat up, keeping her immobile. A slow smile usurped his contrite expression. He gazed down at her, taking note of the way her robe gaped, exposing half of one breast. "Did I hurt you?"

"No." As she gazed up at him, memories of that night in the hotel room in Playa del Carmen flashed through her, spurring her heart into a gallop. The likelihood that he would soon transport her in a similar way made her quake with lust. He could probably hear her heart pounding.

"You were tryin' to kiss me," he accused. His eyes crinkled at the corners as he looked at her lips.

"I was checking to see if you were breathing."

"Uh-huh." Parting the gap in her robe, acting surprised to see one erect, pink nipple pointed up at him, Tristan looked back into her eyes. "If you want something, honey, you're going to have to say it," he informed her. "Wouldn't want you accusing me of forcing you."

Infuriation heated Juliet's blood another degree. Tristan was going to make her grovel just to prove a point. Pride and desire locked horns.

Tristan circled the nipple of her exposed breast with his thumb, and her resentment evaporated.

"I need you," she admitted, in a quick rush of syllables.

He cocked his head. He put his weight on one arm and bent over her. "How much?" he whispered, pinching her nipple lightly and sending a spark straight to the juncture of her thighs.

"Stop teasing." She arched demandingly toward the heat of his hand while craving the feel of his mouth on hers.

"And do what instead?" He brought his lips to within an inch of hers.

Juliet closed her eyes. Was he really going to make her say it? With her face heating, she whispered what she wanted.

She scarcely got the words out before his mouth crushed hers. She welcomed his deep plunder with gusto.

With an efficient yank, he untied the belt on her robe. Tearing his lips from hers, he drew them in a path burning down her neck and over a collarbone to devour her breasts.

For the next tortuous minutes, he palmed, licked, and nibbled them.

Juliet reached for his manhood where it peeked out of the slit in his boxer briefs. She encircled it, reveling in the combination of velvet and steel. With a groan, Tristan pulled free of her hold. Drawing the heat of his mouth over her hipbones, he kissed his way toward her inner thighs.

The memory of her bath the other night set her right on the brink of orgasm. Parting her thighs to him, she slid her hands into his hair, directing him without shame to where she needed him most.

He chuckled at her brazenness. At last, his mouth descended with searing heat onto her core. With skill Juliet didn't care to ponder, Tristan impelled her instantly toward climax. Her cry of repletion filled the hotel room.

Before her orgasm had fully subsided, Tristan lunged upward, found her opening and filled her with one stroke. His fierce possession brought her to wantonness once again. His sensual tempo vaulted her back into a state of rapture and kept her there for an immeasurable span of time. Relishing every moment, Juliet climbed the ladder of ecstasy and tumbled off a second time.

Tristan, who'd apparently been holding himself back, immediately followed suit. Burying his face in her hair, he shuddered over her and groaned. Then, heaving a huge sigh of satisfaction, he rolled onto his side pulling Juliet with him.

Finding her head resting on his shoulder, she regarded the upward tilt of his mouth with mixed feelings. He needn't look so pleased with himself. So she'd broken down and given him what they both wanted. That didn't mean they were in any way committed. That didn't mean she'd agreed to be his girlfriend.

It was just sex—such amazing and fulfilling sex that she already looked forward to the next time. She wasn't letting Tristan get a grip on her heart. She hadn't flown all the way to California because she loved him. She'd come to find her parents' killer.

Or was she fooling herself?

Juliet gulped with sudden uncertainty. Of course not. They were working partners—with benefits—same as they'd been down in Mexico. She had walked away without a care six months ago, scarcely thinking of him afterward–except at night when he'd appeared in her dreams to ravish her. When this present investigation ended, she would walk away again. No worries—right?

She closed her eyes, snuggled into Tristan's embrace, and released the question with a quiver of uncertainty.

9

"Something disturbs me about this artwork."

Tristan's comment compelled Juliet to study the mural-covered wall more closely as they walked alongside it.

"Of course they're disturbing," she said, hugging herself against the chill. A blanket of mist hung over the city, so thick that the alley in which they stood seemed to lead into a mystical alternate universe. "That's the point. They're illustrations of protest."

As it was Sunday, they had slept late before driving into the city for the one tour offered that day, starting at noon. Striking out from the mural center with their guide, they had covered eight city blocks as their guide regaled them with an explanation of the Chicano movement and pointed out ways in which the more prominent murals depicted struggles of a marginalized community.

Juliet had found the vignettes odd but interesting, especially these murals closest to the mural center to which they were returning. She slowed her step to regard one of them more intently. Brown-skinned youths were about to be arrested by white police officers drinking out of "Starsucks" coffee cups.

She pointed it out to Tristan. "Check this out. I wonder if the CEO of the world's leading coffee franchise has seen this."

Tristan frowned at the colorful vignette. "That's not just a protest of the status quo," he stated.

"What do you mean?" She looked back at the vignette and frowned.

"I think it's a call to revolution. See the weapons?"

"No." To her, the painting seemed merely like a harmless cry for change. "Where?"

"Here," Tristan said, stepping closer and pointing out the butt of a pistol jutting from one boy's rear pocket. "Also here." He stepped sideways to indicate a migrant worker in the process of loading a shotgun while, nearby, a well-dressed man prepared to step into a snazzy sports car.

"Oh, come on. He's just angry that the man has a car and he doesn't."

"Then what the hell is this about?" Tristan indicated a robed figure holding something over his head.

Juliet sidled closer to examine the image. "It's a priest displaying the communion bread."

"Right. Why is he standing in the crosshairs of a rifle scope?"

On closer inspection, she noticed the crosshairs centered right over the priest's heart. "Well, the guide did mention the corruption of the Catholic church."

"So violence is the solution," Tristan interpreted. "That's what these murals advocate."

All at once, what appeared to be art depicting social inequality took on a more sinister aspect. Juliet rubbed her arms through her thin sleeves and wished she'd worn something warmer than a lavender blouse.

"Cold?" Tristan threw an arm around her, enveloping her in warmth.

She willed herself to shrug him off but found she didn't want to. Being with Tristan in San Francisco wasn't like being with him back home, she rationalized. This was more like a vacation—a working vacation, not much different than going on a cruise. She'd let her hair down then. In theory, she could do so now and not jeopardize her heart because a vacation wasn't real life.

"Why is it so chilly here?" she groused. "I thought this was sunny California. And where is Goebel's emblem hiding?"

According to Hilary, it was on the wall closest to The People's Eyes Mural Center. But that wall stood ten feet high and a city block long. They could hunt for it all day and never see it.

"Didn't Hilary send you a picture?" Tristan reminded her.

"Oh, yeah." Pulling out her phone, Juliet compared the emblem's placement in the picture to the scenes near where they stood. At last, she spotted it, positioned above a vignette of politicians driving farmers off their land. "There it is."

"Oh, wow." Moving around behind Juliet, Tristan pulled her against him a second time, wrapping both arms around her as they studied the image together.

"Time to talk to Renata Blumenthal?" His voice by her ear gave rise to a pleasant shiver.

According to their guide, the founder of The People's Eyes —just back from her travels abroad—would be at the center shortly after one. After they met with Ms. Blumenthal, Tristan and Juliet would drive seven miles to Russian Hill to knock at the door of the man whose features matched those of her parents' killer.

"It's time," Juliet confirmed. Sudden doubts assailed her. She twisted in Tristan's arms to look up at him.

"Hey, maybe you should do the talking," she suggested.

His eyebrows quirked. "Me?"

"You're far more charming than I am," she insisted, recalling how he'd gotten information out of a pawnshop owner in Merida. "Plus, she's a woman, which means she'll adore you. Flirt with Ms. Blumenthal. Make her like you. Then ask her about the emblem."

He gave an affable shrug. "Sure. If you want me to."

Relief swamped her. "Thanks." She stuffed her phone back into her purse. "Come on, let's go." As they strode toward the mural center, Tristan caught her hand in his. His warmth felt too good to relinquish.

Cars vied for space along the curb that fronted the three-story, Victorian building. With its vivid purple façade and a yellow sign hanging over the entry, the non-profit enterprise was impossible to overlook. More than that, it buzzed with activity. Individuals greeted one another on the sidewalk before proceeding into the building through the glass-paneled door.

"Is this a church, too?" Tristan asked, his step slowing.

Juliet propelled him forward. "If it is, we're just in time for a service."

They entered with the other visitors, only to stand awkwardly at the sales counter in the front room while everyone else continued through a second door into a large room at the rear.

Listening to the warm greetings of people who appeared to have known each other for years, Juliet questioned whether the murals advocated violence or not. The social upheaval depicted in the paintings didn't carry over to what seemed to be happening here—a community potluck, based on the aroma of food wafting from the back room.

She was about to suggest to Tristan that they return later when the treads on the old staircase creaked. They turned to see a woman descending into the front room. Juliet recognized Renata Blumenthal from her online photo.

The founder of People's Eyes moved with the grace of a younger woman. Platinum hair pulled into a tidy bun atop her head complemented her rather austere, long black dress. Spying the guests standing in the lobby, she smiled at them warmly.

"Welcome," she called, coming off the last step to approach them. "I'm afraid you missed the only tour we have on Sundays."

"We just did the tour," Tristan countered. "It's the reason we came to see you."

"Oh?" The woman's pale blue eyes jumped to Juliet. She

regarded her closely for a second, blinked, and looked back at Tristan.

"But if you're busy, we can come back later," Tristan said, as the door to the back room closed, sequestering its occupants.

Renata dismissed his offer with a wave. "Nonsense. We are never too busy for guests. I'm Renata." She extended a hand devoid of rings. "CEO and founder of The People's Eyes."

"John Whitby," Tristan answered, startling Juliet with his glib lie. "This is my wife, Jeanette."

Renata released Tristan's hand and firmly squeezed Juliet's.

"We're from North Carolina," Tristan emphasized his Southern drawl.

Renata chuckled. "I hear it in your speech."

The woman's own speech, Juliet noted, betrayed the faintest German accent, reminiscent of Juliet's mother's.

"How did you like the tour?" Renata asked, forcing Juliet to answer as she held her hand in a grip that bordered on crushing.

"Fascinating," she admitted, rather relieved when the woman let go.

"Did it engage your empathy?" Pale blue eyes rested intently on Juliet's face.

"Absolutely," Juliet replied, even as she categorized Renata as a bit of a fanatic.

"We had a question about one painting in particular," Tristan inserted.

Renata showed polite interest. "Then I hope to answer it."

"My wife and I bought a painting recently," he continued, "marked by the artist with a symbol instead of a name. We saw that same symbol on the mural around the corner."

Juliet masked her surprise. Her own method of questioning people tended to be direct. Tristan, on the other hand, found indirect ways of extracting information. If Renata knew anything about Goebel's art collection, she'd surely want to share what she knew, given the line he'd fed her.

However, the woman's beautiful face betrayed only interest and puzzlement. "What's this symbol look like?" she inquired.

"Show her your picture of it, honey." Tristan turned to Juliet and gestured at her purse.

Taking out her phone, Juliet accessed the online image Hilary had sent. Then she held it out so Renata could see it. The woman's arctic eyes considered the emblem without a trace of recognition.

"I'm afraid I have no idea," she apologized. "Over a hundred artists have expressed themselves with their murals, so naturally I have trouble keeping up with all of them. But, if you like, I'll research the matter further. Why don't you leave me your contact information, and I'll do some digging and get back to you?" She nodded at Juliet's cell phone.

"That'd be great," Tristan answered.

"Yes, thank you," Juliet agreed.

"Just write your number here," Renata instructed, sliding the guest ledger down the counter toward Juliet, "and I'll give you a call. How long are you in the area?"

"Only a few more days," Tristan supplied as Juliet picked up a pen and jotted down her phone number, remembering at the last instant to append the names Tristan had given them— John and Jeanette Whitby.

If Renata was going to call her, Juliet needed to change her voice mail message right away as it currently identified the name of her practice.

Putting the pen down, she cocked an ear to the sound of singing coming from the adjacent room. "Do you run a church here, too?" Juliet asked, curious to know what was going on.

"A community center," Renata explained. "You're welcome to join us," she added, gesturing toward the closed doors.

"Thank you," Tristan declined the offer graciously. "We don't have much time left to sightsee, so we'll pass."

"Well, enjoy your stay." Reaching out, Renata squeezed Tristan's arm admiringly. "Do come back if you're ever in the area again."

"We will, thank you," Juliet replied.

Tristan put a hand under her elbow and steered her toward the exit. "Bye, now."

"I will call as soon as I have information," the center's owner promised, waving a hand in farewell.

At the door, they nearly collided with a young man rushing in with a carton of fast-food. The delectable aroma of fried chicken reminded Juliet that they'd skipped lunch since their breakfast was so large, and now she was ravenous.

Walking back toward their parked car, Tristan broke the silence. "She was pleasant enough."

"Had a grip on her like a linebacker," Juliet answered.

He slanted her a sidelong look. "Ready for phase two?"

Her stomach tightened at the reminder of what they were going to do next. Go to the current address of retired police officer Hans Coenen and casually inquire whether he'd murdered her parents. Longing for some caffeine and calories to fortify her first, Juliet eyed an upscale bistro across the street.

"Need a snack?" Tristan guessed.

"Yes, please."

Together they pushed into a cozy eatery filled with enticing scents. The venue offered comfortable-looking furniture, and the menu's selection of drinks and edibles rivaled the notorious "Starsucks." A woman with Middle Eastern features took their order, promising to bring it to their table right away, as they were the only customers.

"Is everyone at the community meeting?" Juliet inquired as she paid for their order.

The faintest pursing of the woman's lips conveyed disapproval. "Most likely." Averting her dark gaze, she swiped Juliet's card then turned away to blend their drinks.

Juliet and Tristan selected a booth by the window, both of them sliding toward the wall to peer up the street. The doors to the mural center were closed and the blinds, pulled. Juliet took out her phone and promptly deleted her voicemail greeting, in case Renata Blumenthal gave her a call.

"Are you nervous?"

Tristan's question caused her to look at him with her most impenetrable expression. That morning, she'd advised him of her intent to interview Coenen but had left out certain details—mostly because she knew he wouldn't like them.

"'Bout what?" Having worked with police and lawyers, she'd learned to keep the ins and outs of her investigations to herself. She put her phone away.

"Come on, honey." He leaned over the table, pitching his voice on a soft, silky note that did funny things to her insides. "You have got to be nervous about ID'ing this guy."

When, exactly, had she become so transparent to him?

"For all we know, he could have been an assassin in his past life, working for Goebel. What if he did kill your parents?" Tristan's eyebrows pulled together. "You look a lot like your mother, you know."

The fact that his thoughts closely mirrored her own made her swallow hard. Juliet wasn't about to admit to Tristan that she was counting on Coenen to recognize her.

The proprietress of the shop saved her from having to reply as she marched up to their table. "Pumpkin spice latte, a large café mocha, and two cream-filled donuts," she announced, placing each item on their table.

"Smells amazing," Tristan complimented her.

Juliet's gaze rose to the woman's name tag. "Shaza." She sent the shop keeper a winning smile. "What is it about the community meetings you don't approve of?"

Shaza shot a wary glance out the window before looking back at them. "You're not from here, are you?" she asked.

"No, we're from…North Carolina," Juliet answered, remembering to stick to Tristan's story.

Shaza chose her words carefully. "Let me just say that I came from a destitute district of Pakistan in Southern Punjab. There was no way to get ahead, no way to improve one's social situation regardless of how hard one worked. But here in America, things are different. If you are smart, get a good education, you can work your way up. Capitalism has fed my family. I have sent my oldest to the university," she added proudly.

The reference to capitalism caught Juliet off guard. She darted a look at Tristan who seemed equally perplexed.

"Does Ms. Blumenthal not hold with capitalism?" she inquired.

Shaza's lips tightened. "She does not," she answered shortly. "There is more sugar and creamer if you need it." She gestured to a table against the wall, putting an end to their conversation. "And should you have need of the restrooms, the key is next to the cash register in the red cup. Enjoy."

With a professional smile, Shaza turned her back on them and retreated behind the counter.

Juliet sank her teeth thoughtfully into her donut. "I think we hit a sore subject there," she mused around a mouthful of pastry.

"Sounded like it," Tristan agreed. His phone, which was sitting on the table, lit up. Peeking at it, he took a swig of his café mocha, and announced with satisfaction, "Hack's driving up to meet your assistant, as we speak."

Juliet tore into her donut "Seriously? He told you that?"

"I thought they'd hit it off." Tristan saluted himself with his cup. "Hilary is exactly the type of woman he needs. Hooyah," he added, cheering them on.

"What type is that?" Juliet asked, though she already knew.

Tristan's eyes danced with merriment. "Let's just say Hack hasn't been laid in about a year. He's shy with women."

"Oh, and you think Hilary's going to do all the talking and tear his clothes off, do you?" She demolished the rest of her donut.

Tristan grinned. "Don't you?"

Juliet chewed until she could talk again. "Most likely. Maybe Hack can help her dig up history on Coenen. I need to link him to Goebel if I'm going to establish a motive for murder."

"Aw, leave Hack and Hilary alone. Let them get to *know* each other." He imbued the word with all its baser meanings.

She had promised her assistant Sunday and Monday off, but Juliet was only in California for a few more days. "Can't.

I'll need information now. It'll give them something to do besides—you know," she added, washing down what was left in her mouth with a swig of her latte.

Tristan shrugged. "Have it your way." Polishing off his donut in two bites, he wiped his mouth with a napkin. "You can call her in the car. Ready to head out?"

Juliet's heart rate sped up at the prospect of paying Coenen a visit. "Almost." She concealed her anxiety by licking the tips of her fingers. "I think I'll use the restroom first." Slipping out of the booth, she picked up her purse and went to fetch the key from the red cup.

Once in the restroom, she shoved a magazine, loaded with hollow-point, 115 grain, brass-fitted cartridges, into her Ruger until she heard it lock. As she washed and dried her hands, she took a good hard look in the mirror. From her coloring to the slight cleft in her chin, she did resemble her mother.

It would be interesting indeed to see if Coenen recognized her.

Hilary fussed around her living room, plumping pillows, to ensure that her apartment looked as tidy and welcoming as possible. Stuart Rudolph would arrive at any moment. Excitement fizzed in her as she envisioned how the day could end. Turning toward the mirror hanging beside her coat closet, she assessed her appearance with a practiced eye.

Too sexy? *Too orange?*

The cashmere sweater hugged her well-supported double D's, making them look like a pair of matching pumpkins. The fuzzy top, paired with a black skirt and black fishnet stockings, screamed Halloween, which was only two weeks and a couple of days away.

What she wore beneath the ensemble was even sexier—a mega push-up, leopard-print bra, with matching thong panties. Designed to drive a man wild, she'd put them on with the calculated intent of blowing Stuart Rudolph's rational mind—

and maybe some other part of his anatomy, should the opportunity *arise*.

Of course, she wouldn't rip his clothes off as soon as he walked through the door. She'd let the tension build over a bottle of wine and the latest *Star Trek* movie running on Netflix. At the peak of the action, when it looked like Jim wasn't going to make it, she would shift closer to Hack and hug his arm between her breasts. Her breathing quickened as she pictured what would happen after that.

Suddenly, her cell phone jangled, startling her from her reverie. Oh, God, he had better not be calling to cancel. She ran to her kitchen table and snatched the phone. Wait, why was Tristan Halliday calling her? Maybe Hack had put him up to it.

"Hello?"

"Hey, Hilz." Juliet's greeting made Hilary purse her lips with annoyance. "I knew if I called you from my own phone, you wouldn't answer."

"I can still hang up," Hilary pointed out.

"Please don't." Juliet's urgent tone kept her from doing just that. "I need you to give me Coenen's address again. And I have a favor to ask. If he's positively the guy I saw, I need you and Hack to try and link him to Goebel. Or at least dig up some dirt on him."

"You said I could have today and tomorrow off," Hilary reminded her.

"I know. But this is important."

Hilary's plans for a wicked, sexy afternoon started to disintegrate.

"Fine," she snapped, whirling toward her laptop to find the information. "Here's the address." She read it to Juliet. "I looked up the property in Russian Hill. Oddly enough, the deed names Irena Kapova as the owner. You know, the famous Russian ballet dancer. Ring a bell?"

"No."

"Kapova defected from the USSR in '81, then ran a dance studio in Russian Hill for the next two decades. Perhaps she leases out rooms or Coenen lives with her."

"Good to know. Thanks, sweetie."

"Be careful," Hilary told her, relieved that at least Tristan was with her boss.

"Always am," Juliet replied and hung up.

Putting her phone away, Hilary stepped through her sliding glass door onto the third-story balcony to await Stuart's arrival. A crisp autumn breeze took the edge off her annoyance about Juliet reneging on her promise. It carried the comforting hum of highway traffic from the Beltway. What the hell. Working on a project with Stuart might be a handy way to break the ice.

The appearance of a burnt-orange, all-electric car zipping through the parking lot prompted her to lean over the railing. She guessed it was Stuart's before he even pulled into her spare parking place. Who else would drive such a fuel-efficient vehicle? With a held breath, she waited for him to get out. And waited. And waited.

What the heck?

She was about to run down to the parking lot to fetch him when the car door opened. The driver emerged with the caution of a Navy SEAL infiltrating an enemy compound, his dark head swiveling as he scanned for threats. Seeing none, he ducked back into his car and pulled out a laptop bag, shouldering the strap as if slinging an assault rifle over one arm.

"What a nerd," Hilary breathed in admiration.

His head jerked back. He'd apparently heard her whispered words from three stories below. He looked straight into her eyes, and heat flooded Hilary's body. Her girlie parts tingled.

She sent him a slow smile. "Hi, Stuart," she sang out.

He neither smiled back nor returned her greeting. His free hand remained glued to his open car door, making her worry that he might jump back in and take off. To her great relief, he slowly closed it and activated the lock with a swipe of his thumb on a keypad.

Hugging his laptop bag like a drowning man clutching a flotation device, he moved resolutely toward the breezeway and the stairs that would take him to her front door.

Hilary watched him disappear from view.

"Huh," she mused, reordering her expectations. Stuart Rudolph didn't strike her as the type to have sex on the first date.

Oh, well. Hilary shrugged off this impediment to her plans. She would simply have to seduce him.

10

"Wow. Ballet dancers must make good money," Juliet mused, eying Irena Kapova's two-story stucco townhouse as Tristan parked on the other side of the street. Located at the height of a steep hill, the beige home's large-paned windows overlooked San Francisco Bay.

"She was famous," Tristan reminded her, turning the wheel into the curb and setting the brake to keep the car from rolling down the steep incline they had ascended. "I can't believe you've never heard of her."

Juliet shrugged. "I wasn't into ballet as a kid."

"Let me guess," he drawled. "Emma was the dancer."

"Yep, pretty much."

Tristan cut the engine and reached for her arm. "What are we going to say to Coenen if he's here?" he asked.

"*You're* not going to say anything," Juliet corrected him lightly.

His grip on her arm tightened. "What do you mean?"

She pretended to consider his attire—well-worn jeans and a navy blue sweatshirt. "You're not dressed for the part," she said apologetically.

"What part?"

She handed him the business card she was already clutching. "This is how I approach potential witnesses or

137

suspects. By the time they realize who I really am, I've had the opportunity to look around and size them up."

Tristan studied the glossy photo and job title printed beneath it. "This says you're an insurance broker for a big name insurance company."

"My foot in the door," she explained, taking the card back. "I've done this a million times, and I know what to say." Juliet studied his broad shoulders and muscle-hewn thighs. "Even if you changed your clothes, Tristan, you'd look nothing like an insurance salesman. I have to do this alone."

His expression predictably clouded over. Quick as a flash, he caught her jaw between his thumb and forefinger and leaned toward her until they were nose to nose.

"When are you going to learn, Juliet, that operating all alone is dangerous?"

Her eyes widened at his sudden vehemence. His hot fingers seared the sensitive skin beneath her chin.

"The last time I left you to your own devices, you dove into the middle of a gun fight, drawing fire from Mexico's most notorious drug lord. Hell, no, you are not going solo."

"You admitted afterward that I was a help to you!" She jerked her chin from his grasp.

"You were. But you don't just run into a fight without a buddy to cover your back." He gestured toward Kapova's townhouse. "I'm not letting you confront a potential killer on your own. We're teammates," he reminded her firmly. "We do this together or not at all!"

"OK!" She ought to have known he would protest her independence. "I'll call your cell right now and put mine on speaker. That way you hear everything, and if Coenen pulls me into the house and starts strangling me, you can break the door down and kick his ass. Happy now?"

Tristan's glower let her know that he was anything but happy. He gave a grudging nod. "Call me now."

She quickly accessed his number. The instant his phone buzzed, she put her own on speaker and slid it into the pocket of her purse, microphone up.

Then she withdrew the digital recording device she always wore into interviews and fastened it over the button of her blouse where it peeked out over her sweater.

"Is that a camera?" Tristan asked.

She lowered her hand so he could see it. "Can you tell?"

He regarded the device with a critical frown, then shrugged. "Not really. It looks like a button."

"Exactly. I'll be all right, Tristan." But sudden doubts assailed Juliet as she reached for the door handle. She would miss Tristan's reassuring presence as she faced Coenen alone. "Aren't you going to wish me luck?" she asked.

With a softening of his grim expression, Tristan bent toward her and brushed a sweet, encouraging kiss across her lips. "I'm right inside your bag," he reminded her.

Sending him a brave smile, she climbed out of the car, shouldered the strap of her purse, and followed the steeply rising sidewalk to the beige house.

Apparently, Irena Kapova enjoyed gardening. That or she'd paid someone to plant a vivid cactus garden in her front flower bed. Approaching a wide green door, Juliet noted the security camera and intercom mounted on the wall next to it.

Her heart thudded against her breastbone as she rang the doorbell and waited. The prospect of coming face to face with the man in her nightmare caused her to break into a cold sweat.

As heavy footsteps sounded on the other side of the solid wooden door, Juliet used her thumbnail to activate the digital recording device on her button. The security system mounted on the wall next to her clicked as the homeowner examined her through the lens of the camera.

Juliet's mouth turned dry.

Whoever was inside was looking at her. She braced herself for the door to swing inward, but it didn't. A second later, footsteps retreated from the door. She released her held breath as disappointment punched her in the gut.

Had that been Hans Coenen? Had he recognized her? The sound of hushed voices came to her ears. Determined not to be ignored, Juliet raised a hand and knocked again.

At last, a lighter step approached the door, and it swung open. Even knowing it wasn't Coenen this time, Juliet's pulse still thrummed. A stern-faced woman with beetling eyebrows and dark, dyed hair glared at her. Was this Irena Kapova or Coenen's housekeeper?

"Yes?" the woman demanded. Her brisk, unfriendly voice carried a distinctly Russian accent suggesting she was, in fact, the ballet dancer herself.

Juliet summoned a professional smile. "Good afternoon— Mrs. Coenen?" she asked, making certain she stood in such a way that her camera caught the woman's reaction to her intentional error.

Kapova's scowl deepened. "No. My name is Kapova. There is no Coenen here."

"Oh, I'm sorry," Juliet said, pleased to have identified her correctly. "I was told Hans Coenen lived here. He made an online request for information about our life insurance." She held out her business card, forcing the woman to take it.

Kapova accepted the card grudgingly, glanced down at it, then back at Juliet. "You have the wrong address," she insisted.

Juliet sent her a confident smile. "I'm sure this is the one he gave our office. If you'll please give that card to Mr. Coenen, I'd appreciate it. He can reach me at the number listed on it, and we can meet at his convenience."

The former ballet dancer's eyes glinted with suspicion.

"Well, good day." Tipping her head in farewell, Juliet turned and retreated down the walk. "Lovely garden," she called over her shoulder.

Arriving at the sidewalk, she pivoted in the opposite direction from Tristan's Camaro and added in a voice that only he could hear, "I'm going to walk around the block. Pick me up one street over."

At the corner, Juliet glanced back casually to see Kapova gone and the green door firmly closed. Movement at a large second-story window above the door had her glancing sharply upward. The face looking down at her turned her blood to icewater. Coenen stepped abruptly out of view, but not before she recognized him as the man at the site of her parents' death.

He *did* live here. He *was* the man she'd seen that night.

Shock reverberated to the ends of her fingers and toes, drowning out the sights and smells of the well-appointed neighborhood as she walked like an automaton, past houses and high-end shops, to the next street. There, she was relieved to see the yellow Camaro, idling in wait for her. Only then did she remember to flip the switch on her button recorder to OFF.

With her heart still hammering, Juliet dropped into the passenger seat and shut the door, promptly locking it. "It's him," she stated, with less composure than she would have liked. Catching a glimpse of the mystery man after all these years had shaken her more than she'd thought possible.

Tristan stared at her. "You OK?"

"Yeah. Of course. Drive," she pleaded, drawing a deep breath to steady herself. As Tristan drove down the block, she removed the tiny camera from her blouse. She tried to subdue the tremor in her hands while returning it to the special pocket in her purse.

"You can hang up on me now," Tristan reminded her, turning at the intersection.

She'd completely forgotten about their phone connection. Locating her phone, she pushed the end button on her screen and sat back. "I saw him looking down at me from a second-story window. He looks exactly like he did eleven years ago, just older."

"Question is, did he recognize you?" Tristan shot her a grim, sidelong glance.

Juliet thought back to Coenen's reaction. "I don't know."

A beat of silence passed. "What happens now?" Tristan asked.

"Now I wait for him to call my messaging service." She explained how she employed a service to take messages any time someone called the number on her insurance business card. "If he's curious about why I'm looking for him, he'll call."

"You think he will," Tristan stated.

When she didn't answer, he looked away from the congested street to quickly assess her. She fought to look relaxed, but she was trembling, and no doubt he could see it.

"You sure you want to do this, Juliet?" His concern only strengthened her resolve. She'd never reacted to danger in such an obvious manner. It was all she could do to keep her teeth from chattering. What was wrong with her?

"Of course." Clenching her molars, she averted her face, pretending to take in the view. Heavy clouds had impaled themselves on the Oakland Bay Bridge's tallest spires. It cloaked Treasure Island in a blanket of mist giving it the appearance of a scene straight out of a movie.

"Where are we going?" she asked, as Tristan, cued by the car's GPS, waited for a trolley to roll by before following the prompt to turn right.

"Sightseeing," he replied.

The explanation scarcely registered in her fogged mind, let alone aroused her interest. Seeing Coenen through the window of his home validated having seen him through the car window of her nightmare. His intent regard that night as he'd stared at her dead mother was suddenly so vivid, Juliet couldn't believe she'd allowed herself to forget it at all. Let alone for more than a decade.

In her distracted state, she was vaguely aware that Tristan was driving them downhill toward the waterfront. As they passed a park with a public beach, he pointed out a man in a wetsuit carving through the choppy water near the shore.

"Now that's a cold swim," he stated as he turned onto Beach Street. "Wouldn't want to trade places with him."

Completely self-absorbed, it took Juliet a moment to realize they had arrived at Fisherman's Wharf. The seafood restaurants and souvenir shops gave away their location. Even in mid-October, tourists crowded the streets. An open-air, double-decker bus laden with sightseers rumbled past, headed out for a tour of the city and the Golden Gate Bridge.

Tristan turned into a parking lot, took the automated ticket to raise the bar, and nosed into one of the last remaining parking spaces. Juliet just gazed at him unable to focus.

"Might as well have a look around." Pushing his door open, he got out and rounded the car to assist her.

With jerky movements, Juliet followed his lead. Taking her hand, Tristan directed her toward the nearest street. In seconds, they merged into the flow of pedestrian traffic cruising the storefronts and eateries.

Tristan paused in front of a shop with rental bicycles while he considered Juliet's pale face. She was still envisioning Coenen's rectangular head behind his window.

"Want to ride bikes over the Golden Gate Bridge?" Tristan asked.

Juliet regarded him blankly.

He pointed to the map displayed on the shop window. "We could bike to Sausalito—get something to eat then continue around the coast to Tiburon, where the ferry brings us back to Fisherman's Wharf. That sounds fun, doesn't it?"

She would ordinarily have relished the opportunity to tour the area from the vantage of a bicycle. Searching her feelings in that moment, however, all she felt was a cold emptiness, as if she'd died along with her parents that long-ago night.

"Maybe another day," Tristan decided when she didn't answer. "Let's hit up the Ghirardelli Chocolate factory." Murmuring something under his breath about chocolate fixing everything, he caught her hand again and walked toward the park.

Even in her numb state, Juliet recognized what he was doing—acting as if nothing were out of the ordinary, giving her time to thaw. It occurred to her that if anyone understood what it felt like to come face to face with the enemy, it was Tristan.

Half an hour later, with a square of salted caramel melting in her mouth, Juliet left the Ghirardelli gift shop, relieved to be feeling like herself again. A glance at her phone showed that her messaging service had yet to receive a call from Coenen. Maybe he wasn't her parents' killer. Maybe he was just some man who looked exactly like her memory of that monster. In which case, she'd been freaking out for no reason whatsoever.

"Want to do a city bus tour?" Tristan asked as they passed the Taste of the Town Tours and Activities counter.

She paused to look at the colorful poster advertising various tours. "Sure," she agreed. "Might as well see as much of San Francisco as we can."

"There's my girl," he murmured before pulling her into a hug.

Submitting to his embrace, Juliet had to quash the affection that billowed in her like a kite in a stiff breeze. She wasn't *his girl*, but they were on vacation, so what difference did it make?

"Don't let Coenen get to you, honey," he murmured in her ear. "He'll have to go through me first, and I'm not going to let that happen."

Inhaling Tristan's scent while resting her cheek on his soft sweatshirt, it was oh-so tempting to accept his assurance at face value. Relying on him now, however, would weaken her in the long run. What if she found herself needing him all the time? Then what? She would have to be like Emma, relinquishing her man to the constant brushes with death and trusting in fate to bring him safely home again.

She squirmed free of Tristan's embrace.

"I'll buy my own ticket," she insisted, reaching into her purse. "They're pretty expensive."

He visibly swallowed his protest. As they joined the line, Tristan examined the sky with the experienced eye of a navigator. "Maybe you should pop next door and buy a couple of ponchos," he suggested. "I think it's going to rain."

Seeing through his ploy to purchase both their tickets, Juliet leveled him a look. Nevertheless, since she didn't relish getting wet, she left him in line to head into the adjacent shop.

When she emerged five minutes later, Tristan had moved closer to the front of the line but was still waiting to purchase their tickets. Given the number of people queuing at the curb for the bus, she decided if they wanted a seat on the upper deck, she had better wait with them. Catching Tristan's eye, she signaled her intent and found herself next to a harried mother reassuring her squirming child that the bus would be there soon.

As if on cue, the big red tour bus swung around the corner and headed in their direction. At the same moment, a yank on Juliet's purse brought her head around. Expecting to see some young child hanging on it, she was startled to find a teen with multiple facial piercings tugging her bag from her grasp.

"Hey!" In her surprise, Juliet nearly let go. However, remembering her loaded pistol, she dropped the ponchos to grab her purse with both hands. Tristan, with his back to her, had no idea of her plight. Juliet had to defend herself. Shifting her weight to her left foot, she went to kick the kid's ribs. In that same instant, he let go.

At the sudden cessation of his opposing pull, Juliet lost her balance and stumbled off the curb, directly into the path of the approaching bus.

Denial vied with the instinct to live. Purse clutched to her chest, she threw herself into a backward somersault, tucked and rolled, all the while bracing for the bone-crushing impact of a ten-ton vehicle. The oversized bus's hydraulics hissed forcefully. With a chorused shout, passengers toppled from their seats as the driver slammed on the brakes.

Miraculously alive, Juliet lay in the middle of the street, one yard away from the cable rail that ran down its middle. The metal hummed, signaling a cable car's approach. Clambering shakily to her feet, her gaze went to the spot where she'd toppled off the curb. The bus was now idling over it. One tenth of a second slower, and she'd have been terribly injured, at best.

The whey-faced bus driver slid his window open. "Lady, are you OK?" he yelled as she sat up.

She stared back, furious that some petty thief had nearly gotten her killed.

"Juliet!"

Tristan appeared next to her, looking every bit as ashen as the driver.

"What the hell happened?" he asked, crouching to help her up.

Strangers hovered close, their expressions pictures of concern.

Back on her feet, Juliet searched the crowd for the would-be thief, but he'd obviously fled. "Some kid tried to steal my purse," she said. "I went to kick him and he let go."

To her immense gratitude, Tristan didn't state the obvious. If she were any less fit, if she didn't work out as hard as she did, the bus would have hit her.

He looked her up and down. "Did you break anything?"

Aside from her stinging pride, she couldn't feel a thing. "No."

He led her back to the curb where the crowd made room for them. Traffic on the street had slowed to a crawl. People hung out of the approaching cable car to get a better look at Juliet.

She continued searching for the miscreant teenager. Swear to God, if she saw the kid, she'd sic Tristan on him. "Anybody see where he went?" she asked the bystanders, but nobody spoke up.

"Clear a path." A police officer elbowed his way through the crowd to get to her. "Ma'am, are you all right?"

Juliet heaved an inward groan. Now she would have to file a report. "I'm fine," she snapped. "Some kid tried to steal my purse."

As she explained that she'd lost her balance when the purse-snatcher let go, the officer opened an iPad. "What did this kid look like?"

With a dozen tourists listening in, she described his hair and his facial piercings. Two onlookers spoke up, adding details she hadn't noticed, like the gauges in his earlobes and the clothes he was wearing. Juliet sent them grateful nods.

"May I see your driver's license?" the officer inquired. "I'm obligated to make a report," he explained. "We don't tolerate purse-snatching around here. In fact, I have a fair idea who the perp might be."

A shiver rolled through Juliet as she fished inside her purse for her wallet—belated shock. As they waited for the officer to transcribe the information from her ID, Tristan put an arm around Juliet as if aware of her sudden lightheadedness.

"You want to sit down, honey?" he asked.

She locked her knees to keep them from folding. "No, I'm good."

The onlookers lost interest and began boarding the bus.

"Ma'am," the officer said, handing her ID back, "I'm sorry this happened to you. I hope you won't judge our city by the actions of one misguided kid. I think your bus is about to leave. I hope you two enjoy your stay. Take care."

With a tight smile, he zipped his iPad into the case strapped to his belt and walked away.

"Excuse me. Here are your ponchos." The words drew their attention to a young girl who'd gone to the trouble of retrieving Juliet's recent purchase from the sidewalk.

"Thank you." Tristan took them from her.

The girl looked like she might say something more, but with a glance at the retreating officer, she turned away and climbed aboard the bus.

Tristan turned his gaze on Juliet. "You still up for a tour?" he asked.

Juliet balked at the notion of getting on a bus that had almost killed her. "Did you buy the tickets?"

He pulled two tickets out of his pocket. "Yes, but I'll get our money back."

She didn't doubt that he would. "I'd like to go back to the hotel if that's OK." She winced at how pathetic she sounded. "I'm sorry. Maybe tomorrow." She'd had enough ups and downs for today.

Without another word, Tristan led her to the kiosk. The people in line yielded to him as he approached the counter to request a refund.

Enveloped in shock, Juliet waited for him to complete the transaction. At last, Tristan took her hand in his, and they headed back toward their parked vehicle.

11

Sliding toward the center of her sofa, Hilary focused on the laptop balanced on Stuart Rudolph's long, muscular thighs and gaped at the identifying logo on the top left corner of the screen.

"Oh my God, did you just hack into Homeland Security?" She verified the logo on the website then sat back to regard him in awe.

In the two hours he'd been in her apartment, they'd barely spoken a word. Stu, as she'd begun calling him, had powered up his laptop, jumped onto the internet using his hot spot, and gone straight to work fulfilling Juliet's request for more background on Hans Coenen. Hilary had figured they might as well get that chore out of the way since casual conversation had proven more than Stu could manage so far. Working side-by-side ought to break the ice, at which point Hilary could proceed with her seduction.

Eyes fixed on his laptop, Stu shrugged his wide shoulders. "It's not that hard." His deft fingers alternated between the keys and the mousepad, moving so quickly she hadn't been able to follow his strategies.

"They have way too many systems with trusted relationships," he added, hitting the enter key and waiting for the next screen to open. "Once you're in one, you can daisy-chain all the way to the target."

Stu made it sound easy, but Hilary had tried many times, unsuccessfully. "But how'd you get past their firewall?"

A twitch of his handsome lips indicated that such devices were merely knee-high hurdles to him. "I used a zero-day exploit."

His hacking strategies couldn't have sounded any sexier. In fact, everything about Stuart Rudolph from his long, clever fingers to his dark eyes and the profound thoughts in them entranced her. He was tall, socially awkward, and reminded Hilary of Clark Kent in the way he hid his superhero physique under a purple turtle-neck sweater and corduroy pants.

A certain sexy SEAL needed help with his wardrobe.

She'd like to take him shopping right then. First, they would do their job since Stu was relentless in getting it done. He'd declined Hilary's offer of a glass of wine. Like a SEAL on reconnaissance, he wanted to keep alert lest he overlook something critical. Hilary sensed that, short of tearing her clothes off in front of him, there'd be no distracting him.

If you can't beat them, join them, she'd decided, opening her own laptop.

At first, she'd attempted to compete, trying to find something, *anything,* about Coenen's history before Stu did, but it quickly became apparent he would beat her every time. Not wanting to look incompetent, she'd set her laptop aside to watch him work. Under the pretense of needing to see his screen better, Hilary had shifted closer and closer until her right breast brushed his left arm.

"You are a freaking genius," she breathed as he poked around in Homeland Security's server.

He sent her a quick, distracted glance, which dipped momentarily to her breast resting on his arm. A hint of color appeared on his sharp cheekbones. Was it her comment making him blush or the fact that he could feel her nipple grazing him?

"If I were a genius, I would have found something incriminating by now," he replied.

What they'd found so far made Coenen sound like an all-American hero. The man had devoted twenty years to law enforcement—coincidentally kicking off his career in Juliet's parents' home state of Virginia serving with the Arlington Police Department. In 1995, he moved to San Francisco to continue police work with the SFPD. Not a single traffic violation existed on his record at the DMV. After five short years with the San Francisco Police, he'd risen in rank to Commander of the Youth Services Unit, a program devoted to providing juvenile delinquents with alternatives to gang-life. He had earned the Silver Medal of Valor in 2010, and the Meritorious Conduct Award in 2014.

The one and only thing unusual about Coenen was that he wasn't an all-American hero. According to the DMV, he'd become a naturalized citizen in 1995.

That revelation prompted Stu to breach Homeland Security's website so they could find out Coenen's country of origin. Hilary watched in amazement as he skirted the defenses at U.S. Citizenship and Immigration Services.

"Here we go," he said, hitting the enter key with a confident tap.

Hilary's eyes widened at the warning that appeared on the screen. *You are accessing a U.S. Government (USG) Information System (IS) that is provided for USG-authorized use only.*

"You did it," she marveled. "You got in. Oh, my God you totally have to teach me everything you know," she added. Her plans to seduce Stu moved to the backburner. It set her mind on fire to imagine what she could do with his skill set.

Intent on finding Hans Coenen in a database, Stu didn't reply to her comment. He located the month and year Coenen was naturalized and clicked the hyperlink to download a spreadsheet from the website to a virtual storage area—one that no one could trace to his laptop, just in case Homeland Security noticed the breach.

"Here he is," he said, pointing out Coenen's name on the list.

She followed his finger across the spreadsheet to the column naming the country of origin.

"South Africa." Hilary's tone conveyed her disappointment. "I thought Coenen was a Dutch name."

"The Dutch colonized South Africa," Stu reminded her. "And just because his documents were South African, doesn't mean he was born there. The Stasi would have had access to all kinds of false papers."

"True," Hilary agreed, pleased with Stu's insight. "If he gained citizenship in '95 and you have to live in the States for five years before becoming a U.S. citizen, he would have had to arrive here around 1990, right after German reunification."

"Which proves he can't be Dieter Goebel because he was still in prison then."

"Not to mention Goebel is twenty years older."

"Oh, hey, looks like Coenen had a sister," Stu exclaimed.

"What?"

He pointed to the new information. "Says here that the brother and sister arrived in the country at the same time, and they received naturalization papers on the same day."

Hilary gasped. "What if they're Anya Ausfeld's friends, the ones she mentioned in her letter?" Hilary had produced a copy for Stu to read at the outset of their research.

Stu made a thoughtful sound in his throat. "Hans was older by seven years. I don't remember the letter mentioning that."

"It doesn't, but he would have to have been older in order to influence Anya and his sister so profoundly. While they were young and impressionable, he was already a man of the world."

Stu lifted his gaze abruptly. "How old are you?"

The personal question made her heart beat faster. "Twenty-nine." Hilary shrugged self-consciously. "I'm older than you, aren't I?"

"Two years," he confirmed. He looked back at his laptop,

and his fingers danced on his keys, letting her know he'd forgotten her already.

"What are you looking at now?" she asked.

"Standard procedure," Stu replied. "I'd like to know if Coenen ever leaves the country."

"You're going to hack a dozen airline networks?"

"Nope, just need to look at TSA's."

With her respect soaring, Hilary watched Stu pit himself against TSA's security. When the Transportation Security Administration's logo appeared, she clapped a hand over her mouth to stifle her gasp.

A smile hovered over Stuart's lips, but he didn't look at her.

"What did you do?" she demanded a second time. She'd never tried hacking into TSA, as that first required getting into Homeland Security's server.

Stu shook his dark head. "Can't tell you."

Hilary grabbed his arm, astonished to discover his biceps were as dense as steel. Stu was built like a demigod. "I swear, I won't tell anyone," she promised.

Shaking his head again, Stu accessed a database of passengers taking international flights in the past year. Having copied Hans Coenen's driver's license number from the DMV website, he pasted it into a graphical user interface and proceeded with his search.

"Please. You have to teach me what you know," Hilary begged. "I'll do anything you ask me to—*anything*." Her tone gave the final word a sexual connotation.

Stu's fingers froze over the keys of his laptop. His eyes swiveled toward her rapidly heating face. With dismay, she knew she'd gone too far. Stuart Rudolph wasn't used to forward women. He wasn't used to women, period.

Instead of the lust that Hilary expected, his eyes darkened with compassion. "You don't have to do that, you know," he replied.

Her cheeks flamed even hotter. "I was joking!" she insisted, doing her best to look affronted.

"You're worth more than that," Stu insisted.

Stu's quiet assertion touched something in Hilary that she hadn't felt in a long, long time. A distant memory surfaced of running to meet her father as he emerged from the arrivals terminal at the airport. *My girl!* He'd swept her twelve-year-old self into his big, burly embrace where she had felt so safe.

Grief pressed against the back of Hilary's eyes. God, she missed her father, even after all these years.

Relieved that Stu had gone back to his laptop, Hilary swallowed hard and pushed the memory away. Most men were happy to accept what she offered. Did Stu not find her attractive? Oh, God, was he gay? Had she read him all wrong?

"Well, well," he muttered, unaware of her sudden insecurities.

"What?" She jerked her gaze to the screen and recognized a flight itinerary.

"Looks like Hans went to Chile just last week."

"Chile?" Something knocked at the back of Hilary's mind, but she was too caught up in the mystery of Stuart Rudolph to chase down the fleeting thought. "What's in Chile?" she wondered out loud.

"A lot of former communists," Stu replied, proving thoroughly knowledgeable about recent history. "Several key figures of the German Democratic Republic, including its leader Erich Honecker, fled there after reunification."

"Seriously?" Hilary's thoughts percolated. "Everything we've found suggests that Hans might be the older brother mentioned in Anya's letter."

"But it doesn't prove it." Fingers poised over his keyboard, Stu's thoughts turned inward.

Hilary kept quiet for as long as she was able. "What are you thinking?" she finally whispered.

Stu closed his laptop with a snap. "I've got a friend who might be able to help us." He sent her an inscrutable smile. "Mind if I use your restroom?"

In other words, he wanted to place a private phone call.

"Oh, sure. It's that door," Hilary divulged, "across from my bedroom." Where she had thought they would be by now.

Stu patted her knee and stood up. "When I'm done we can watch that movie," he promised, taking his laptop with him as he walked away.

Staring at the spot on her leg where his hand had been, Hilary listened to Stu lock himself in her bathroom to place his super-secret call. She heaved a sigh of confusion while reordering the events in her head that she'd assumed would happen that afternoon. Something told Hilary she and Stu would not be having wild monkey sex anytime soon.

Hilary reminded herself there was still the movie to get through. She could point out the scenes that exemplified Jim and Spock's *bromance* and maybe get Stu to talk about his buddies on the Team. After the movie, she would whip them up a delicious pasta dinner and get him to drink a little wine. Maybe he would tell her how he'd hacked into Homeland Security. And maybe following that, he'd be willing to indulge in a little romance of their own.

Pinning her hopes on that eventuality, Hilary texted Juliet their latest findings.

"You know, *Rise of the Planet of the Apes* takes place in San Francisco."

Tristan's comment as he inserted the card key into the lock on their hotel room door was meant to draw Juliet out of her funk, she knew. Unfortunately, she was still too shaken by the afternoon's events to show any interest. Walking straight into the room, she sat on the king-sized bed without comment.

"So watching the movie will be just like taking the tour," Tristan continued, pulling off his sweatshirt and lobbing it toward his suitcase. The sleeveless tee he'd worn beneath it emphasized the breadth of his shoulders.

Juliet managed a crooked smile for him. Tristan's attempt to humor her only increased her guilt over ruining their plans to explore the city. "Sure it will," she replied.

"I saw it advertised on Pay-Per-View." Snatching up the

remote control, he turned on the TV, set it to the proper channel, then lowered the volume on the background music. "But first you get a massage," Tristan added, putting down the remote, "since you have to be hurting after pulling that stuntwoman move."

The very thought was an invitation to relive that afternoon's close call.

Juliet glanced toward the window. A fine drizzle misted the glass pane. "Why me?" she asked, as the incident unfolded in her mind's eye.

Tristan came to stand in front of her. "What do you mean?"

She shook her head. "Why would some punk try to snatch my purse and not that of a little old lady, or a mother whose hands are full with her kid?"

Tristan tipped his head to consider her question. "Maybe he just didn't think it through. You're beautiful, so he grabbed yours wanting to know more about you."

"Maybe." Except the only person who'd ended up learning more about Juliet was the cop, who'd been polite and profusely apologetic. "I wonder if that police officer ever worked on the force with Hans Coenen."

Tristan's eyes narrowed. "You're not thinking Coenen had anything to do with that kid grabbing your bag."

Juliet shrugged one shoulder. "I'm finding it a bit of a coincidence that the thief would target me, specifically, and when he failed, there was the cop—who may or may not have worked with Coenen—asking for my driver's license."

Tristan sat beside Juliet and threw a casual arm around her. "That's what cops do, honey. How would Coenen have known we went to Fisherman's Wharf?"

"Maybe he followed us. It's not like our yellow Camaro is hard to see," she drawled.

"True, but I think you're stretching the limits of plausibility."

She expelled a breath. Tristan was probably right. Given her rough day, Juliet allowed herself to lean into him. She even laid her head on the plane of his pectoral and closed her eyes. That felt better.

"I'm sorry." Tristan followed his soft apology with a kiss on her forehead.

She pulled back to look at him. "For what?"

"I said I would protect you, but I let some kid almost rob you and a bus almost run you over."

"Oh, please." She frowned at him. "None of that is your fault. I can't believe I fell off the curb."

At that moment, her phone chimed, signaling the arrival of a text. Springing out of Tristan's embrace, Juliet went to collect it.

"It's a text from Hilary," she announced, resuming her seat next to him.

Tristan leaned closer, trying to read the small print.

"She and Hack have found something." As she skimmed the long text, Juliet's enthusiasm immediately waned only to lift again when she reached the end. "OK, so get this." She summarized the highlights. "Coenen emigrated from South Africa around 1990, accompanied by his little sister, Bergit. They lived in Arlington, Virginia, where Coenen was hired by the police soon after becoming a U.S. citizen. But in 1995, a warrant was issued for Bergit's arrest involving a homicide. Oh, wow. There went big brother's prospects for promotion. That same year, Hans moved to California after being hired by the San Francisco Police Department. He worked for them for the next twenty years, retiring only ten months ago. Interestingly, he left the country last week to visit Chile, where key figures of the German Democratic Republic happen to have fled following reunification!" Juliet looked at Tristan, amazed at how neatly the pieces of the puzzle were falling into place. "Hilary thinks Hans and Bergit were my mother's friends," she finished. "If they were, they had every reason to seek revenge."

"It sure took them a long time to find her," Tristan commented.

Her parents had been in witness protection for almost two

decades. "That's the reason WITSEC didn't suspect foul play," she agreed.

"Know what I find interesting?" Tristan turned on the bed to face her. "That Hans and Bergit lived in Arlington before Hans moved here. That's where your grandmother lives, where your father was from. I bet they watched his parents' house for years, hoping to find Anya that way."

Juliet swallowed hard at the frightening thought. "I wonder why Hans went to Chile last week." A sudden thought occurred to her. "Wait a minute. A while back, Hilary mentioned one of Goebel's paintings was up for sale at an auction house in Santiago, Chile. You think he went there to buy it?"

"Why would Coenen want Goebel's artwork?"

Tristan's skepticism slowed her runaway imagination. True, it was Goebel who loved his art collection, not the spies who worked for him. Looking at her phone, Juliet skimmed Hilary's long text a second time, formulated a response, and texted her back.

Find out who bought Goebel's painting at the auction in Santiago last week. And see if Bergit Coenen ever showed up in any records after the warrant was issued.

Juliet's phone chimed as she sent her reply. It was Hilary, adding one more piece of information.

"Stu—that must be Hack—is trying to find out where Goebel went after the CIA offered him asylum," Juliet relayed.

When Tristan didn't answer, she looked up to find him frowning. "What are you thinking?"

"That we should get out of the area."

His surprising answer had Juliet lowering her phone to her lap. "Why?" How could she leave now when all evidence pointed to Coenen being her parents' killer?

"If you're right about Coenen masterminding today's purse-snatching—and I'm not saying you are," Tristan was quick to qualify, "he had to have recognized you as Anya's daughter. Which means he must have known your mother. Naturally, Coenen would want to know more about you. He could have asked some thug he once arrested to grab your bag. And it would be easy for a former cop to ask a colleague to make an appearance at the scene to get your personal information."

"So now you think it's plausible," Juliet pointed out.

"I don't know. After hearing Coenen's history, though, I'd rather err on the side of caution. Is the information on your driver's license current?"

"Unfortunately, yes." She'd been living in her current apartment for some time.

"Damn. Coenen might have your name, license number, and street address. He could easily find out everything about you."

Worry sprouted roots in her mind.

"If he murdered your parents, Juliet, he's going to want to take measures to protect himself," Tristan added on a grim note.

She swallowed hard at the thought.

"Let's do something different." Tristan pushed to his feet to drive his point across. "Coenen has connections here. Let's go somewhere else—like Monterey, for instance. He's got your fake insurance card. If he wants to communicate, he can call your messaging service."

The mention of Monterey reminded Juliet of Tristan's father, whom he was anxious to meet. She'd been so caught up in tracking down her parents' killer she'd forgotten all about Gary Sigmund. Guilt made her quick to agree to Tristan's suggestion. "That's a great idea. Let's go to Monterey and meet your dad."

"Great." Tristan looked ready to walk out the door right then. "Should we pack?"

"Um, I'm already stuck with the bill tonight," Juliet hedged, cringing at the thought of how much money she would forfeit if they left right then. Her body also felt too stiff and sore to sit in a car for several hours. "How about we leave first thing in the morning? We still have to get our tour of the city," she added, nodding toward the television.

"Right." Tristan visibly wrestled with the idea of staying where they were.

"Tell you what." Juliet stuck her phone back in her purse and pulled out her Ruger. "I'll leave my gun loaded and ready. If Coenen tries anything tonight, I give you permission to defend me." Slapping the magazine into place, she laid her pistol on the nightstand. "Good enough?" she asked, turning to face Tristan.

"I'm going to need some more incentive," he said, shaking his head. "Can you take your clothes off for me?"

"Hah." Tristan's innocent question made her laugh. "You take *your* clothes off," Juliet countered. "I don't strip for just anybody."

"You'll pay for that." He shook a finger at her, but his eyes twinkled devilishly. "Lucky for you, I have no such reservations. Want to see?"

Of course she did, but she wouldn't appease his ego by telling him so.

Not waiting for an answer, Tristan started swaying to the cheesy music on the Pay-Per-View channel. Proceeding to strip, he lifted his T-shirt slowly over his abs, spinning it over his head before sending it flying. With a look of exaggerated sexiness, he freed the button on his jeans and tugged the zipper down slowly.

In spite of herself, Juliet started to chuckle. "Oh, my God. Please tell me you don't moonlight as a Chippendale dancer."

"Oh, but I do," he insisted. "Because I have so much free time." With the fly hanging open, Tristan worked his pelvis back and forth until his jeans dropped to his ankles. He kicked them away.

Juliet doubled over, wiping a tear of mirth from her eye. But when Tristan's stance morphed from that of an entertainer to a predator, she straightened. Her laughter abated suddenly.

"Pay up time," he whispered.

With a squeak of alarm, Juliet tried scrambling across the bed to safety. Quick as a whip, Tristan caught her by the ankle and dragged her back. Seizing her waistband, he flipped

Juliet over, deftly dodging the foot she raised to push him away.

With the look of a satisfied buccaneer clad only in cotton jockey shorts, Tristan straddled Juliet's hips and proceeded to undress her, releasing the buttons of her blouse to expose her cream-colored bra. Her pulse raced at the prospect of a sex marathon like they'd enjoyed in Mexico. The aches and pains in her body mysteriously disappeared.

"God, I love you," Tristan rasped as he gazed down at her.

The unexpected words made Juliet's ears ring. *Wait, what? Did he just say "I love you"?*

But he was already bending over her, freeing her breasts in order to suckle their tips, and Juliet allowed her pleasure to distract her from what he might have said.

If he'd said the L-word, he'd probably uttered it in the heat of passion, and it didn't mean anything. Besides, Tristan had probably said it to a hundred women.

Thrusting that unwelcome thought aside, she concentrated on the present moment, humming her approval as Tristan transferred his attention from her breasts to her lips, plundering her mouth in a way that portended a slow and thorough ravishing. Her very bones seemed to melt.

The man could do things with his tongue that ought to be illegal. As if to illustrate, he worked his way slowly down her body, licking and nipping as he went. The traces of adrenaline still lingering from her close call that afternoon seemed to enhance every sensation. It felt so good to be alive, to have Tristan's hands gently shackling her to the bed as he forced her to endure his unique brand of torture.

Freeing one hand, she finally managed to assert herself, using her lips, tongue, and teeth to make him groan.

By the time Juliet climbed atop Tristan, impaling herself on his straining sex, it only took the feel of him filling her for her to come undone. He smiled at her loss of control, letting her melt over him. As Juliet floated down from bliss, Tristan flipped her onto her back and launched her into another frenzied state, where more of him was never enough.

It could have been fifteen minutes later—or an hour—before they fell into an exhausted stupor. Lingering sparks of pleasure flitted over Juliet as she hooked one thigh over Tristan's smooth hip and pulled an errant pillow under her head. Hearing his rhythmic exhalations, she turned her head to study his handsome visage in the late afternoon light and realized he'd fallen asleep.

God, I love you.

The memory of his out-of-the-blue declaration warmed Juliet like a summer's rain shower. Why would it please her to hear him say those words? She wasn't his girlfriend. She'd never been in a long-term relationship with anyone, and she wasn't about to start now.

"Please don't love me," Juliet whispered, too quietly to disturb him but just loud enough to let her conscience say she'd warned him. The last thing she wanted was to hurt Tristan when their lives went back to normal. With a heavy heart and a soft sigh, she yielded to her physical contentment and slid into slumber.

12

"So what's your story, Stu?"

They sat on Hilary's sofa, slouching comfortably in the movie's aftermath. With the lights off, she had to rely on the amber glow of the lights in the parking lot to see him. They had analyzed the movie's plot, the futuristic technology, and the players. Stu's insights had filled Hilary's head with ideas about future innovations and the fate of Planet Earth. She found herself wanting to mind-meld with him, the way Spock had done with Kirk on the Delta Vega. However, being fully human and not Vulcan, the only way for Hilary to get to know Stu was to ask questions. Unfortunately, Stu, who stroked the cat comfortably settled in his lap, didn't answer.

The fact that Mitzie had cozied up to him, when any other human made her run and hide, made up for his reticence. Still, Hilary needed to know more. She had hoped the one glass of wine he'd consumed with the lasagna she'd baked earlier would loosen his tongue.

"Where are you from?" She tried again, reframing her question to make it more innocuous. "You have an accent I can't put my finger on."

"Vermont," Stu answered, swallowing the "t," in what was apparently a dialectal trait.

"Brrr." She pretended to shiver. "I bet you can drive in the snow, can't you?"

"Oh, sure," he said. Mitzie purred beneath his stroking fingers.

Getting the man to open up was like pulling teeth. Hilary tried a different tactic—talking about herself first.

"I grew up in Europe, mostly," she volunteered. "Germany and Italy, so I'm pretty good at skiing but not driving in the snow. Can you ski?"

"Somewhat. We didn't do it often, though. Skiing is expensive."

She pounced on the morsel of information, inferring from the comment that he'd grown up poor. "Who's we?"

Stu hesitated. "Mom, me, and my three siblings."

"Four kids," Hilary exclaimed, noting the absence of a father though not commenting. "I'm an only child," she confessed.

"Must have been nice."

She twisted onto her side to study him more intently. He had yet to touch her, not even to hold her hand during the movie. Oddly, after spending the entire afternoon and evening with him, Hilary felt more at ease in Stu's company than she'd felt with any man she could name. Even the dozen or so men she'd had sex with, some of whom she could not name.

"Nice?" she queried. "What makes you say that?"

"Peaceful, I mean," Stu amended. Because she'd requested clarification, he added, "No brothers and sisters fighting over stuff."

The loaded statement gave her sudden insight into his childhood. "Being an only child is lonely, actually," she corrected him. "My dad was gone a lot, so it was just my mom and I most of the time. I wish I did have siblings."

"No you don't," he said with certainty.

Hilary frowned at Stu. "Why not? What was it like?"

He heaved a rather desolate sigh and kept quiet.

Fearing Stu would stonewall her, Hilary backtracked and

broke her questions into more manageable units. "Were you the oldest?"

"The youngest."

That surprised her. She had envisioned Stu as the protector.

"And the genders of your siblings?" she pressed.

"Two brothers, then my sister, then me."

She imagined him, small and spindly, observing his older siblings through the eyes of a genius. "What happened to your father?" she asked softly.

Stu's hand stilled over the cat, which bumped his palm, urging him to continue.

"Took off when I was a baby," he finally replied, resuming petting Mitzie.

Hilary sat up straighter and searched Stu's shadowy profile. "You don't remember him?" Considering how lonely it had been when her own father was away, she could imagine the burden Stu's mother had borne.

Stu shook his head. "No."

At least he didn't miss his father the way she still did hers, although..."That must have been so hard on your mom."

"Yeah." The single gruff syllable conveyed deep empathy for his mother's plight. Hilary waited, wishing Stu would elaborate, and he suddenly did, in a quiet voice that had her straining to catch every word.

"My older brothers weren't much help. They got into fights at school, in the neighborhood, and with each other. They broke things in the house. My mom was afraid of them, so she never did anything about it."

"Oh, my God." Hilary could picture it so clearly—Stu cringing as one of his big brothers broke a chair over the other brother's head.

"What about your sister?" she asked.

He was quiet for so long she thought he might not answer. Meeting her gaze in the dark, he said, "She slept around, got pregnant. Married and divorced. I think she's on her third marriage now."

The fact that he didn't know for certain implied that Stu

and his sister weren't close. No wonder he'd been reluctant to talk about his dysfunctional childhood. And suddenly it made sense why Stu turned out the way he had. Being the youngest and blessed with his incredible intelligence, he had likely retreated into a world of his own, if only to escape the chaos and to give his hardworking mother a reprieve.

"You didn't get into trouble, did you?" Hilary asked, wanting her assumptions corroborated.

Stu's mouth quirked with amusement. "Well, I'd like to say I didn't but, I'd be lying."

Disappointment tugged at Hilary. Served her right for idealizing the man.

"In high school, I hacked into the local gas company and altered my mother's heating bill so we wouldn't get our service turned off. I didn't know how to cover my tracks back then, and the juvenile courts sentenced me to house arrest. But the good news was, I managed to delete the records of my mother's usage, so she didn't have to pay her bill."

Her faith in Stu's heroism came surging back. "Yay!" Hilary cheered his vigilante efforts.

"The courts confiscated my computer, so I ordered used parts and built myself a new one."

"Of course you did." Hilary expected no less of him.

"All that time at home certainly gave me more time to think. I'd heard rumors about the mayor, so I hacked the server at the municipal building and found some seriously incriminating photos he was storing there. I tried to finger him anonymously. However, since the cops knew my MO and I had a rap sheet, they got a warrant for my arrest and seized my new computer, which was all the evidence they needed. Luckily, the judge took into consideration that I'd caught the mayor distributing child pornography. He gave me a choice—go to jail or join the military. I chose the military, and it changed my life for the better."

Stu fell suddenly silent as if realizing he'd said more in a minute than he usually did in the course of a day. Also, Hilary was grinning at him, which had to be making him self-conscious.

"So you are a bad boy," she concluded.

He gave a self-conscious shrug.

"You're a modern-day Robin Hood," Hilary added, warming to her rose-colored vision of him.

Stu snorted at her assertion. "Hardly."

"Wow," she said, resting her head against the back of the couch and gazing at him with a fresh perspective. "I've never met anyone like you."

He avoided her gaze, staring at the digital clock on her DVD player. "It's past midnight," he pointed out. "You should probably get some sleep."

Was he packing her off to bed or suggesting they go there together?

"You go ahead," he said, providing an answer to her unspoken question. "I'll be fine out here." Reaching for the Mac he'd stowed beneath her couch, Stu startled Mitzie into abandoning his lap.

Hilary blinked at Stu as he roused his Mac with a tap. "You're seriously going to work at this time of night?"

"Just for a bit. I'll crash here when I get tired."

How could he not be tired now? Her eyelids were as heavy as sandbags. "I'll fetch you a blanket and a pillow," she offered, hurrying to her bedroom to retrieve the proffered items.

Returning to the living room, Hilary hesitated. "Here you go." She placed the bedding on the cushions next to Stu.

The glow from his laptop illuminated his intent expression as he pursued his mission. "Thanks," he said, not bothering to look up.

Vexed that he was ignoring her, Hilary pursed her lips and turned away. Shutting herself inside her bathroom, she studied her reflection while she scrubbed her face and brushed her teeth.

Very seldom had any man rebuffed her sexual advances. There were only two reasons she could think of why Stu persisted in doing so. One, he wasn't attracted to her flamboyance—though he had called her pretty when they'd Skyped. Some men preferred their women mousy and spineless. In short, they were fools. Reason number two was a stretch, something she could scarcely comprehend. Maybe he put women on a pedestal. Considering how he'd witnessed his mother's struggles to raise a family, then watched his sister throw away her innocence in her quest to find the right man, that was a distinct possibility.

Don't ever give yourself away. You're worth way more than that.

Stripped of her makeup and jewelry, she looked young and innocent. The truth was, though, Hilary had given herself to just about any man who'd shown her the slightest bit of attention. Not because she was a nymphomaniac. Not because she was a slut. Hilary simply wanted male attention, and she could never get enough.

Having Stu in her living room, taunting her with his powerful male body, so near yet so unattainable, was driving her nuts. Did he want her or not? She had to know if she was wasting her breath on him.

After putting away her toothbrush, she returned to the living room. Totally engrossed in whatever he was looking at, he didn't even glance at her.

Undeterred, Hilary walked up to him, furrowed her fingers into the soft waves of his short hair, and waited. He looked up —startled but not repulsed. Watching him for the slightest sign that he objected, she leaned over him, unmindful of her gaping robe.

He glanced down at her breasts, hanging like ripe fruit, then jerked his gaze back to her face. Nothing in his expression begged her to stop.

Touching her lips to Stu's, Hilary found them warm and smooth. He responded sensually and gently. The slightest suggestion of bristly six o'clock shadow on his chin rasped her cheek as she lingered, savoring the sweet promise of desire as it flowered between them.

When Hilary severed the kiss and straightened, there was no mistaking his hooded stare for anything but appreciation.

Triumph beat back Hilary's uncertainty. Stu wanted her—hah! Maybe she hadn't managed to seduce him, but it was certainly going to happen one day. All in good time. Oh, yes, she was going to witness Clark Kent turning into Superman, and she couldn't wait for that unveiling, yet wait she would, if he preferred.

"Good night, Stu," she purred, biting her lip to keep from smiling like the Mona Lisa. He didn't need to know how much his interest pleased her.

Profound silence accompanied her as she padded to her bedroom. At her door, Hilary glanced back to catch Stu staring. He jerked his attention back to his laptop.

He wouldn't take her up on her invitation tonight. She'd already guessed he wasn't the type to have sex on the first date. And that was OK. Hilary was exhausted anyway. Stepping out of her robe, she hung it up, snapped off her light, and slipped naked between her silk sheets. In less than a minute, she was asleep.

At six in the morning, Stu roused from a light slumber on Hilary's couch, helped himself to her bathroom, showered and shaved. He kept his movements stealthy so as not to wake Hilary. He figured she deserved to sleep in after he'd kept her up so late.

Entering her tiny kitchen, he poked around to get his bearings. Mitzie appeared from some hiding place to weave circles around his ankles. Locating the cat food, he fed her first, then brewed a fresh pot of coffee. Finding eggs, bacon, and bread in the refrigerator, Stu set about making breakfast.

Hilary's kitchen, with its kitty cat canisters and matching dish towels, struck him as cozy. Stu hummed tunelessly beneath his breath. When he was a kid, he'd wanted to fix his mother breakfast in bed, but she'd always been up and out of the house before he and his siblings even woke for school. The opportunity to pamper a woman rarely came Stu's way. Sure, occasionally, he'd left a bar with a woman, mostly just to appease his teammates who'd set him up with dates. But he'd never stayed the night with any of them. And Hilary was nothing like those other women.

For one thing, he could talk to her almost as comfortably in person as over the phone, and when he did, she understood him! She even challenged Stu's assertions by suggesting possibilities he'd never considered. Best of all, Hilary looked at Stu like he was more than a freakishly intelligent person diagnosed with a mild case of Asperger's.

Stu hoped, if he played his cards right, Cat Lady would let him visit her again—even if they never caught and held Anya Audfeld's murderer accountable.

Over the sizzle of the bacon, he heard Hilary's bedroom door click open. As he glanced up, she emerged, tousled and impossibly sexy in the same satin kimono she'd worn while she kissed him last night. The memory of her sizeable, creamy breasts swaying before him made Stu's mouth water.

"Morning," she called, as she stretched her arms up overhead a moment, reminding him at once of Mitzie. Placing her glasses on her nose, she smiled up at him, her eyes enormous, turquoise pools.

"Hey." Stu dragged his attention to the stove before he burned the bacon.

She glided closer, wearing that hero-worshipping look that made him feel bigger and stronger than any other man. "Did you even sleep?" she asked.

"Oh, sure." He transferred the bacon onto a paper towel-covered plate. "Caught a few hours on the couch."

She blinked at the pan he held. "You're making breakfast."

She made it sound like he'd hacked into North Korea's nuclear weapons program.

"Do you mind?" Maybe she was territorial when it came to her kitchen.

"Are you kidding?" she beamed at him.

Phew. "Hope you like your eggs over easy." He cracked two open on the side of the pan.

"My favorite," Hilary declared, padding across the kitchen to pour a cup of coffee.

Stu tried to remember what he wanted to tell her. "Oh, I found something interesting last night."

She whirled wide-eyed to look at him. "What?"

"The painting at the auction house in Santiago—it was bought by a woman."

Hilary gasped with excitement. "Bergit Coenen?" she guessed.

"Yes. How'd you know?"

"Logic," she replied. "According to Anya's letter, Bergit fancied herself in love with Goebel. Bergit, more than anyone, would have an interest in reassembling his collection. Now, if that's not confirmation of the Coenens' association with Goebel, I don't know what is!" Hilary paused to add cream and sugar to her coffee.

Stu gingerly turned the eggs, careful not to break the yolks. "I found something else interesting."

"What?" Hilary's spoon chimed against the lip of her mug.

"Irena Kapova might have defected from the USSR, but she's a registered Socialist."

Hilary carried her coffee closer. "Oh, that *is* interesting," she crooned. "What, exactly is the difference between socialism and communism?"

He paused to think. "Well, according to Marxist theory, first there's feudalism, like what existed in the Dark Ages. The bourgeoisie gain power and feudalism gives way to capitalism. That works for a while, until the rich get richer and the poor get poorer. That's when the working class revolts. They advocate socialist ideals that spread wealth around to everyone because everyone is supposed to own everything jointly with no private property. After those ideals become legislated and enforced, a communist state arises." Stu cracked open two more eggs. "So communism is just an advanced form of socialism where some group, usually a political party, becomes the government, owns everything and controls the wealth."

"God, you're smart." Resting her mug on the counter next

to him, Hilary watched Stu. Her assertion, paired with her intense scrutiny, made him fumble the fork. He nearly dropped it in the hot oil.

"We need to tell Juliet what you discovered," she declared, producing her cellphone from the pocket of her kimono. Thumbing a swift message, she put her phone away, and lifted her big, beautiful eyes. "You make me look good," she declared, giving him a cheeky grin. Her gaze fell to his puce-colored sweater and lower, to his brown corduroy pants. "But you have absolutely no fashion taste," she asserted.

One moment Stu felt invincible. The next, he wanted to hide under the table.

"That's OK." She patted his arm consolingly. "Because I'm taking you to Tyson's Corner today to do a little shopping."

Hilary's announcement made Stu's heart sink. He would rather be waterboarded or repeatedly tased than forced to mill around with strangers in a public location or to try on clothes. But with Hilary at his side, he supposed he could suffer through it.

"I think we've earned a little shopping therapy," she added, blithely unaware of his dismay.

13

"You gotta admit, the view is gorgeous," Tristan said, following Juliet's gaze out the passenger-side window.

California's Coastal Highway offered an unparalleled view of the Pacific Ocean, stretching as far as the eye could see. Bright sunshine had replaced the previous day's clouds. A stiff breeze ruffled the water's steel-blue surface and kept the birds above gliding on a perpetual current. Juliet's sweet profile as she took in the scenery completed Tristan's contentment.

"It looks a little inhospitable," she replied in the dry tones of a realist.

"For people," Tristan agreed, even as a breeze buffeted their vehicle. "But the marine life loves it. Hooyah," he added, expressing his happiness.

Their plan to visit Monterey's famous aquarium while they were in the area further bolstered his spirits. They had left Hans Coenen and his murky ties to Cold War espionage far behind. He and Juliet would enjoy this adventure together as they had down in Mexico—at least until all hell broke loose. By the time their impromptu vacation drew to an end, Juliet would realize heaven meant for them to be together.

First Tristan had to take her thoughts off Coenen, which wouldn't be easy, considering Hilary had just texted with news that Irena Kapova was a registered Socialist and that Coenen's sister, Bergit, had bought Goebel's painting in Chile the week before. It looked more than ever as though Hans and Bergit were the brother and sister pair mentioned in Anya's letter. What's more, Bergit was still obviously allegiant to the spymaster if she was buying pieces of his art collection. Whether that gave any of them a motive for seeking vengeance after twenty-two years was still debatable.

Intent on drawing Juliet into the present moment, Tristan turned up the volume on the country music station they were enjoying. He promptly joined the artist in belting out a line about no shirt, no shoes, no problem. Juliet tossed him a tolerant smile and he thought he had her, but then her cell phone rang. She pounced on it, gasping as she read the number.

"It's my messaging service!"

As tension tightened her face, Tristan's hopes for a carefree getaway went straight out the window.

Coenen had taken the bait. Disappointed, Tristan watched Juliet's reaction as she listened intently to the message. Her gaze went to the road ahead of them. She began to peer around as if expecting to see something.

"He wants to meet," she relayed when the message was over. "At a town called Rockaway Beach, just south of San Francisco. And it's obvious he knows I'm not an insurance agent because he didn't even bring that up. Do you know where Rockaway Beach is?"

Tristan's mood abruptly darkened. "Yeah," he affirmed. "We're almost there." He had glimpsed the quaint, seaside village on his way to the airport to pick up Juliet. In fact, he'd planned to stop there for a quick meal this very day. Coenen had just ruined his and Juliet's lunch date.

"He wants me to meet him there at noon," Juliet added, her expression tightening, "on the path that goes out to the point."

The update had him spearing a suspicious look in his rearview mirror.

"He's following us, isn't he?" Juliet said in a voice taut with strain.

"Yep." For Coenen to expect a rendezvous outside of San Francisco in ten minutes, he had to know exactly where they were, just like he might have known yesterday that they were at Fisherman's Wharf. Obviously it was time to find another set of wheels.

Tristan scrutinized the cars behind them, looking for one that a retired cop might drive. "You're not going to talk to him without me," he insisted. He'd be damned if he'd sit in the car again, like he had the day before, and let Juliet face a possible murderer on her own.

She considered his ultimatum a moment before casting him a look of apology. "I have to be alone. He's not going to admit to anything with you standing there."

"What are you planning to say to him?"

She had already thought this through. "I'm going to tell him I saw him at the scene of the accident."

"What?" A black Charger trailing three cars back caught his eye. "Are you crazy?"

"Listen." Juliet tried to reason with him. "Sometimes to incriminate a perp, you have to catch them off guard. When I tell him I know who he is and what he's done, Coenen will either deny my accusation or walk away. Chances are good that he'll do or say something incriminating."

"And you'll be filming with your button again," he guessed.

"Of course." Juliet withdrew the device from her purse and attached it to the lightweight jacket she wore. It looked just like the other buttons on her outerwear. No doubt she had bought the jacket with that fact in mind. Coenen would never know the difference. Still, he could only have some nefarious purpose for wanting to talk to Juliet so privately.

Tristan didn't want to scare her, but…"Look, the path to the point where he's asked to meet you is probably right next to a cliff. Doesn't that make you nervous?" It made his skin crawl.

Juliet considered the question. "Not really. He's not going to try to kill me knowing you're watching us."

Her words relieved some of the tension building in him. "Then I'm coming with you."

"Not exactly. You'll be close enough to shoot him if you have to, but far enough away to give us privacy."

Juliet's comment pulled a reluctant laugh out of him. "Honey—" Leery of trampling her pride, he weighed his next words carefully. "This isn't the kind of investigative work you usually do. There's a political history here that neither one of us can fully appreciate. I think the FBI needs to question Coenen. Not you."

"Agreed," Juliet said, proving herself reasonable. "But no agency will believe my story without more evidence. Trust me. I have the advantage here. Coenen never saw me at the scene of the accident. When he finds out that I saw *him* there, that should shake him, and I'll be filming his response. If he tries to hurt me, by all means shoot him but don't kill him. That's a totally defendable action, especially if we're standing on a cliff."

Tristan groaned and shook his head. "I can't believe I'm agreeing to this."

"It'll be all right," she said in a calm voice meant to reassure him. A glance at her lap, however, revealed she was gripping her purse with white-knuckled hands.

This insanely dangerous meeting wasn't the adventure Tristan had in mind when they'd set out that morning.

As Rockaway Beach came into view on a straightaway, a cold feeling dropped into the pit of his belly. Two hotels, a couple of restaurants, and a quaint village of touristy shops comprised the village by the sea. Signaling his intent to exit the highway, Tristan watched in the rearview mirror as the black Charger slowed and moved into the right lane to follow. A hundred bucks said Coenen was driving that car.

Parking proved scarce, even on such a blustery day. Tristan zipped into a spot as someone vacated it, putting them directly by the bulkhead of boulders. Waves battered the rocks, and a fine sea spray immediately filmed their windshield. He looked in his mirrors for the Charger, but the driver must have pulled into a different parking area.

Adjacent to the parking lot, a worn path followed the rocky bluff, enticing tourists to a grassy overlook that jutted into the ocean two hundred yards distant.

"There's the path." Tristan pointed it out to Juliet. "You sure you're up to this?"

Her expression as she took in the cliff's edge betrayed no fear. "I'll be fine," she repeated. "Here, take this." She reached into her purse and produced her Ruger, placing it in his palm.

Tristan checked the magazine and found it loaded. Smaller than the weapons he was accustomed to, the 9-millimeter felt like a water pistol. Without practice firing it first, he doubted he could hit a target past fifty feet.

Taking one last look at Juliet's set features, he felt the words *I love you* rush to the tip of his tongue. But since she hadn't responded the last time he made that confession, he kept the words in check and, instead, brushed a quick kiss across her lips.

"Okay, let's do this." Hiding the pistol in the front pocket of his hoodie, he rounded the back of the car to get Juliet's door.

"Do you see him anywhere?" Juliet sent a nervous glance over her shoulder then looked back at the group of tourists thronging to the point ahead of them.

"I think that's him right there." Tristan nodded toward a man seated on a boulder tying his shoe laces.

As the man straightened, the shape of his silvery head caused Juliet's innards to lurch. "It is," she affirmed, switching on her surveillance device.

Tristan's grip on her other hand tightened. "I'll leave you here with him and walk ahead," he said, his voice gravely with reluctance.

"Thank you. I'll be fine," she promised.

As they drew parallel to Coenen, he looked up at them.

Tristan leveled him with a distinctly chilling glare, released Juliet's hand, and continued to forge the path alone. A bracing breeze rocked Juliet as Coenen pushed to his feet and closed the distance between them.

The glimpse of his face at the window the day before had prepared her somewhat for the visceral shock of meeting him face-to-face. Still, his pale gaze seemed to run her through.

"Hello," she said, managing a cool smile.

With a scant nod of recognition, he cataloged her features wordlessly. Juliet imagined he was comparing how she looked to his memory of her mother.

"Do I look that much like her?" She seized the opportunity to broach the real purpose of their meeting.

Coenen's gaze jumped from her neck to her eyes. "I'm sorry?" He pretended not to know what she was talking about.

"Like Anya, your old friend, the one you recruited for the Directorate."

His pale eyes narrowed, concealing any reaction to her words. "I don't any Anya."

Dismay pinched Juliet. She had hoped to startle a stronger reaction out of him, but his self-control was superb. Even his German accent was nearly gone. Juliet managed a condescending smile. "I know all about you, Mr. Coenen. My mother left copious notes," she added, exaggerating grossly.

Thoughts might have flickered behind his carefully blank expression. He kept quiet, forcing her to fill the strained silence.

Juliet's heart began to thud. She had only one more chance to startle a reaction out of him. "I was there when you murdered my parents, Mr. Coenen. I saw you look through the car window." She had meant to sound like a cool-headed interrogator, but the pent-up horror of witnessing her parents' deaths got the better of her. She heard herself continue to accuse him, all the while fighting to keep her voice steady and waiting for Coenen's stony expression to crack.

"You see, I was there in the back seat. You looked right at me, but you never saw me. You didn't call for help, either. Why would you? It was you who masterminded the accident, jamming my mother's seatbelt, disabling the airbags. You thought of everything, didn't you?"

The only indication he'd heard her was the subtle creasing of the lines on his broad forehead. Otherwise, Coenen held perfectly still while his trench coat snapped in the wind and his thin white hair fluttered. Juliet pressed on, determined to get a response that would betray his guilt.

"You must have been monitoring their phones for some time to know their destination that night and when they'd be on that road. But you didn't know about a last-minute change in plans. You didn't know that I went with them. I saw *you*, Mr. Coenen. I know what you did."

At last, a muscle twitched in his cheek, indicating she had struck a nerve.

Juliet paused, sucking in the air needed to feed her hammering heart.

"Sorry, miss." His voice could have frozen running water. "You've mistaken me for someone else."

With those dismissing words, Coenen inclined his head and stalked past her, retracing his steps to the village in a swift but unhurried stride.

Swallowing a scream of pure frustration, Juliet whirled and watched him retreat. Her fingernails dug into her palms as she battled the impulse to chase after him and pummel him until she exorcised her fury. Her thoughts went to her gun, which was, fortunately, in Tristan's hands.

Turning to look at the point, she found Tristan heading her way, his gaze fixed and worried.

With Coenen putting more and more distance between them and needing a moment to collect herself, Juliet started for the parking lot. As she walked, she switched off her recording device, crushed that what she'd filmed had in no way advanced her investigation.

She had underestimated Coenen's professionalism. He had arranged for them to meet so he could feel *her* out while revealing nothing about himself, a skill he'd clearly perfected as an East German mole and later a police officer. All she'd managed to do was alert him to potential murder charges. Her calculated risk had backfired. Now that he knew why she was after him, he had time to manufacture an alibi, to find a good lawyer, maybe even flee the country, joining his sister in Chile, where Bergit might well still be, given she was wanted for murder in the states.

Tears of frustration blurred Juliet's vision as she allowed herself an emotional moment. The shivering that had wracked her the day before started up again, forcing her to clench her jaw.

"Juliet!" She could hear Tristan calling, so she slowed her step, composing herself as he caught up to her.

She had just smoothed her features when he tugged her around. Taking one look at her face, he swept her into a consoling embrace.

"You did great," he praised, hugging her so hard the pistol in his pocket gouged her belly.

"I said too much," she admitted, suddenly angry with herself. "I only meant to rattle him, but I couldn't stop talking. Now he knows everything I know."

She squirmed free of his embrace, but Tristan kept hold of her shoulders.

"Give yourself a break, OK? What you did took some serious balls."

His choice of words drew a short laugh out of her.

"We'll call the FBI over lunch. We'll tell them what you witnessed as a kid and why you're sure Coenen was responsible."

He sounded so eager for her to hand over her investigation that she nodded with reluctance. "OK." It didn't look like she'd be able to implicate Coenen on her own anyway. Worse than that, the man might feel compelled to hinder her investigation permanently—by quietly murdering her. A shiver of concern snaked through her. "What if he keeps following us?" she asked.

"Already thought of that," Tristan answered. "We're going to change vehicles."

"How do we do that?" she asked.

"Easy." He pulled his cell phone from his back pocket. "I call Hertz, and they bring me one."

She watched him thumb his keypad. "Why would they deliver a car to you?"

Tristan winked at her. "'Cause I'm special."

Listening to him introduce himself and spin a yarn about how the Camaro wasn't handling well, Juliet guessed that the people at Hertz still thought of him as the famous NASCAR racer. He even had the gall to request an Audi TTS.

"Hour and a half?" He glanced at his tactical watch. That's perfect. "We'll meet you in the front parking lot. See you then. Thanks." He grinned at Juliet as he put his phone away.

"Well, I guess you *are* special," she relented.

He raised an inquiring eyebrow. "Are you mocking me?"

As much as she wanted to keep him in his place, she had to admit she couldn't have faced Coenen without Tristan nearby. "Not this time," she replied.

His smile grew as he waited for her to say more—possibly even to admit that she loved him. Yes, he was special, but there were limits to how close she could let him get.

Tristan chuckled at her reticence. "Good enough," he decided. "You ready for lunch?"

The thought of food turned Juliet's stomach. However, a quiet moment in an ocean-side restaurant was exactly what she needed to regain her poise.

"Sure," she agreed. "And then I'll call the FBI."

Two hours later, Tristan eased their sleek silver Audi TTS onto California's CA-1, pointed in the direction of Monterey.

"Why an Audi?" Juliet had asked him when the Hertz employee first pulled up in it.

"Used to own one," he'd explained. "I like the way it

handles." He hadn't told her the real reason—that he was worried Coenen might come after them. If Juliet's life was in Tristan's hands, he wanted to have the fastest vehicle at his disposal, one he knew how to handle.

He pictured a scene straight out of *The Fast and the Furious*, in which he executed a drifting maneuver around a deadly road bend, while the villain chasing them smashed into the guardrail, then over it, splashing into the ocean below.

There was no sign of Coenen following them. All the same, Tristan wasn't going to ignore the cold sensation in the pit of his stomach. Jeremiah had taught him to pay attention to it. Hence a vehicle with a six-speed dual clutch and 292 horses under the hood.

Glancing at his quiet companion, Tristan wondered if Juliet realized exactly how dangerous Coenen might be. If he'd worked for Goebel, he'd probably killed for him more than once.

Sitting straight as a board in the bucket seat next to him, Juliet white-knuckled the purse on her lap. The vigilant look in her gray eyes suggested she was every bit as aware of the dangers as he was.

If only she'd managed to speak with an actual FBI investigator. The call center had connected her with the voicemail of an agent where she'd left a concise but powerful message. Like every other federal employee in the country, however, the investigator was out of the office in observance of Columbus Day.

Since the call, she'd turned tense and pensive. Tristan tried to think of something to lift her spirits; the best he could do was to deliver them as speedily as possible from Coenen's sphere of influence. Edging his speed to five over the posted limit, he hoped to convey them to Monterey by twilight.

The terrain grew steep. Sunlight glanced off the hood of the vehicle as it zipped uphill, following the edge of a precipitous cliff. They came to a section of the highway called the Devil's Slide, named thusly for the eroding sandstone. A few years back, the state had transformed the most dangerous portion of the highway into a walking path. Two brand new tunnels funneled travelers safely through the crumbling escarpment to the other side.

The north and southbound lanes split, each disappearing into their own brightly lit, one-way tunnel, with only a single lane of traffic. Tristan sped into the southbound passage. Hearing Juliet's indrawn breath, he looked over to find her glued to her seatback, eyes fixed on the curving cylinder ahead.

What the hell? "You OK, honey?"

"Claustrophobic," she bit out.

Well, damn. The woman had a chink in her armor, after all. Wanting to alleviate Juliet's distress, Tristan accelerated, shifting into a higher gear until the lights along the side walls turned into a solid line.

Within seconds, they tore out of the enclosure and back into the sunshine. Juliet heaved a sigh of relief. Tristan felt good for having rescued his damsel in distress, until a glimpse into his rearview mirror banished his satisfaction. Tucked into the shadows right outside the tunnel's exit, sat a black and white patrol car just waiting for some hotshot like him to come screaming out of the tunnel at well over the speed limit.

14

Tristan weighed the benefits and drawbacks of a high-speed chase. Not even a turbo-charged police cruiser could keep up with him in the TTS. Tantalizing images about what he could do around turns tempted him to outrace the cop. Unfortunately, the plates on the rental would lead straight to Hertz, and then to him. He'd be charged with evading the law, which meant Tristan's task unit commander would call him into the office and chew him out until his ears singed. Totally not worth it.

"Oh, crap." Juliet had noticed their predicament.

Tristan prayed for the cop to let him go. Of course not. Blue lights flashed, and a siren split the quiet as the cruiser pulled out in pursuit.

Tristan slowed and looked for a safe place to pull off.

"It's my fault," Juliet stated, taking the blame for his speeding.

"Relax, honey," he soothed, dropping two tires onto the soft sand at the side of the road. "Sometimes I can talk my way out of a ticket." He kept the car idling in the expectation of being able to do precisely that.

"Wait, how do we know this guy's not a friend of Coenen's?" she asked, clutching her purse tighter and craning her neck to peer out the small back window.

Tristan considered the possibility and dismissed it. "Coenen is SFPD," he reasoned. "This is California Highway Patrol—you know, like the seventies TV show, CHiPs. Watch Eric Estrada come walking up to my window and tell me I was going ninety in a forty-five," he added, hoping to humor her.

Juliet didn't even crack a smile.

A uniformed officer bellied up to Tristan's car door— literally. Standing maybe five feet tall, the man was no movie star. Barely an adult, with smooth cheeks devoid of facial hair and a build like the Pillsbury Dough Boy, the young officer regarded Tristan through a pair of dark sunglasses before scrutinizing Juliet.

"You know why I pulled you over?"

"Yes, sir." Tristan found it hard to use the respectful title for this boy officer. "How fast was I going?"

"Eighty-six in a forty-five."

"Ouch." That was going on his driving record. Pleading chivalry wasn't going to cut it with the frowning Dough Boy.

"Is this your car?" the young officer asked.

"It's a rental." Tristan pulled his driver's license from his wallet. "Honey, can you look in the glove box for the rental agreement?"

"You in the military?" Dough Boy had caught a glimpse of Tristan's other ID.

"Yes, sir." Tristan handed them both over. Sometimes a military ID got him off with only a warning, but it was never as effective as his old NASCAR membership card. Too bad he'd had to turn it in when he gave up racing.

The officer studied both cards. "What do you do in the Navy, Petty Officer?"

Tristan found it grating to be grilled by a man ten years his junior. "I'm a radar tech on a destroyer," he lied.

Out the corner of his eye, he saw Juliet look at him sharply.

"Where are you based?"

"San Diego," Tristan said. Why make Coenen's job easier if this kid was, in fact, his puppet?

"You're a long way from home," Dough Boy stated, taking note of Tristan's North Carolina driver's license.

"Yes, sir."

Plucking a pen from his breast pocket, Dough Boy scratched something onto his clipboard. He handed back both of Tristan's IDs, eschewing the rental agreement Tristan started to give him. "You can keep that. Better slow down, Petty Officer," he counseled. "There are some tight turns up ahead."

Tristan just looked at him. "Yes, *sir*," he finally said. "Thank you, *sir*."

If Dough Boy recognized his sarcasm, he didn't show it. Giving them a swift nod, he turned and waddled back to his car. Tristan watched him in his side mirror. It wasn't the first time his military service had gotten him out of a speeding ticket, but something felt different about this particular incident.

Juliet sat stiffly back in her seat. "I can't believe he let you go like that."

Tristan couldn't either. No patrolman worth his salt would have let him get away with breaking the law so flagrantly. Or maybe the officer was still so inexperienced, he hadn't known how to handle himself. Maybe Tristan's superior size had intimidated him. Tristan didn't think so.

Dough Boy may have been tasked with finding out more about Juliet's partner. For all Coenen knew, Tristan could be working for the FBI.

Keeping his suspicions to himself, Tristan boasted in response to her comment, "Hey, they don't call me the Golden Boy for nothing." Shooting her a careless grin, he eased their rental off the shoulder and back onto the highway.

"You really are a Golden Boy," Juliet admitted as they pulled away from the gate to the postgraduate school where Colonel Sigmund taught. Tristan had just convinced the guards standing watch that he was paying his father a surprise visit and he needed directions to the colonel's house, as Hilary hadn't been able to dig that much up in her research.

When Tristan didn't answer, she regarded him more closely. "You OK?" she asked as he pointed their vehicle toward Gary Sigmund's home.

"Yeah, sure," he said on a distracted note.

He was scared, Juliet realized. For the first time since she'd known him, he wasn't brimming with his usual confidence. For reasons that she didn't understand, his sudden insecurity tugged at her heartstrings.

"It's going to be fine," she heard herself comfort. "He's going to love you."

The vulnerable look he swung at her prompted her to stretch out a hand and place it on his thigh and rub it encouragingly.

"What makes you so sure?" he asked.

"Tristan." She laughed at the absurdity of his doubts. "Look at you. You're amazing. Anyone would want to claim kinship with you."

Her words met with lengthy silence. Peering at the upcoming road sign, he changed lanes and slowed to make the turn. "What about you?" he finally asked her. As he picked up speed, he shot her a sidelong glance.

She could sense where he was going with his question; still, she tried do dodge it. "We're not related."

"We could be," he answered.

His oblique reference to marriage made her pull her hand back. Her stomach cartwheeled. "We're not talking about us. We're talking about your biological father. Let's focus on him right now."

"Right," he agreed, though his tone suggested he didn't see the difference.

To Juliet's relief, he slowed in front of one of the larger homes in the housing area. Tristan parked along the curb and killed the engine. Dusk had fallen. Lights shone in the house's lower-level windows, and two cars sat in the double driveway, suggesting his father was home and that he wasn't alone.

Without another word to her, Tristan rolled up out of his seat and rounded the car to collect her. He reached for her hand, relieving her worry that he might remain upset with her. Together, they crossed a sparse lawn to the covered porch. Juliet discerned the tang of the nearby bay. A televised sportscast playing in the house sounded over the chirping of crickets. Tristan's palm felt distinctly moist against hers. He blew out an audible breath, raised a hand, and gave the door a knock.

Light steps sounded, and the door swung inward. A fit, middle-aged woman holding a beer bottle sent them both a welcoming smile.

"Well, hi," she said, stepping back to admit them. "Gary, your students are here," she sang out, clearly mistaking Juliet and Tristan for her husband's pupils. "I'm Holly," she added, shaking Juliet's hand first as they joined her in the warm foyer.

"I'm Juliet," she introduced them, "and this is Tristan."

Holly squinted up at Tristan as she pumped his hand. "I think we've met," she said.

With an expression of bemusement, Tristan didn't say anything.

"Well, come on in. Don't be shy." Holly led them into a tastefully decorated living room, where a broad-shouldered, dark-haired man sat, eyes glued to the play unfolding on a flat-screen TV. "Sweetie, I told you some of your students would show up."

A handsome, craggy face swung in their direction. Gary Sigmund did a double take, then pushed to his feet. "These aren't my students." He regarded them quizzically, his gaze homing in on Tristan. "Can I help you?"

Seeing his biological father face-to-face put a stranglehold on Tristan's vocal cords. Everything about Gary Sigmund, from his rugged features to the smile lines fanning the corners of his deep-set eyes struck Tristan as endearing. The impulse to cry, "Dad!" and barrel into the stranger's arms caught him by surprise.

Juliet spoke up into the long silence. "Sir, I'm Juliet Rhodes. I'm a private investigator."

The colonel's forehead creased with concern as he divided his gaze between them.

"I'd like you to meet Tristan Halliday," she added.

Recognition lit the colonel's face, and stepped toward Tristan to shake his hand. "The NASCAR driver?"

The fact that his father had followed his career kept Tristan speechless as their hands connected. A distinct warmth traveled up his arm, and he managed to nod.

"He's a Navy SEAL now," Juliet revealed.

"Even better," Gary exclaimed, gripping Tristan's hand more enthusiastically.

"And he's your son," Juliet added gently.

The colonel's eyes flared. His handshake froze.

Holly cut a sharp look at her husband, her eyebrows shooting up.

"I don't have a son," Gary protested, as he broke the contact, dropping his hand back to his side.

Tristan managed to find his voice. "My mother was Cassidy King," he stated hoarsely. "You had a—a thing with her back in '87."

The silence between the people in the room contrasted starkly with the rousing cheer coming from the television. Gary Sigmund gaped at Tristan. "Holy mother of God," he finally exclaimed. "I never—Cassidy never told me she got pregnant."

Holly's eyebrows remained aloft. She propped her hands on her hips, looking back and forth between the two men.

"Well...she did," Tristan insisted. "I guess she was all about her career, and she didn't want to have to settle down, so...."

"Oh, for the love of Pete, Gary," Holly interrupted on a sympathetic note. "Of course he's your son. Don't just stand there. Give your boy a hug before I do!"

Shaking himself from his trancelike state, the colonel threw open his arms and engulfed his son in an embrace. Tristan melted. He had thought claiming kinship to a pure stranger might feel awkward. But Gary's heart pounding against his chest drove home their blood connection. A bond, unlike anything he'd ever experienced, sealed instantly and effortlessly between them.

At last, the colonel's grip relaxed. Surreptitiously wiping a tear from his eye, he turned Tristan toward the lamp's glow.

"Let me look at you." Hazel eyes, bright with interest, searched his face. "My God, what a sight," he exclaimed, clearly liking what he saw. He shot a grin at his wife. "Look what I made."

"Not exactly by yourself," Holly drawled.

Tristan sent Juliet a bemused smile.

"Told you," she mouthed.

She'd been right. His father had welcomed him.

"Let's all sit down," Holly suggested, gesturing to the wide couch.

The three of them took the sofa while the colonel resumed his seat in the arm chair. His unabashed gaze never left Tristan's face.

"He's got Cassidy's coloring, her blue eyes," he said to his wife. "How is your mother?" he asked Tristan with sudden interest.

Tristan's throat closed up on him a second time. He shot a pleading glance at Juliet.

"Cassidy didn't raise Tristan," Juliet informed the other couple. Their confused response prompted her to explain the circumstances of Tristan's abandonment and subsequent adoption. "He only just found out who you are and who his mother was," she tacked on, glancing at him sidelong.

"She's dead," Tristan inserted roughly.

Dismay wreathed Gary's face as he noted Tristan's sorrow. "Cassidy's dead?" he said in disbelief.

Speaking over the lump in his throat, Tristan described his recent trip to Carmel and the awful news he'd received from his aunt.

The colonel covered his eyes as he listened. "I had no idea. I'm so sorry, son. *Son*," he repeated, lowering his hand to send his wife a wonder-filled look. "I have a son as well as two daughters!"

"Wait, I have sisters?" Tristan asked.

"Caitlyn and Ashley," Gary confirmed, leaping up to fetch the two framed photographs off the wall. "Nineteen and twenty-one." He handed them to Tristan to study. "They're both away at college."

"Oh, my God," Tristan could see a family resemblance between all three of them. Holly leaned closer to explain which girl was which and what they were doing with their lives.

Warmed by the woman's acceptance, Tristan glanced at Juliet and saw a softness in her face he had never seen before. The look eased the irritation he'd grappled with earlier over her refusal to admit to feelings for him. If she didn't care for him at all, she wouldn't be so happy for him right now. Whether she realized it or not, his prickly PI was falling for him.

Gary straightened suddenly. "We need to toast this occasion. Holly, honey, where's that bottle of scotch I've been saving?"

"It's in the cabinet above the refrigerator."

Tristan caught Juliet's eye and sent her a smug smile. His father called his woman "honey," too.

Sitting in the cramped, fragrant restaurant in D.C.'s Chinatown, Hilary noticed a thirty-something career woman giving Stu *the look*. A proud little smile twitched across Hilary's as she considered her date through the other woman's eyes.

Dressed in the knit forest-green crewneck sweater and the designer jeans she'd picked out at the mall that morning, Stu only vaguely resembled the awkward man who'd arrived at her apartment the day before.

They'd spent a fabulous day together—first shopping at Tyson's Corner, then taking the Metro into the heart of Washington, D.C. to visit the Air and Space Museum. There, they had read every placard on every display, absorbing the history of aeronautics like a pair of sponges. While waiting for a virtual ride aboard the space shuttle, Stu had, without any provocation on her part, grabbed her hand and held onto it. The memory of that moment caused Hilary's pulse to skitter. Prior to then, she'd never thought of holding hands as a kind of foreplay.

They'd left the museum ravenous for food and grabbed a taxi into Chinatown. And here they were, enjoying the best General Tso chicken she had ever tasted.

"I had the best day ever." Hilary simply couldn't contain her happiness and saw no reason not to expound on it. Except then she recalled that it was all about to end. They would return to her apartment, and Stu would get into his all-electric Volt and drive all the way back to Virginia Beach, after finding some place to charge it. She might never even see him again. Hilary's smile abruptly faded.

Gazing across the table, she was pleased to find Stu regarding her intently. So often, his thoughts were turned inward, but right then, he was really looking at her. Reaching across the table, he laid his hand over hers and lightly stroked her knuckles with his thumb. The sensation, like his unexpected action, made her stomach whirl like a spinning top.

"I could stay, you know," he offered unexpectedly.

"What?" Hilary sat straighter in her seat.

"I have two weeks of downtime before the next assignment. I don't have to go back tonight."

"You mean you have the same time off as Tristan?"

"Yes," Stu affirmed, watching Hilary's reaction.

"Oh." Delight blossomed within her. "Stay, please! It'll take the FBI weeks to catch up to where we are with this investigation. I bet we can put the pieces together before the Bureau even looks into Juliet's allegations."

Stu's answering smile conveyed confidence. "If that's what you want."

What she wanted was for Stu to lay her across her bed and ravish her, and maybe that would fit right in while they attended to Juliet's problem. After all, two weeks was a long time. "Oh, I do," she said earnestly.

His phone buzzed, interrupting whatever he was going to say. Figuring it was Tristan checking in, Hilary watched Stu pluck his cell phone from the holster on his belt. She hadn't had the heart to deny him that particular accessory.

Pretending disinterest, she applied herself to finishing the food on her plate while straining to hear his conversation over the piped-in music. The call lasted all of thirty seconds, and she'd barely had time to swallow a forkful of rice, before he thumbed it to a close and put his phone away.

"Sorry," he apologized.

"Tristan?" she asked.

"My secret contact."

"Oh." Hilary laid down her fork and leaned across her plate. Curiosity consumed her, but she wouldn't ask who the person was, what they did for a living that made them so secretive, or how Stu even knew the person. "What did he or she say?" she whispered.

"He told me where Goebel was offered asylum, and what name he adopted."

Hilary noted with relief that the contact wasn't female. "And?" she prompted, eager to hear what he'd learned.

"He went by Peter Goyle," Stu relayed. "He was given an apartment in San Francisco and a sizeable monthly stipend to live on. He also passed away two years ago."

Possibilities fired off millions of neurons in Hilary's brain at once. Scooting to the edge of her seat, she pitched her voice so only Stu could hear. "Maybe he had a LinkedIn page like Coenen does, and we can establish a connection between them."

Stu's dark eyes glimmered with excitement. Looking away, he sought to catch the waiter's eye.

Minutes later, they were hustling toward the nearest Metro stop, eager to return to her apartment to research Peter Goyle/Dieter Goebel.

Suddenly, with the sureness of a shadow warrior, Stu

hooked an arm around Hilary's waist and backed her against the marble exterior of a fancy hotel. He searched her expression briefly. In the dark, all she could make out were his eyes as he lowered his head and gently brushed her lips.

A thrill rippled through her like water slipping over a rocky streambed. Stu was finally kissing her. Hilary couldn't believe it.

His kiss was as light as the wind wafting down the dark alley—and it made her sizzle from her head to the tippy toes of her purple high-heeled boots.

Lifting his head, he took in her reaction, then lowered his mouth a second time and kissed her hard enough to coax her lips apart. Hilary fought the impulse to take over. It was obvious he hadn't kissed many women. His instincts, however, were unerring, his tentative foray like the *Enterprise* venturing where no man had ever gone before—except that many had. Stu didn't need to know that, of course.

She'd never been kissed like this—as if every second counted. He wasn't simply making a pit stop on his way to the finish line. He was going to stay awhile, explore the terrain, and even classify the life forms.

As the kiss deepened, Hilary's bones went into a slow melt. Yet their height difference must have troubled him for, without warning, he lifted her off her feet and fused his mouth with hers. Behind her closed eyes, the bright lights of the city seemed to spin.

Under ordinary circumstances, Hilary would have groped her partner boldly. But this was Stu, and she was dangling helplessly, so she coiled her arms demurely about his neck. Instead of grinding her pelvis against his thigh, she rubbed his broad shoulders through the soft fabric of his new sweater.

All too soon, he severed the kiss and slowly lowered her to the ground—though not before she felt evidence of his arousal. "Sorry," he said.

As if he had any reason to apologize.

"That's OK. Anytime," she added, hoping Stu would kiss her again.

Instead, he grabbed her hand and pulled her down the street. "Better keep moving. We have a lot of work to do."

The inference that they would be researching Peter Goyle all night and not exploring new frontiers wasn't lost on her. Oddly enough, she was OK with that. There was something nice about dating at Stu's pace. It was like junior high all over again, when a girl could like a guy and didn't have to do backflips to prove it.

As they caught the Silver Line Metro back to Tyson's Corner, Hilary wondered whether she and Stu could connect Hans Coenen and the so-called Peter Goyle before the FBI returned Juliet's phone call. Hell, Juliet would have to give her a raise if that happened!

15

"Well, you must be one hell of a private investigator," Gary Sigmund asserted, fixing his admiring gaze on Juliet.

The four of them were seated around the Sigmunds' coffee table, holding beer bottles and munching on chips. The clock on the muted football game showed a minute left. Having filled his father in on the highlights of his twenty-nine years, Tristan ended his narrative with an explanation of how Juliet had managed to do what the Wilmington police hadn't—track down his birth mother by identifying the man who'd left him as an infant in the medical center.

"My assistant gets the credit for that," Juliet demurred.

"They are both amazing women," Tristan chimed in, bestowing Juliet with an affectionate shoulder rub.

The colonel took note. "So, you two are a couple?" he inquired.

Juliet kept quiet.

"Yes," Tristan answered. He shot her a wounded look for not answering.

Holly and her husband made eye contact.

"I'm here on business," Juliet clarified.

"She's going after the guy who killed her parents," Tristan explained.

Both Sigmunds look at Juliet to see if Tristan was joking. She met their stares without blinking.

"You mind if I tell them?" Tristan asked.

She didn't see much reason to reveal her story, but Tristan seemed eager to share, so she said, "Go ahead."

"OK, so get this." He propped his elbows on his knees as he leaned in to tell his story. "Juliet's mother was a spy for East Germany."

"No way." Holly's expression conveyed skepticism.

"It's true." Tristan insisted. He sketched them a description of Anya Ausfeld's past—her recruitment by the Main Directorate for Reconnaissance and her subsequent attempts to glean intelligence from an American employee of NSA working in West Berlin.

"Wait a minute," Gary Sigmund interrupted. "You know I teach History of the Cold War at the Post-Graduate school, right?" He looked from Tristan to Juliet.

That was news to her. Juliet shook her head. "No, we only knew that you taught here, but not your subject."

Gary waved a dismissive hand. "Anyway, get back to your story."

Tristan hesitated. "Well, maybe Juliet should tell it."

With the Sigmunds eyeing her expectantly, Juliet found herself describing her parents' marriage, her mother's subsequent defection from East Germany, and the couple's mutual plea for asylum in the States. "WITSEC gave Anya and Gerard new names, new jobs as teachers, and a house. I grew up never knowing what they'd been through," she added.

Holly and Gary regarded her with identical expressions of incredulity.

"My parents were safe for twenty years," Juliet continued, pushing through the sudden constriction in her throat. "But, when I was sixteen, I believe my mother's past caught up with her."

With rising agitation, she described the single-car accident and the mechanical malfunctions that led to the death of both parents. "The car was resting on its side in a ditch. My arm got pinned, trapping me in the back seat, but I saw a man looking through my mother's window."

Holly covered her mouth with one hand.

"He couldn't see me, but I saw him clearly. After a minute of staring at my parents, he just turned and walked away. No one came to help for another four hours. I now believe my mother used to work with that man, in the Directorate. I think he caused the accident."

"Oh, you poor girl." Holly looked like she might get out of her seat to come offer her a hug.

Tristan rubbed Juliet's back consolingly.

"Fortunately—or unfortunately, depending on perspective, after I recovered, I had no memory of the man." Juliet shook her head in regret. "It was only a week ago that I remembered seeing him at the car window."

"Juliet's unconscious mind was trying to protect her," Tristan explained.

"That happened to a friend of mine in the Corp," Gary said. "It's not that unusual."

"I believe I have discovered who the man is." Continuing her tale, Juliet explained how she and Tristan ended up searching in San Francisco for Hans Coenen.

Gary's eyes narrowed. "He's here in the U.S.?"

"Yes. He's a retired policeman living in San Francisco."

"A policeman," Holly marveled.

Juliet caught Gary's eye. "Perhaps you've heard of the man who headed up the Directorate—Dieter Goebel?" she asked.

"Of course," Gary said, even as Holly shook her head. "The Man Without a Face, the world's greatest spymaster. The reunified German courts tried and imprisoned him after the Wall came down."

Juliet nodded, pleased to find Gary well informed. "Yes, but Goebel disappeared from jail in 1992 because the CIA offered him asylum in the States."

Gary nodded gravely. "I'd heard that rumor."

"Guess where they placed him." While Tristan had been sharing the highlights of his racing career with Gary, Juliet had received a text from Hilary that confirmed her suspicions. She held up her phone. "My assistant just informed me that he took the name Peter Goyle, and he lived in San Francisco until his death two years ago."

"Really!" Gary sat back with a look of astonishment.

Tristan sent Juliet a startled look. "That explains why his emblem is painted on the mural there."

At Tristan's comment, Juliet explained that Goebel had also been an artist, and that he'd marked his original pieces with the Stasi emblem. "We found the exact same emblem painted on a wall in the Mission District."

"Oh, we've been there," Holly exclaimed. "The murals are fascinating."

Gary sat forward again, his brow creased with thought. "I take it you think Goebel and Coenen remained in contact all these years."

Juliet nodded. "Yes. If I could prove that, I could establish the motive for my parents' murder."

Gary considered her for a moment. "You know, my neighbor is on loan to the Naval Post Graduate School from the FBI."

Juliet saw Tristan's expression brighten.

"Right now, he teaches criminal justice at the academy," Gary added, "but I bet he could get the ball rolling on a federal investigation. Shall I invite him over?"

Juliet hesitated to impose. "Oh, I don't know. This is a special time for you and Tristan—"

"Call him," Tristan demanded, brushing aside her protest.

Juliet looked at him, surprised by his insistence.

"Juliet spoke to Coenen face-to-face," Tristan told the Sigmunds. "They met at the point at Rockaway Beach. She pretty much told the guy she was onto him."

Self-conscious heat seared Juliet's cheeks. "I was hoping to startle a confession out of him. I was taping the confrontation, but he didn't crack."

"I think we should talk to your neighbor," Tristan said.

"What do you think you're doing?" Juliet whispered two hours later.

Even in the dark and unfamiliar bedroom belonging to Gary Sigmund's eldest college-aged daughter, Tristan's silhouette as he slipped out of the Jack-and-Jill bathroom connecting the girls' two rooms could not be mistaken for anyone else's.

Hushing her, he pulled back the covers and joined Juliet in the double bed.

She protested a second time. "If the colonel wanted us to sleep together, he'd have put us in the same room."

"He probably would have, if you hadn't insisted we aren't a couple," Tristan reminded her. "He's just going along with your story."

"It's not a story," Juliet mumbled. "It's reality."

"*This* is reality," Tristan countered, snuggling up to her and pressing the warm pillar of his sex against her hip.

Ignoring a secret surge of excitement, Juliet whispered fiercely. "We are not going to have sex with your father and his wife right across the hall!"

"Who said anything about sex?" Looping an arm around her waist, he flipped her onto her side, facing away from him, then molded himself against her backside. With his member nudging her derriere, it was hard to fix her thoughts on other matters. She tried her best, though.

"It's a good thing we came here," she admitted.

It had seemed like fate, as a matter of fact, when Gary's neighbor, Kevin McNulty, listened raptly to Juliet's story. An hour later he took with him a digital copy of her conversation with Coenen, and promised to talk to the appropriate agent at the Bureau the very next day.

"I agree." Tristan's hand, gentle but determined, skimmed the plane of Juliet's stomach toward her thighs. "Takes a load off my mind, anyway. Puts it somewhere else," he added under his breath.

She snorted at the pun. "You have a one-track mind," Juliet stated, even as she waited on tenterhooks for Tristan to seduce her.

"Is it on the right track?" He'd begun tracing the stitching along the front panel of her panties in a feather-light touch that affected her lung capacity.

"Maybe," she admitted breathlessly.

"Why don't you kiss me and we'll find out?"

Craning her head back toward him, Juliet parted her lips. Even in the dark, there was no mistaking Tristan's smile. He'd won again. She hadn't wanted to admit they were a couple, yet here she was, capitulating once more because she desired him. To justify her weakness, she told herself she needed to forget her encounter with Coenen. Tristan's lovemaking would be an antidote to the memory of that man's expressionless stare. Besides, she was still on vacation, which meant she could behave any way she damn well pleased. *What happens in California stays in California.* That mantra had worked for her down in Mexico, so why not here?

Cutting off her internal monologue, Juliet surrendered to the feel of Tristan nibbling his way down her neck as he rolled up and over her. At the same time, he nudged the fabric of her sleeveless sleepshirt up and over her puckering nipples, exposing them.

"No moaning," he cautioned before tonguing them into stiffness. "No whimpers of delight," he added, blowing cool air across the tight peaks.

Anticipation rippled over her in the form of goosebumps. "I don't whimper," Juliet insisted, even as the hidden muscles in her body thrilled and flexed.

"And definitely no screaming out my name," he said, ignoring her assertion and tossing back the covers to squirm lower. "Otherwise, they'll *know* we're together."

Digging her nails into Tristan's shoulders, Juliet punished him for his impudence. His open mouth descended over the apex of her thighs forcing her to stifle her approving cry. Pleasure radiated from her core. Her skin heated, giving rise to a sudden cooling sweat. By the time Tristan flipped her onto her stomach and pulled her to her knees beneath him, Juliet's heart was pounding, her body quaking.

"Please!" she whispered, curling her fingers into the sheets.

Tristan drove himself into her, sending a cry of raw pleasure up her throat, which she barely caught back. Rocking against him, she met his thrusts with abandonment, arching toward his touch as he reached around her hips to impel her toward release. In seconds, a shattering climax crashed over her, pulling her into a vortex of bliss that spun on for what felt like forever.

Tristan! His name rang out in her mind, imbued with all the passion she felt for him but refused to acknowledge. With their breaths still gusting, they collapsed onto their sides, their bodies still joined, their limbs damp with exertion.

"Hooyah! And holy hell," Tristan breathed.

The emotion overflowing her at that moment caused her breath to hitch. Juliet searched her heart for assurance that this intense connection she felt wasn't love. It couldn't be! It had to be hormones making her want to turn and face Tristan, to press a tender kiss against his neck.

But hormones didn't explain why, in less than a week, she'd come to think of Tristan as an indispensable part of her team. It was he who'd stumbled onto Goebel's emblem, giving them a lead pointing them toward San Francisco. Since then, even with his depression following the discovery of his birth mother's death, he'd proven a dependable counterpart. Ever cheerful, ever considerate, Tristan kept Juliet from drifting into dark thoughts. He'd humored her when she was down. He had even risked a speeding ticket to get her out of that phobia-inducing tunnel. No wonder she felt so attached to him.

Infatuation! Juliet seized the explanation with relief. Of course, it wasn't love. She had simply fallen for Tristan's charm, like every other person who had ever met him. It wasn't permanent. Infatuation was temporary, born of the heightened emotions from what they'd been through together, first in Mexico, and now, here.

All the same, Juliet needed a moment to come to terms with her sudden sense of vulnerability. Lifting Tristan's arms from around her waist, she separated their bodies and stepped out of bed.

"I'm going to go clean up," she whispered. "I'll bring you a washcloth."

Stepping over her panties, she slipped into the adjoining bathroom and locked the door. Dimming the light first so as not to blind herself, she sent an admonishing glare at her tousled reflection. Flushed and bright-eyed, Juliet looked like a woman in love. Except she wasn't.

"Infatuation," she insisted, reaching for a washcloth. She wasn't the type to fall in love. She didn't do relationships.

All the same, she dared a peek into her future, should she decide to stay with Tristan. The Teams would keep him busy. When he got time off, which was usually for several weeks at a stretch the way it was for her sister's husband, Tristan could drive up to Northern Virginia and help with her investigative work. As he'd once said, he had related skills.

Her thoughts went to Tristan's missions, and her imaginings skidded to a stop. How could she have forgotten, even for a minute, the kind of work he did? The dangers of his job made her occupation look like teaching preschool.

Merely thinking about it made Juliet's intestines cramp and her skin grow cold. Could she handle the stress of dating a SEAL, knowing he could die in the line of duty? Hell, no. She wasn't equipped for dating any man, let alone a Navy SEAL.

And yet, her sister, Emma, seemed to handle it. Emma claimed to have faith in her husband's training. She also trusted in the power of positive thinking, stating if she *believed* Jeremiah would return safely from his missions, he would.

No offense to Emma, but for Juliet, faith like that went by a different word—naiveté.

So, no. Juliet wouldn't entertain the option of continuing to see Tristan after they got back home. Which meant she had to pull away, starting immediately.

God, I love you.

Juliet really wished Tristan hadn't said those words the other day. Knowing he had feelings for her made it even harder to break away and hurt him. Then again, he'd gotten over his girlfriend, Mariah, the instant he'd met Juliet on the cruise ship the previous April. With all the women in the world waiting for a man like Tristan, chances were good Juliet would be replaced in his affections about as quickly as the unfortunate Mariah.

Jealousy sank its fangs into her at that thought. Damn it. She had suspected this would happen, which was why she'd gone out of her way to avoid him.

Now, to save them both any more heartache than necessary, Juliet would have to sabotage the bond they had forged. There was no other way—not for her, at least.

With regret filling her heart, she ran a washcloth under the water and proceeded to tidy up.

Sipping from the mug of hot coffee in his hand, Stu looked down at the angel sprawled across the sofa. Mitzie lay curled up in the gap between her legs. Sunlight slanted through the blinds at the window turning Hilary's hair to vermillion. She had tried staying up late with him, fighting back yawns in their mutual quest to discover every bit of information they could on Peter Goyle, looking for one thread connecting him to Hans Coenen.

Too bad they hadn't found it. Around midnight, Hilary had rested her cheek on Stu's shoulder to watch him work through half-shut eyes. Minutes later, he glanced down and found her fast asleep. He'd let her stay like that. She was less distracting when she was asleep, for the looks she'd been giving him all night let him know she was his for the plucking.

But he hadn't plucked. Or even tried anything that rhymed with that word.

Instead, Stu had reminded himself that what Hilary really wanted was the same thing his sister had been looking for—a man to fill the void of her missing father. He wasn't going to be like most men and take advantage of her desperation.

He must have made some kind of sound for Hilary came abruptly awake, sending Mitzie leaping away from her as she sat up to blink at him.

Remembering the glasses he'd taken from her nose the night before, Stu retrieved them off the coffee table, handing them wordlessly to Hilary. She slid them up her nose, took note of the blanket he'd draped over her, and beamed up at him with such a look of adoration that he was tempted to renege on his avowal to cherish her before he bedded her.

"I guess I fell asleep on you," she observed in a sweet, sleepy voice. Swinging her feet to the floor, Hilary stretched languidly, drawing his gaze to the straining fabric of a plaid pajama top that had still had a tag on it when she put it on. "I haven't been much help. Did you find anything?"

Stu had hoped to surprise her with a breakthrough, yet in spite of his persistent efforts, he'd found nothing whatsoever linking Hans Coenen to Peter Goyle. "No, I didn't. Sorry."

Her smooth forehead furrowed. "Don't apologize. You thought of everything," she soothed.

As it turned out, Peter Goyle had never established an online presence with social media accounts, making their quest to find his network of friends exponentially harder. The most Stu had managed was to hack Goyle's credit history, locate his credit card statements from right before his death, and see what kinds of purchases he'd made.

The man's address placed his apartment mere blocks from the Mission District and seven miles from Coenen's townhome, which suggested the two men might never have crossed paths. Tellingly, though, Goyle had eaten out a lot, spending sufficient sums to indicate he'd been buying someone else's meal, as well as his own. Not surprisingly, he'd bought art supplies at a craft store in San Francisco. He'd paid off his credit card monthly with the CIA's generous stipend.

"How'd you sleep?" Stu asked as Hilary worked a kink out of her neck.

"Good. But I had the strangest dream," she replied, visibly recalling it.

"About what?" Stu asked.

"I was at my father's funeral, standing next to his coffin, except my mother wasn't there. And the body didn't look like Daddy's. I think my mind substituted in Peter Goyle for my father."

Her words had Stu easing onto the couch next to her and putting down his coffee mug. The gears in his head began to turn. "That *was* a weird dream."

"All of my father's friends were there to pay their respects, just like they'd been at Daddy's funeral, only it wasn't him in the casket. I kept expecting someone to point it out, but no one did."

The confusion and loneliness in Hilary's voice broke him down. Stu put an arm around her, and she immediately snuggled closer, soaking up his comfort with dizzying abandon. He could press her back against the couch and demand virtually anything of her, and she would do it, all in the hope of filling the hole in her heart caused by her father's death.

Stu forced himself to picture Hilary, young and devastated, standing by her father's coffin. Deep down, she was still that lonely girl.

Suddenly, he envisioned Peter Goyle lying in a coffin, and a thought pierced his consciousness. "Oh," he exclaimed, thinking it through. Releasing Hilary, he reached for his laptop. "That's it."

She searched his face in bafflement. "What's it?"

His pulse quickened. "Someone would have had to make the arrangements for Goebel's funeral, right? Maybe it was Coenen. At the very least, if they were friends, Coenen would have come to pay his respects. Funeral homes keep electronic guestbook ledgers. If we can access the one for Goebel, we'll know at least some of the people who considered him a friend."

"That's brilliant!" She gripped the muscles of his upper

arm. "Let's find his obituary. The name of the funeral home should be in it."

As Stu logged onto his laptop, Hilary hugged him in anticipation. In his excitement, he caved in to the urge to kiss her though, targeting her cheek instead of her lips. "You are brilliant, Cat Lady," he praised.

"Right," Hilary scoffed. "Like this wasn't your idea." All the same, she blushed prettily at his compliment.

The wave of lust that crashed over Stu made his heart race and his blood simmer. They couldn't afford to get sidetracked now, though, not with Coenen fully aware that he was being scrutinized.

Surely those who'd spent their lives devoted to Dieter Goebel's vision had come forward at his death to pay their respects. Hopefully, they could find proof that Hans Coenen was one of them.

16

Watching the giant Pacific octopus make its way toward them across the rock wall at the back of the display, Juliet caught herself about to lean into Tristan, who stood next to her. She shouldn't do that anymore, she realized, squelching her remorse.

The rosy-hued cephalopod held their attention as it drifted closer. Roughly the size of a house dog, its eight long tentacles extended and retracted, each with an agenda of its own. Flaps on its bulbous head pumped rhythmically, propelling it toward the transparent pane of acrylic glass separating its home from the human visitors.

"Look, she's coming to see you," Tristan murmured. His sidelong glance told Juliet he knew something had changed and had decided to give her space.

Juliet's thoughts went to the moment she'd awakened, tangled for the last time in his embrace. She'd allowed herself to watch Tristan sleep, marveling as she had down in Mexico at the fact that he didn't snore; admiring the way tawny stubble glinted on his jaw, how he seemed to smile in his sleep when his face relaxed. A pang of loss had pierced her heart, but it was nothing compared to the pain she'd feel if he died in the line of duty after she'd inextricably linked herself to him.

Determined to save herself from future torment, she'd slid from his embrace and scarcely touched him since.

She had yet to tell him their affair was over, though. Tristan wasn't stupid. He would figure it out by the time they flew home. She almost hoped he would act desperate and clingy, arousing her annoyance and giving her incentive to shake him off. He hadn't. Not yet anyway. He'd been the perfect companion, cheery, stable, and concerned.

Caught up in her circuitous thoughts, Juliet watched with half an eye as hundreds of suction cups rippled delicately over the rocky aquarium floor. The eyes on either side of the octopus's head appeared to study them intently as it glided closer.

"How do you know it's a she?" she demanded just to be contrary.

"By the sexy way she moves," Tristan whispered in her ear.

The rippling motion of the tentacles did strike Juliet as rather sensuous. And the gruff tenor of Tristan's voice sent a pleasant shiver down her body.

"Actually, the guard just told us," he amended with a chuckle. "That one over there is male." He gestured to the tank adjacent to where they stood. "This one's female. She's got more *suckers*," he added, imbuing the word with a sexual connotation.

Elbowing him for his lewdness, Juliet glanced toward the male counterpart in a tank twenty feet away. Seeing her and Tristan's full-length reflection on the tank's acrylic wall, she was struck by how right they looked standing next to each other. Anyone glancing in their direction would see a couple who belonged together.

She noticed a reflection in the glass of someone standing well behind them. The sparse shock of white hair, the distinct shape of the man's head, caused Juliet to suck in a breath. She whipped around to find the person she'd just glimpsed. *Hans Coenen?*

All she saw was the back of a head as someone strode out of sight behind the staircase. Ignoring Tristan's puzzled call, she gave chase, her heart thudding in the expectation of confronting Coenen for a second time. Had he followed them? Seriously, was he stalking her even now?

Rounding the staircase, hearing Tristan right behind her, she drew up short, searching the aquarium's crowded lobby. The man she'd seen had disappeared into the crush of visitors.

Maybe she'd imagined him. After all, there'd been no indication Coenen had followed them farther than Rockaway Beach. He would have had to linger long enough to see them swap out vehicles.

Tentacles of fear reached into Juliet's brain.

"Hey." Tristan curled a hand around her elbow, pulling her around. He searched her distracted face before looking around the lobby. "Did you see something?"

Her imagination had to be running amok due to lack of sleep. No one in the crowd remotely resembled Coenen. "No."

The feel of her phone buzzing in her purse provided an excuse not to discuss the matter. Pulling it out, Juliet noted the unfamiliar number. "I think this is the FBI getting back to me." Glancing around for a quiet place to answer the call, she spied a set of glass doors behind them leading to a quiet patio overlooking the bay. "I'm going to take this call out there."

Tristan had caught sight of the touch pool just inside the doors. "I'll be right here," he said, causing her to glance at the stingrays circling the shallow water. "Stay where I can see you."

She nodded at him, answering the call at the same time. "Hello," she said, pushing through the door onto the sunlit but chilly terrace. The breeze from the bay threatened to snatch her voice away.

"Mrs. Whitby? This is Renata Blumenthal from The People's Eyes Mural Center."

Renata's accent, so like Juliet's mother's, stirred her emotions.

"Oh, yes. Hello, Ms. Blumenthal." Juliet hadn't honestly expected the woman to call.

"How is your vacation going, my dear?"

"Great, thanks."

"Sorry it took me so long to identify the artist who painted the mural you inquired about."

Anticipation pulsed through Juliet as the door clicked shut behind her. She pressed her phone to her ear to hear over the cries of seabirds. "You found him?"

"It's the work of a local artist who passed away two years ago. His name was Peter Goyle."

Victory buoyed Juliet's spirit at the confirmation that they'd located Dieter Goebel's final stomping grounds. Now if only they could connect the spymaster to Hans Coenen, they could attribute a motive to her parents' killer. "Sorry to hear he passed away. He must have touched the lives of many people through his artwork."

"Oh, I'm sure he did. I also discovered some of the other murals he painted. Why don't you come back this way, and I'll point them out to you in a private tour."

"Oh, that's so sweet of you." Juliet paused to consider the woman's intent. Why would she go out of her way to appease the Whitbys' curiosity? Would it gain Juliet and Tristan anything to look at Goebel's most recent paintings? "We might do that."

"Lovely," Renata exclaimed. "I'll put you down for the day after tomorrow in the morning. Would that work for you?"

"Um…sure." Juliet figured she could always cancel if neither Hilary nor Tristan saw any benefit to meeting the woman again.

"I'll see you Thursday, then. Shall we say ten in the morning?"

"Yes." Juliet made a mental note to put it on her calendar. "Thank you," she tacked on.

"You're most welcome, dear. See you soon."

"Bye." Thumbing the call to a close, Juliet let the wind whip her loose hair as she reflected on Renata's invitation. The woman had confirmed the intelligence Hack had gleaned from some mysterious source. All the pieces of the puzzle were coming together.

Hearing someone approaching behind her, Juliet mustered a polite smile and stepped aside to allow access to the door. A powerful hand closed without warning around her upper arm. Turning her head, she gasped her dismay as Hans Coenen plucked her cell phone from her grasp and nodded toward Tristan.

"Look."

Following Coenen's gaze through the glass, Juliet realized that Irena Kapova was standing close behind Tristan, who watched in fascination as the stingrays were being fed. Returning Juliet's mystified gaze, the woman drew a glinting stiletto from the pocket of her fawn-colored jacket then tucked it out of sight again. The message was clear. Tristan was not to be involved.

"Let's talk," Coenen suggested, tugging Juliet away from the door and windows, out of sight from Tristan, who was reaching to pet the stingrays. "No need to provoke, my comrade. She's a tad unstable, that one." Coenen's conversational tone struck Juliet as entirely at odds with his reticence the day before.

"What do you want?" she demanded, refusing to budge another inch beyond the corner of the building. "Why are you following me?"

Coenen slanted her a chiding look. "I've come to warn you, Miss Rhodes." His expression as well as his voice conveyed concern for her safety.

As the same time, his casual use of her surname caused a chill to sweep through Juliet.

"I'm a reasonable man," he continued affably. "Having considered the allegations you made yesterday, I am compelled to take countermeasures."

His words implied the subtlest of threats.

"The accident that befell your parents was most tragic," he acknowledged.

Juliet's thoughts flew to her surveillance device, lying useless in the pocket of her purse. If only she were wearing it now, for his words suggested he was well aware of precisely what had occurred, in spite of his denial at Rockaway Beach.

"Yet you waste your time trying to prove my involvement." Coenen sounded like a father giving advice. "Should you persist in persecuting me," Coenen paused, turning his head and making her realize that from where he stood, he could still see Tristan and Kapova. Looking back at Juliet he added, "Let's just say the consequences wouldn't be worth it. My friend would take great delight in slitting the throat of a U.S. serviceman. She's also a crack-shot with a pistol."

A buzzing filled Juliet's ears. Good God, Coenen *had* been behind the traffic stop the previous day. Worse than that, he'd just threatened Tristan's life! She felt her cheeks grow cold as the blood drained from her head toward her fast-pumping heart.

Leaning toward her, Coenen whispered as if they were conspiring together, "She used to be KGB."

That statement slid into Juliet's psyche like a ghost walking through a wall. The KGB hadn't existed since 1991, yet even today the acronym invoked fear and mistrust.

Too shaken to respond, she stared at Coenen through dilated pupils.

"I've kept you long enough." He started to hand her cell phone back, then appeared to reconsider.

A cry of denial escaped Juliet as he hurled it over the railing. The sound of plastic shattering on the rocks below assured her the phone was now useless.

"Have a good day, Miss Rhodes." With a nod, Coenen turned and walked casually toward the crowd thronging the outdoor steps to the Great Tide Pool.

Dismissing him as he disappeared behind a troupe of teenagers, Juliet whirled back toward the glass doors. *Tristan!* However, Kapova had already vanished. Tristan still knelt at the pool's edge, thoroughly engaged in playing with the sea creature, blithely unaware of the threat that had just been issued.

Seeing him unharmed, Juliet's knees went weak. She

tugged at the door but found herself suddenly too feeble to haul it open. Belated shock rendered her lightheaded. She clung to the door's handle, drawing deep breaths to compose herself.

To think that Coenen had braved the popular tourist attraction's security cameras to issue an ultimatum! If she persisted in her investigation of him, Tristan could wind up killed. And what if he found out about Emma and Sammy?

Coming from anyone else, Juliet might have dismissed such a threat as a ruse. After all, Tristan was more than capable of defending himself. But Coenen had been trained by the ruthless Goebel, so why would he bluff? As for Kapova, if she was ex-KGB, she might, in fact, be capable of slitting Tristan's throat if she caught him by surprise. She could more easily shoot him from across a parking lot. All the training in the world couldn't protect a body from a bullet.

Tristan's job was dangerous enough as it was. The thought that she might be responsible for his death was unthinkable. "Hell, no," she breathed. Coenen didn't get to take the life of anyone else she loved.

Oh, so you love him now?

Oh, my God. She drew a sharp breath at the realization that —yes, she did. She'd probably loved him since the cruise. But in her stubborn refusal to get involved with him, she'd fooled herself into thinking otherwise. Looking at him now as he grinned down at the stingray he'd befriended, her heart swelled with emotion.

He must have realized how much time had lapsed, for he straightened off the ledge and looked for her. Glimpsing her expression, his smile of fulfillment faded. He leaped off the ledge and hurried in her direction.

What the hell would she tell him? Not the truth—she couldn't.

If Tristan learned that Coenen had threatened her, he would stick to her like white on rice, if only to protect her. The possibility that Kapova might target him at some unexpected moment wouldn't even phase him. He'd be more concerned about Coenen coming after *Juliet*, whether she ceased her investigating or not.

Opening the door between them, Tristan searched her pallid face. "You OK, honey?"

The concern in his voice made her heart melt with love for him. Her nose tingled as the urge to cry overwhelmed her. Not trusting herself to speak, she nodded.

He stepped outside, letting the door fall shut behind him. "Was it the FBI calling?"

She shook her head and sought a normal-sounding voice. "No, it was Renata Blumenthal."

"Oh, her." His eyebrows came together. "What did she say?"

"That an artist named Peter Goyle painted that emblem."

Tristan shrugged. "OK, so we were right."

"She invited me up to look at some of Goyle's other paintings, but I don't see the point. I think I'm done," Juliet added with a shaky breath. "I think I'm ready to leave now."

His expression reflected confusion. "Already? We haven't even seen the IMAX movie about the rescued otter."

He sounded so let down that she nearly relented. But realizing how hard it was going to be to push him away made staying any longer impossible. "I'm sorry, Tristan. I need to leave."

She caught herself glancing in the direction Coenen had disappeared. The man would certainly be somewhere close, watching her response to their conversation.

"What's going on, Juliet?"

Tristan was watching her through narrowed eyes. His tone demanded honesty. The impulse to tell him everything rose within her with the force of a geyser. Still, she managed to repress it. Tristan would never back out of her life if he knew of Coenen's threat. He'd hover ever closer, making it impossible for her to ensure his safety while also resisting his effect on her emotions. She'd wanted to break up with him anyway. Now she had good reason to.

"I'm done," Juliet repeated, forcing the words through a tight throat.

He frowned and cocked his head. "Done with the aquarium?" he asked carefully.

She licked her suddenly parched lips. "Done with my investigation," she said, searching for a reason to excuse her change of heart. Tristan had to believe his help was no longer necessary. "I've thought about it, and I don't see the purpose of going after Coenen anymore. It was Goebel who put him up to it. Coenen was merely the messenger. And Goebel is dead so...that's it."

Tristan's eyes had turned to slits as he pondered Juliet's explanation.

"There's no point to my being here," she persisted, desperate to make him believe her. "I have work to do at home. I think I'll head back today."

Watching Tristan's face freeze over like ice on the surface of a pond, Juliet's heart gave a spasm of protest.

"Seriously?" he demanded. Anger colored his voice. "I thought you were enjoying yourself."

She had been—way more than she wanted to. "I did," she admitted.

"What about us?"

The question made her waver—until she pictured blood gushing from a bullet wound in his chest. She forced an answer through her aching throat. "I told you this from the beginning, Tristan. There is no *us*. I don't do relationships. Nothing can change that. Please take me to your dad's to get my bag. I'll take an Uber to the airport."

Disbelief swam in his gaze as he stared down at her. "You can't do this," he finally said.

"I'm sorry." She reached for the door, intending to haul it open.

His palm struck the glass before she got the chance. "Wait."

Startled by his vehemence, Juliet gazed up into Tristan's thunderous countenance and quailed. In her peripheral vision, she could see people watching curiously.

"If you go through with this, I'm not going to come crawling on my knees, begging you to change your mind. This'll be it. You won't see or hear from me ever again."

His words hit her like a fist to the gut, driving the air from her lungs. It was all she could do not to throw her arms around him and sob *I don't want to!*

Terror for his safety locked her trembling knees and grappled her emotions into submission. His safety took precedence over justice for her dead parents. After all, nothing would bring them back, not ever. Tristan, though, was very much alive, and she intended to keep it that way.

"I understand," she managed.

An expressionless mask usurped Tristan's frown. His lips thinned, and his eyes turned hard as marbles. "Let's go." He clipped the words out, pulling the door open and gesturing for her to precede him.

His cold tone made her want to cry. However, sensing Coenen's gaze on her person, Juliet lifted her chin and walked back inside the building. Her vacation with Tristan had come to a sudden, heartbreaking end. It was better this way. He could move forward unaware of the threat against him. Sure, he'd be sad for a while. He might even hate her. But she had to believe he wouldn't be alone for long.

She'd done the right thing. If only it didn't contradict every emotion pulsing through her body. So much for protecting her heart by keeping her distance. That rational about love not being real when it happened on vacation? She couldn't have been more wrong.

"Which airline?" Tristan asked as they neared Monterey Regional Airport.

Juliet didn't respond right away. "United," she finally answered, her voice barely audible over the roar of a plane taking off.

The tension was thick enough to carve. The two of them

had scarcely exchanged a word since leaving the aquarium. He had driven Juliet to his father's house to get her stuff but had refused to make up some excuse for her abrupt departure. His silence forced Juliet to explain to a baffled Holly that her sudden decision to leave was because she'd decided to suspend her investigation. Listening to Juliet's excuse, Tristan wondered why on earth she would do that.

Between their time together in Mexico and the last few days spent non-stop in her company, he'd thought he'd gotten to know Juliet fairly well. She wasn't the type to let an injustice pass. Nor was she flakey or flighty or prone to sudden changes of mind. So what the hell was going on? Something had happened that was making her act this way, only he had no idea what.

"I'll call an Uber," she'd insisted when she'd come out of her bedroom with her suitcase. He'd watched her grub in her purse for her cell phone, stop, and look like she'd just remembered something.

"Where's your phone?" he'd asked since she obviously couldn't find it.

"Doesn't matter." Juliet shook her head, refusing to explain. "Maybe I can use the house phone."

Her closed attitude made Tristan's temples throb. "How can it not matter?" he'd demanded, chasing her down the hall. "You use your phone for work. If you left it at the aquarium, I'll take you back to get it."

She'd kept her back to him, schlepping her suitcase down the stairs. "I accidentally dropped it off the patio. It's gone. Broken."

What the hell? Her excuse was so blatantly a lie. Half an hour later, it still mystified him. How could she have dropped her phone off the patio and not mention it? Exactly what had he missed in those ten minutes he'd been petting stingrays?

Had he said something earlier that she'd taken the wrong way? He wanted to ask, but he was sick and tired of her pushing him away. Damn it, he'd been celibate for six months simply to earn the right to date her. He'd helped with her investigation with the hope that time spent together would remind her of how great they got along. He had never felt as much chemistry with any other woman as he had with Juliet, and he probably never would.

Nevertheless, neither his sacrifices nor his actions had gotten him what he wanted. Why should he further dent his pride by demanding an explanation?

Slowing next to the curb at the terminal, he slanted her one final look. She had donned a pair of sunglasses and was gazing out the passenger window, her face averted.

As Tristan popped the lever to open the trunk, she reached for the door handle, about to scramble free. In spite of his pride, he found himself grabbing her arm to delay her.

"If I did or said something wrong, I just want to say I'm sorry." His gruff apology was a last-ditch effort to bridge the gap.

She froze. Watching her profile, he saw her lower lip quiver. For a second, he believed she might turn to him and tell him it was all her—that she needed time to adjust to being with someone. Juliet's chest rose on a shaky breath. As she turned her head and looked him in the eye, he was pleased to see tears glimmering behind the lenses of her sunglasses. At least she was feeling *something*. His heart went into free fall.

"Good-bye, Tristan."

With her words, his optimism nosedived. She thrust her door open and sprang from her seat. By the time he arrived at the back of the vehicle, she was lifting her suitcase out of the trunk. Without so much as a glance in his direction, she set it on the curb, turned, and strode away, wheeling it behind her.

Tristan stared at the back of her head until she disappeared through the automatic doors. Recalling that she'd lost or destroyed her cell phone, he wondered how she was going to communicate with anyone—most importantly Hilary, who would be equally as dumfounded as Tristan to hear that her boss was finished with investigating Coenen.

At that precise moment, Tristan's cell phone buzzed, and he snatched it from his pocket. Speak of the devil. "Hey," he said.

"Hi, Tristan." Hilary's bright greeting contrasted sharply with his gloomy tone. "Juliet's not answering her phone for some reason, and I have something really important to tell her." Juliet's assistant sounded like she might burst with excitement.

A driver behind him beeped his horn, urging Tristan to move out and make room for others. "She destroyed her phone somehow," he explained, slipping back into his car.

"How'd she do that?" Hilary asked.

"No idea." His glum terseness finally got her attention.

"Is everything OK?" Now Hilary sounded worried.

"Not exactly." Putting his phone on speaker, Tristan set it in the cup holder and concentrated on merging back into traffic. "I just dropped her off at the airport. She said she was pulling the plug on her investigation and she wanted to leave."

Hilary's silence was a replay of his earlier disbelief. Then she exploded. "What? I mean, seriously! What. The. Hell! We have been busting our butts back here for hours upon hours. Not only that, we just had a breakthrough on our end," she reported.

Tristan's curiosity flickered. "What kind of breakthrough?" he asked, changing lanes and accelerating.

"You'll never guess who arranged and paid for Peter Goyle's funeral."

He took a stab at it. "Hans Coenen?"

"Nope, Renata Blumenthal."

"What?" Renata had been speaking to Juliet during those ten minutes that changed everything.

"Renata knew all along who painted that emblem. She and Peter Goyle were a couple. They'd been together for decades before he died," Hilary relayed.

"Are you kidding me?" Tristan was briefly distracted by the road signs he was approaching while trying to discern which way to go. "Isn't she like twenty years younger?"

"Twenty-five," Hilary corrected. "You can tell by the condolences written in his funeral register that people considered her his common-law wife."

Tristan gave a thoughtful grunt. "It's all moot now," he decided. "Juliet's made up her mind that, with Goebel dead, she's not going after Coenen."

"I can't believe that." Hilary's denial was just as fervent as Tristan's had been.

"Yeah, me neither. Listen, I gotta go so I can use my map app. I think I took the wrong exit."

"Oh, sure. Sorry. Are you OK, Tristan? You sound really upset."

Self-pity was a noose around his neck. "I gotta go," he repeated hanging up on her.

Upset was an understatement. The thought of never holding Juliet again, never spending time with her, sucked every drop of joy out of him. He'd known for a while that he was in love with her—though he hadn't realized until then how much he'd been relying on her falling in love with him, too.

No, he wasn't upset. He was fucking devastated.

17

Standing in the breezeway outside of Hilary's quiet apartment, Juliet strained her ears for evidence that her assistant was up and moving at eight o'clock in the morning. All Juliet could hear was the light patter of rain in the parking lot. She could always wait for Hilary to come rolling into the office around 10 a.m. and give her new phone number to her then, but no doubt her red-headed techno wonder had to be worried about her. Besides she wanted to make sure Hilz knew they were still definitely on the case of her parents' murderer.

By now, Hilary would have most certainly called Tristan, which meant she would have heard about her boss's decision to suspend the investigation. Juliet couldn't wait to set her straight. Coenen had threatened her because she was on to him. If she could link him somehow, some way to Goebel, she could establish his motive for murdering her parents.

Silence followed Juliet's firm knock. Hilary was definitely still sleeping.

Damn it, this wouldn't be necessary if the woman didn't get herself a new cell number every time she broke up with a boyfriend. Juliet would have simply texted her already, using the cheap flip phone she'd purchased at a kiosk at Monterey Regional.

The scraping of the chain lock preceded the door swinging

open. Juliet blinked in surprise to see the SEAL who'd manned a laptop in his part of a search-and-rescue team in Mexico gazing down at her. She hadn't heard his footsteps, but then, of course, he would have moved swiftly and silently.

"Oh. You haven't left yet," she exclaimed. No wonder Hilary was still in bed then.

On the other hand, Hack was fully dressed and, given the scent of bacon wafting out of the apartment, he'd been up for a while now.

"Remember me?" she prompted when he simply stood there, saying nothing.

"Juliet." He stepped back and let her in.

"Thanks. Um, sorry to show up like this, but I need to talk to Hilary." A blanket and pillow stacked on the couch in the living room caught her eye. "Is she awake yet?"

Hilary's door swung open. "I am now." There she stood in a pair of plaid pajamas, her hair sticking up in all directions.

All signs suggested the couple had not slept together. Juliet divided a speculative gaze between them.

Hilary propped her hands on her hips. "What the heck is going on?" she demanded of Juliet. "Tristan said you'd destroyed your phone or something, and you were pulling the plug on the investigation."

Aware of Hack's acute interest, Juliet hesitated to make her reply. "Can I speak with you alone?" she asked uncomfortably.

"What?" Hilary exclaimed with predictable affront.

"I'll take a walk," Hack offered, pivoting toward the door.

Juliet shot him a grateful look. For a man described by his teammate as socially inept, Hack proved himself surprisingly astute.

"Ten minutes," she called as he stepped outside the door, shutting it behind him.

Juliet met Hilary's baffled gaze. "Can we talk in your bedroom?" She couldn't take the chance of Hack overhearing their conversation.

Hilary shrugged and led the way, flicking on the light. The half-made bed affirmed Juliet's ealier guess. Curiosity made her want to ask what their status was, but she stuck to the matter at hand.

"You can't tell Hack any of this." With sudden exhaustion, Juliet dropped onto the edge of Hilary's bed and scrubbed a hand over her eyes. In spite of arriving home late the night before, she hadn't slept so much as a wink. Tristan, who had once avowed he loved her, had to hate her now. She would never again feel his arms around her, never know the sweet bliss of his kisses.

Hilary gazed down at her, visibly confused and concerned. "What's going on, Jules?" she demanded.

Juliet dropped her hand and sat up straighter. "Coenen caught up with me at the Monterey Aquarium yesterday."

Hilary gasped. Her eyes seemed to fill her face. "Tristan didn't tell me that."

"He doesn't know. And that's the way it's going to stay." In a ragged voice, Juliet related what had happened the previous morning, including Coenen's threat and his assertion that Kapova had once been KGB.

Hilary wrung her hands. "You really think they would target Tristan?"

Her skepticism was understandable. Tristan could probably take on Coenen and Kapova at the same time with one arm tied behind his back. No man, however, could stop a bullet coming unexpectedly out of nowhere. Juliet wasn't willing to take any chances.

"I know it sounds improbable, but we can't underestimate Coenen. And who knows what Kapova is capable of if it's true she was really KGB. Maybe she only pretended to defect so she could spy on the U.S. and report back to the Kremlin."

"I suppose that's possible," Hilary relented. "I can't picture any woman slitting Tristan's throat though. Shooting him, maybe. How would they even know where to find him? Special Ops protects their warriors. It's not as if his address is listed online."

"Exactly. As long as Tristan's down in Virginia Beach, he's safe. But not with me."

"Oh." Comprehension dawned in Hilary's eyes. "So that's why you broke up with him! Oh, Juliet, that's so sweet!" Throwing herself down on the bed beside her, Hilary gave Juliet a heartfelt hug.

Pain wrenched at Juliet's heart. "No, I broke up with him because I don't need or want a relationship," she insisted. "It was going to end anyway. The situation just enabled me to do it before he became too invested."

Hilary sat back to regard her sadly. "And you're not?" she gently queried.

Tears promptly rushed into Juliet's eyes. Ignoring the question, she sprang up to pace around the bed and back. "I don't want Hack knowing any of this. You can't tell him in confidence, either. SEALs are tight. They have this teamwork philosophy that's drilled into them. If Tristan finds out about Coenen's threat, he's not going to stay away. He'll be back in my life, all concerned that Coenen's going to come after *me*."

"Wait." Hilary clapped a hand to her chest and came to her feet. "You haven't even heard the latest, have you?"

Juliet stopped prowling. "Heard what?"

"Renata Blumenthal and Dieter Goebel, who became Peter Goyle, were a couple for at least two decades."

"Are you kidding me?" Juliet's head spun at the unexpected news.

"Not kidding. Renata paid for his funeral, and according to the condolences written in the online guest ledger, people thought of her as his wife, even though they never married. She knew him intimately, Juliet! She *knew* he'd painted the emblem when you asked about it, only she pretended *not* to know, perhaps to protect him."

"She called my cell yesterday while we were visiting the aquarium," Juliet recalled, viewing that exchange from a new perspective. "Oh, my God, she invited me to come visit The People's Eyes on Thursday morning so she could show me more of Goyle's murals!"

Hilary's eyes narrowed. "Why would she all of a sudden trust you?"

Suspicion crawled along the nape of Juliet's neck. "Who said she trusts me? Maybe she was trying to lure me back so she could probe my intentions."

"Do you think she worked for Goebel, too," Hilary asked, "like Coenen did?"

Juliet considered the question. "I don't know. She's a little young to have been a spy during the Cold War."

"No younger than your mother was."

The tired neurons in Juliet's brain sparked anew. "It's possible. I guess we need to find out."

Hilary clapped her hands gleefully. "Then we're not pulling the plug," she concluded.

Juliet spared a thought to Tristan's safety. As long as he was nowhere near her, he'd be safe. "No. I never intended to stop this investigation. We need to connect Hans Coenen to Peter Goyle, the same way we connect Renata to him."

"I knew you weren't really giving up," Hilary declared.

"Tristan doesn't need to know that," Juliet reminded her. "Again, I'm sorry, but Hack can't know either."

Her assistant's smile faded.

"I swear if he knows anything about what really happened yesterday, he's going to tell Tristan, and Tristan will show up at my door demanding to know why I lied to him. I really can't face him right now," Juliet added, revealing the depth of her vulnerability.

Hilary just looked at her boss, unable to reply.

"Listen, I'm not saying that you can't continue to see Hack," Juliet hedged, "but it would be better if you'd wait until after we find a way to get Coenen arrested."

"That could take months!" Hilary protested.

"I know, but how will you feel if you say something to Hack, who tells Tristan, who starts hanging around me and winds up getting killed? Coenen knows my address, remember? He arranged that purse snatching so a cop had a reason to ask for my ID. He knows where I live."

"Doesn't he know where Tristan lives, too?" Hilary argued. "Didn't he arrange for that cop to pull him over?"

Juliet had suspected as much, but Hilary was the first to articulate Coenen's involvement. She nodded thoughtfully. "Yes, only his driver's license is from North Carolina. Like you said earlier, SEALs keep their whereabouts secret. Coenen can't find him if he's not hanging around me."

"Look." Hilary lifted her chin in the air to make a point, "I'm not going to stop seeing Stuart, and I'm not keeping this information from him. However, I will swear him to silence," she offered. "We need his help, Jules. We're not going to implicate Coenen or find out anything more about Kapova without him. He's a freaking genius."

Juliet's shoulders slumped. Too exhausted to pursue her argument, she let it go. She would simply have to trust Hilary to do what was best for all of them.

"Fine," she conceded. "Whatever. Just try to keep Hack quiet." She turned and exited the bedroom. "I've got to get to the office and catch up on stuff. Please join me as soon as you can. The FBI's not going to consider my allegations if we don't give them more. Oh, and I have a new cell phone number. I'll give it to you when you come to work."

Hilary chased after her. "You're being careful, aren't you, Jules?"

"Of course." She'd changed the passcode on her apartment door, and she kept her pistol either on her person or in her purse at all times. She paused with her hand on the doorknob. "You're sure you can swear Hack to silence?" she asked her assistant.

Hilary nodded definitively. "Absolutely sure," she stated.

Mollified, Juliet let herself out of the apartment and started down the zigzag steps that led to the parking lot. Halfway down, she encountered Hack on his way back up.

"Sorry about that," she muttered by way of apology.

With a slight nod in her direction, he continued wordlessly past her.

Juliet shrugged and rolled her eyes. He certainly was a man of few words. In her present situation, that was a trait that could save Tristan's life—provided loyalty to his teammate didn't take precedence.

"Good God, son, you're going to kill me." Gary Sigmund slowed to a stop at the scenic overlook at the top of a sand dune and propped his hands on his knees to catch his breath. "I thought I was in shape," he panted as Tristan slowed next to him. "This is humiliating."

"For a marine, you're in great shape," Tristan ribbed, taking in the view of the beach below them. A veil of morning mist hovered over the blue-gray bay, keeping them from seeing very far beyond the waves that lapped softly onto shore. A gentle breeze ruffled the hardy wildflowers at Tristan's feet and dried the sweat from his skin, lifting away a portion of the depression that had shackled him since Juliet's departure the previous day.

It was only at Gary's insistence that he'd dragged out of bed at dawn. Now, he was glad he had given in. Halfway through their five-mile run, he could feel the endorphins kicking in.

"Gorgeous view, isn't it?" his father asked, straightening to take it in.

"Hooyah," Tristan agreed, but it would have been better if Juliet were present to admire it with him.

"Ready to head back?" Gary asked.

Tristan mustered his enthusiasm. "Yeah, sure."

They set off at an easy lope, following the reverse imprints of their sneakers, left along the sandy path. Down the face of the dunes and through an abandoned WWII artillery range they trotted, arriving at a barbed wire fence that kept the range off-limits to non-military personnel. They had passed beneath the highway and were making their way along a row of crumbling barracks when a dark Buick turned at the intersection ahead and sped downhill toward them.

Tristan braced himself for trouble as the vehicle slowed, but a familiar face appeared behind the lowering driver's window. Kevin McNulty waved them over.

"Morning," he said as they crossed the deserted street to greet him. "Holly told me you'd gone for a run. I'm glad I was able to catch you before I headed to work." Excitement shone in his brown eyes as he directed them at Tristan. "What you told me last night caused a stir at the Bureau."

Tristan shared a look with his father. The previous evening, with Hilary's latest intelligence nagging at him, he had excused himself from Holly and Gary's dinner table to walk next door and advise McNulty of Renata Blumenthal's relationship with the former head of the Stasi.

Kevin reached inside of his suit jacket and pulled out an index card. "Renata Blumenthal is apparently already under investigation. She's been on a watch list for some time due to her radical political views. She's been promoting Marxism and gaining popularity with disgruntled millennials for some time. Everyone agrees she's a kook, though no one really thought she was dangerous until you told us who her boyfriend was. The CIA, in their infinite wisdom, hadn't shared Goyle's history with the Bureau—typical power play. Knowing Goyle used to be Goebel makes Ms. Blumenthal's agenda seem a little more ominous."

Tristan used his T-shirt to wipe the sweat off his forehead.

"Long story short," Kevin continued, "an interagency task force already has dibs on Blumenthal. They've been watching her for years. When they got word of your intel, they wanted to invite you or Juliet to the National Counterterrorism Center in Northern Virginia, to speak with them. I tried calling Juliet, but I couldn't get through."

"Her phone got destroyed yesterday," Tristan explained. "I'll get the message to her," he promised, thinking he could tell Hack, who could relay the message to Hilary, who could then tell Juliet. "What about Hans Coenen? Did his name ring a bell, too?"

"Nope. Only Blumenthal." Kevin handed Tristan the index card. "This is the name and number of the task force lead," he said. "Make sure Juliet gets that and calls him today."

Tristan glanced at the information and frowned. Isaac Calhoun. Didn't he know that name?

"Thanks." Tristan shook Kevin's hand through the open car window. "I won't let you down." If a task force took over Juliet's investigation, he wouldn't have to worry so much about Coenen trying to silence her. That gave him one less thing to fret over.

"Better get to class." With a parting nod, the agent drove off.

Gary threw an arm over Tristan's shoulder. "You want to tell me why she took off on you?" he prodded gently.

"Not really." The pressure filling his chest suggested he might start crying if he did.

"Hey, but now you have a reason to talk to her. Maybe you could mend things," Gary suggested.

Tristan's thoughts went back to the way Juliet had rejected him on the patio of the aquarium. His pride stung all over again. "Nah." He'd get the message to Hack, who would pass it along. Looking down at the card in his hands, he frowned at familiar-looking name.

Gary squeezed his son's shoulder, went to say something more, and said instead, "Let's sprint the rest of the way. I've got to get to class by 0900."

"Stuart, I need you to promise me something."

Stu was busy noticing that the meals listed on the menu were printed both in alphabetical order *and* by price, from least to most expensive. The statistical odds of those two criteria coexisting had his brain crunching numbers to determine the exact ratio.

"Sorry, what?" he asked, dragging his attention to his lunch companion's earnest expression.

They'd ordered drinks already, and Hilary was clutching a

sangria the same color as her hair. Sunlight shone through the umbrella overhead, bathing them both in a soft blue light.

She spared a glance for the other professionals enjoying lunch in downtown Fairfax, a block from her office. Stretching her small hand across the table, she covered Stu's and said again, "I need you promise me something."

Hilary's intensity made him instantly wary. As infatuated as he was, he'd agree to anything, which wasn't the best scenario for making reasonable choices. "Promise you what?"

Hilary worried her lower lip. "I can't tell you until you make The Unbreakable Vow."

The allusion wasn't lost on Stu. He'd read all the Harry Potter books over the course of his childhood. "How can I do that if I don't know what I'm promising?"

She frowned in disapproval and released his hand. "Then I'm not telling you anything," Hilary retorted.

Stu's curiosity niggled. He tried to guess what it was she wanted him to promise. "Can I get a hint?"

"No. If you don't make The Unbreakable Vow, you can't help me anymore with my work. You'll have to go home."

Her words both startled and dismayed him. Leave now when their relationship was just beginning? Was that what Hilary wanted? Both the drooping corners of her mouth and the pleading look in her eyes assured Stu it wasn't.

He reconsidered her request. Keeping information confidential was practically second nature to him, so why not agree? "OK, I'll promise," he said.

Relief lit her face, and Hilary reached for him again, seizing his wrist in the manner that J.K. Rowling described in *The Half-Blood Prince*. Mirroring her grip, Stu engulfed her wrist in his hand and let her turquoise gaze ensnare him.

"Do you, Stuart Rudolph, solemnly vow not to tell Tristan Halliday that Juliet is still investigating Coenen?"

Stu could sense a trap about to spring. He'd learned from Hilary that Juliet and Tristan were no longer seeing each other. He could only assume Juliet didn't want Tristan knowing her business anymore. He could respect that, so he said, "I do."

Hilary eyed him more severely. "Do you swear never to tell Tristan that Coenen approached Juliet in secret at the aquarium in Monterey?"

And there was the snare. Tristan would probably want to know that. "How could that have happened?"

"Juliet went outside to take a call from Renata Blumenthal. Tristan stayed inside by the touch pool, so he could pet the stingrays. He never saw Coenen. Swear it," Hilary added, "or else we probably shouldn't see each other until after Coenen goes to jail."

Considering the odds against Coenen ever going to jail, Stu figured he had better quickly swear, though he needed more information first. "What did Coenen say to Juliet?"

"He threatened to unleash Kapova on Tristan if she didn't leave the past alone."

"Kapova?"

"She was inside the building, standing near Tristan holding a stiletto in her hand. Coenen told Juliet his girlfriend used to be KGB. He said Kapova would either shoot Tristan or slit his throat if Juliet continued to investigate him."

Uneasiness settled in Stu's intestines. He was confident Tristan could hold his own against two aging Cold War operatives. Still, his teammate ought to be made aware of a threat against his life. "Is Juliet going to tell him?"

"Of course not. If Tristan knows Coenen threatened Juliet, he's not going to stay away, regardless of any risk to himself. He could end up getting hurt, or worse, killed, and she doesn't want that. That's why you can't say anything."

Stu stared at Hilary, suddenly torn.

Her grip tightened. "Do you ever want to have sex with me or not?" The question compelled a woman at the next table to turn and stare at them. Hilary promptly blushed.

Oh, Stu wanted sex. Being denied at this point would probably result in his slow death from sexual frustration. "I won't tell Tristan," he promised, hoping he never regretted those words.

Hilary beamed at him. "Thank you." Releasing his hand,

she sat back just as a college-aged waiter ducked under their umbrella to take their orders.

"What can I get you?"

Stu glanced at the menu. Distracted by his buzzing phone, he selected the first entrée on the list before checking to see who was calling. Tristan, of course. Glancing up at Hilary's watchful gaze, he decided he'd better let Tristan leave a voicemail.

"Was that Tristan?" Hilary asked as soon as the waiter departed with their orders.

He wasn't going to lie. "Yes," he admitted. Stu's phone chimed, letting him know Tristan had left a voicemail.

Hilary glanced down at it then back at him. "Aren't you going to listen to that?"

At her urging, he accessed the message, keeping his expression as blank as possible while absorbing its lengthy content.

"What did he say?" she prompted when Stu pulled the phone from his ear.

"That there's a task force keeping watch on Renata Blumenthal already. The lead wants Juliet to call and talk to him. Tristan's going to text me the contact information."

Hilary's eyes widened behind her lenses. "I knew it!" she exclaimed. "Blumenthal is one of Goebel's minions."

His phone chirped as the text message arrived.

"Let me see that?" Hilary requested, pulling out her phone to copy the name and number of the task force lead. "Juliet's going to freak when she hears this," she asserted. "Did Tristan say anything else?"

"Not really." Stu kept the second part of Tristan's message to himself. The Golden Boy would be flying into Dulles Thursday evening. Tristan was hoping Stu could pick him up at the airport, then hang out with him and Jeremiah at a popular Irish pub in Fairfax.

Stu was planning on it.

Having a band of brothers who enjoyed spending time

together was the best part of being a SEAL. Why shouldn't he spend a night out with the boys while he was on leave?

But what if Hilary didn't see it that way? What if she automatically assumed Stu was breaking his promise by hanging out with Tristan? At the risk that she would end up denying him his boys' night out, Stu kept the invitation to himself.

Uneasiness caused him to break into a light sweat. Damn it. He was already regretting that vow.

18

"Were you a SEAL?" Juliet asked the man behind the massive mahogany desk. The trident, prominently displayed in the military medals case behind him, had caught her eye as she lowered herself into one of the armchairs facing his massive desk.

Isaac Calhoun, the Taskforce lead, had "invited" her to the National Counterterrorism Center to discuss what she knew about Hans Coenen. His ruggedly handsome features betrayed a hint of respect for her awareness. "Yes," he said, but his tone did not invite more personal questions.

He looked like a SEAL, ultra-alert and in terrific shape. But whereas a certain other SEAL would have put Juliet at ease by smiling and saying something humorous, Isaac Calhoun struck her as super serious. He was likely also a devoted family man, given the number of framed pictures of a pretty woman and a toddler, and his apparent disinterest in Juliet's looks.

"Let's talk about Renata first," he began, opening a thick file on his desk and flipping through it. The day before, when she'd called Calhoun at Hilary's urging, he'd made it clear Renata Blumenthal was his primary target. However, since her boyfriend Goyle/Goebel may have directed both Renata and Hans Coenen's actions, Calhoun agreed to look into Juliet's allegations that Coenen had murdered her parents.

He handed her several pages from the file. She set them on her lap, tucked the facility badge that dangled from a lanyard around her neck out of the way, and skimmed the contents. They appeared to be observation notes, dating back to 2015.

"We've been monitoring Blumenthal's activities for a couple of years. Nine months ago, we placed an agent on the inside to attend her community meetings. He keeps us informed of developments."

Juliet nodded. "She was holding a meeting the day we toured the murals."

"There's one every second Sunday," he confirmed. "Attendance at Renata's gatherings has tripled in the time our agent's been in place. At every meeting, she extolls the virtues of Marxism and encourages social protest—nothing illegal about that. Our Constitution guarantees freedom of speech. What's alarming, however, is the number of juvenile delinquents participating in the program. They get a kick out of painting their struggles with society on the walls of buildings. Apparently, 'beautification' of the city qualifies as community service."

Calhoun's derision was so understated, Juliet wondered if she'd imagined it. "The courts have funneled dozens of young offenders her way, but they don't leave once they've completed their service hours. They flock to her center every second Sunday. Now and then, they rally for a protest. It all looks very commendable on the surface. With more than three hundred disciples, though, she's starting to make the local law enforcement nervous."

A thought shifted in Juliet's mind at the mention of juvenile delinquents. "Wait. Before his retirement from the SFPD, Hans Coenen won an award for getting gang members off the streets. I wonder if some of them wound up in Renata's program?"

Calhoun tipped his head the same way Tristan did when pondering a new piece of information. "We'll talk about Coenen next," he promised, trading the pages he'd given her for another set. "Have a look at Blumenthal's bio."

Calhoun gave her a moment to skim the pages before

commenting, "Nothing about her upbringing explains her political extremism. Parents emigrated from West Germany right after World War II. They settled in western Illinois, and she grew up on a farm, attending public school and a Lutheran church."

Juliet tried to picture Renata's childhood as he'd described it. "You mean she was born in the United States?"

"Affirmative. July 15, 1958."

Juliet mulled that over. "Why would she speak with a German accent if she's a native English speaker?"

Calhoun's green eyes narrowed at her question. "She has an accent? Our agent never mentioned it."

"Probably because it's faint. If you don't know what you're listening for, you may not hear it, but I can. My mother spoke the same way."

He sat back, crossed his arms, and gestured for her to finish reading.

Juliet flipped the page to find a group photograph on the last page. "Do you have any more pictures? I'd like to see Renata as a child."

"That's the only one, taken from a yearbook published by the school she attended. Apparently, her parents' home burned down, destroying all the photographs from her childhood."

"How convenient," Juliet murmured, holding the page closer to her eyes to focus on the girl's face circled in red marker. A boy at the front of the group held a sign identifying the children as Mrs. Markle's fifth-grade class. Renata would have been about ten. Seeking some similarity between the unremarkable girl in the photo and the striking proprietor of The People's Eyes, Juliet saw that while the girl pictured was fair-haired, her eyes were far darker than the pale orbs that had regarded Juliet so keenly the weekend before.

With rising excitement, Juliet looked up at the lead's watchful expression. She brandished the photo. "If this child is Renata Blumenthal, the woman calling herself by that name has stolen her identity," she asserted.

Her words didn't seem to surprise Calhoun. "We've suspected as much," he admitted. "Question is, who was she before she became Renata?"

The gears had been turning in Juliet's head since the mention of the juvenile delinquents in Renata's program. "Well, I have an idea," she said, drawing the envelope she'd brought with her out of her purse and handing it to Calhoun.

He opened it and pulled out the contents. "This is the letter you told me about," he said, referring to their phone call. "And your parents' marriage certificate." Calhoun looked up at Juliet. "I have to tell you, I looked into your story, and it checks out."

He'd spoken with the U.S. Marshal's Service, then, about Anya Ausfeld and Gerard Brause, just as he'd said he would.

"Good." At least he would know Juliet had been honest and upfront with him. Watching Calhoun peruse the letter, she directed his attention to the pertinent information. "In the second paragraph, my mother describes how the older brother of a college friend recruited her. Mom's friend became a spy, as well. The older brother mentored and protected the two young women. He took them through the Wall at least once to visit Dieter Goebel.

"Mom wrote that her school friend fancied herself in love with the spymaster. Two years later, when Anya confessed her espionage to my father and the intelligence authorities, she warned her colleagues so they could flee to the East and avoid imprisonment. In spite of her forewarning, I doubt they viewed her defection as anything but the deepest betrayal. They had every reason to want to kill her."

Calhoun looked up from the letter. "And you think Coenen was the older brother of your mother's friend?" he guessed.

Juliet had considered that possibility for some time. However, the realization that Renata Blumenthal was likely Bergit Coenen had only just occurred to her. "Yes, except the last name of Coenen is probably an alias. He and his sister, Bergit, came to the United States with South African papers.

My mother never named them in her letter, although she would have identified them to U.S. intelligence officers when they debriefed her. I have a thought," Juliet added, scooting to the edge of her seat to articulate her latest suspicions. "I think Bergit may have taken on a second alias."

Calhoun's green-as-grass eyes narrowed with interest as he waited for her to proceed.

"If Hans and Bergit are the brother and sister pair she described, immigration shows them coming to the States just before the Wall fell. Goebel was already in prison. Suppose, at his behest, they settled in Arlington, where my father's parents lived, so they could hunt my mother down and take revenge for her betrayal. Being in love with Dieter Goebel, naturally, Bergit would have wanted to follow his orders.

"While in Arlington," Juliet continued, "Coenen found a job with the police. His sister, Bergit, on the other hand, got into trouble and was accused of murder. Rather than face the justice system, she disappeared, possibly fleeing to Chile, where she recently bought one of Goebel's paintings at auction. Did you know he was a painter?"

"No," the Taskforce lead admitted.

"That was something he, my mother, and Bergit all had in common. They were all artists. Anyway, I assumed Bergit Coenen was in Chile all this time. Now I realize she wasn't." A tingle of excitement skittered up Juliet's arms to crawl across her scalp.

"When Goebel gained asylum and moved to San Francisco, she would have wanted to join him there, assuming she still loved him. By adopting the identity of a girl with scarcely any record of her childhood, Bergit arrived in San Francisco as Renata Blumenthal. Together she and Goebel could spread their Marxist ideals, with him keeping a low profile and her in the leading role. Are you with me so far?"

Calhoun's expression hadn't changed one iota. "I'm with you," he agreed, causing Juliet's burgeoning excitement to expand. "Especially since the real Renata may have perished in the fire that destroyed her home."

Juliet's excitement mushroomed. Proving Hans and Bergit Coenen murdered her parents seemed suddenly attainable.

"She called me," Juliet continued, relaying the gist of her conversation with Renata two days earlier while at the aquarium in Monterey. "She was expecting me to show up at the center this morning so she could show me the rest of Peter Goyle's murals. I guess I missed our appointment."

"She has your number?" A crease appeared between Calhoun's silver eyebrows.

Juliet's thoughts went briefly to how ingeniously Renata had acquired it in the first place. The woman must have recognized her as Anya's daughter and quickly sought a way to follow her movements. Specialized equipment for tracking the global positioning of a cell phone was easy enough to purchase. As a P.I., Juliet owned such equipment herself.

"Well, not anymore," she assured him. "Hans Coenen threw my phone onto the rocks at the aquarium. I haven't replaced it yet."

Calhoun sat forward, betraying an interest in her statement. "The aquarium? I thought you met with him at Rockaway Beach. McNulty forwarded your digital recording."

"I did. But Coenen followed me to Monterey. Renata must have given my number to him, which enabled him to find me —on more than one occasion," she added, kicking herself for not realizing it earlier. "He showed up seconds after my call with Renata." Recalling Coenen's seeming friendliness even as he'd sought to blackmail her, Juliet shivered involuntarily. "He told me if I didn't stop persecuting him—those were his words —he would unleash his girlfriend on Tristan."

"Tristan Halliday, right?" Calhoun interrupted.

The weight of regret pressed upon Juliet's breastbone. She'd been doing her best not to think about Tristan, let alone draw him into her story. "Yes, he's a SEAL, actually, a friend of my sister's husband." Her gaze darted to the trident in Calhoun's display case.

"I think I know him." The lead sat back in his chair and reflected.

Seriously? This man knew Tristan? Dismay vied with illogical relief.

"I was his platoon leader, my last tour in Afghanistan. I think it was his first. Anyway, back to Coenen's warning. Who is the girlfriend he mentioned, and was she there, too?" He sat forward again.

"Yes, she was, standing next to Tristan and clutching a stiletto while he watched the stingrays get fed," she added shortly. "And then, of course, he had to pet them. Her name is Irena Kapova—you know, the famous ballet dancer who defected from the Soviet Union in the mid-eighties?"

Calhoun had covered his mouth with a hand as though to stop himself from commenting on Tristan's deplorable lack of awareness.

"Coenen told me Irena used to be KGB."

The lead's silver eyebrows shot to his hairline, and he dropped his hand. "KGB?" He looked like he might laugh.

"I don't know if he was just trying to scare me, but it makes sense that Renata and Coenen would have ties to a Russian agent, right? Coenen lives with her in the Russian Hill neighborhood. Maybe they've known each other since the Cold War."

"Did she act like she would knife Tristan right there in public?"

Recalling the smirk on Irena's face, Juliet relived the fear she'd felt at that moment. "Yes. She momentarily showed it to me. Coenen said Irena would take great pleasure in slitting his throat or just shooting him." Juliet barely masked her shudder.

"What does Tristan say about that?"

"He doesn't know," she admitted after a slight pause.

"Why not?"

She had asked herself that question at least a hundred times in the last two days. "I don't want him getting hurt, that's all. As long as Tristan's not around me, he's safe," Juliet insisted.

Her attention was drawn to Calhoun's long fingers as he drummed them on the edge of his desk. "If someone threatened to slit my throat, I'd sure as hell like to know about it," he stated.

She swallowed down her rising guilt and didn't answer.

Picking up a pen, Calhoun scribbled a note on a yellow notepad before looking up at her. "You've been very helpful, Ms. Rhodes." He laid down his pen and pushed his chair back.

Realizing the interview was over, she handed Renata's bio back to Calhoun, shouldered her purse strap, and stood up. "Thank you for working on this."

"I'll be in touch," he said, following suit and shaking her hand. "In the meantime, if there's anything you remember later, please don't hesitate to call." His firm grip conveyed a depth of concern and a sincere willingness to help. "Like I said, our primary suspect is Renata Blumenthal, but we'll look into your allegations and see what we can piece together."

"Thank you." With a parting smile, Juliet retreated through the closed door to pick up the escort who'd waited patiently in the outer office. That woman walked Juliet through the process of turning in her badge and returning to her car in the visitor's parking area.

As Juliet drove away from the facility, she had to admit it was nice to have the help of an inter-agency task force. Honestly, though, Hack and Hilary would probably find proof of Renata's connection to Hans Coenen before anyone else did.

Standing behind her office chair, Hilary watched in admiration as Stu filled all four of her monitors with photos and data pertaining to Irena Kapova. Not wanting to distract him, she kept her mouth closed and her eyes open. The tan length of his sturdy neck distracted her. Lured toward the clean scent emanating from his skin, she inclined her head and drew a deep breath. Stu tensed, then tipped his head to give her better access.

They were supposed to be seeking evidence of Renata

Blumenthal's and Hans Coenen's familial relationship. Upon her return from the NCTC an hour earlier, Juliet had delegated them that task and promptly departed for the gym to work out.

Stu had balked. Pointing out that nothing short of an SNP-based autosomal DNA test could prove consanguinity, he'd suggested they test Coenen's assertion that Irena Kapova had worked for the KGB. He had promptly set about reconstructing Kapova's history.

Hilary found the work tedious. She would much rather brush her lips over the jugular vein pulsing at the side of Stu's neck. Yielding to temptation, she flicked her tongue over the sensitive spot, pleased to find his skin both sweet and salty. At his sharp inhalation, she raked her teeth along the path she'd licked and felt him shiver. Her confidence soared. Tonight would be the night, Hilary decided. She had played the demure maiden long enough. Stu had overcome his inherent shyness. Their consummation of passion was inevitable.

Taking advantage of Juliet's absence from the office, she ran her fingers through his thick hair and sighed. His dark gaze rose from the monitors to gauge her intent.

"Sorry. Am I distracting you?"

His gaze dropped from Hilary's eyes to her mouth, driving a shaft of desire through her. The air seemed to thicken as he realized, perhaps, that her restraint had reached a snapping point. Juliet would be at the gym for at least another hour. They could have sex right there.

"I don't think Kapova was ever KGB." Stu clung to his purpose with commendable tenacity. "She wouldn't have had the time. All she ever did, from the age of four on, was dance."

Nothing could deter Hilary from her sensual exploration. Moving her hand to the front of Stu's shirt, she released the top button, then the next one. "Maybe the Irena who defected is an imposter."

"Doubtful." Stu's voice deepened. "She looks the same at sixty as she did at age ten."

Sliding a hand under his shirt, Hilary zeroed in on a stiff

male nipple and circled it intently. "Maybe the real Irena had an evil twin who took her place."

Stu's concentration visibly disintegrated. Without warning, he hooked an arm around Hilary's waist and hauled her across his lap. She gave a squeal of approval. The chair rocked beneath their combined weight but didn't fall over.

His impulsive response aroused her beyond bearing. "Stu," she exclaimed, planting fevered kisses along the hard line of his jaw, "I really can't wait much longer. Please take me!"

His grip tightened. If the hard column riding the curve of Hilary's thigh was any indication, Stu couldn't wait much longer either. Capturing her lips with his, he bestowed a kiss so blistering her toes curled, and her panties became wet.

"Lay me down," she whispered. "Lay me on the carpet and take me." Peeking through her lashes to measure Stu's response, Hilary caught him sneaking a peek at his watch.

He lifted his head with a look of raw regret. "I have to go," he said.

"What?" Surely she had misheard.

"I told Tristan I'd pick him up at the airport. His flight lands in thirty minutes."

Hilary froze. Stu hadn't mentioned Tristan's name since making the Unbreakable Vow. "You waited until now to tell me this?" Her voice rose in proportion to her plummeting disappointment.

"I'm sorry." But Stu's tone made it clear he was sticking to his plans.

Suddenly indignant, she struggled free, gained her footing, and planted herself before him, arms akimbo.

"Have you forgotten what you promised?"

He shook his head, avoiding her gaze. "Nope."

"What are you not supposed to tell Tristan?" Hilary demanded.

"That Coenen threatened Juliet."

"Right." A portion of her indignation waned.

"I won't tell him," Stu pledged.

Mollified by his calm assurance, Hilary reconsidered the evening's potential. "So you're just picking him up at the airport and taking him somewhere, and that's it?"

Stu hesitated. "Not exactly. First, we're meeting Jeremiah for drinks. When we leave, I'll drive Tristan to Juliet's to get his motorcycle. He left it in her parking garage."

Hilary pressed a fist to her aching stomach. "You're going out with the guys," she stated.

When all Stu did was sit there, she whirled away from his gaze to conceal her devastation. The wishing stone on Juliet's file cabinet resembled a couple locked in a passionate embrace.

Behind her, the office chair squeaked as Stu rolled out of it. Coming up behind her, Stu tentatively encircled Hilary with his arms. Tears sprang to her eyes.

"I have to go," he said.

Part of her wanted to yell *Don't bother coming back*, but Hilary wasn't ready to end their affair before it even began. "Remember your promise," she begged him.

Glancing at the tears that rimmed her lashes, Stu dropped a kiss on her lips and released her. On his way to the door, she saw him check that his phone was in his belt clip and his keys were in his pocket.

"How am I supposed to get home?" she asked as he reached the door.

Given the look on his face, he hadn't considered her need for transportation.

"Forget it. Juliet can give me a ride. Just go, or you'll be late." Hilary waved him away so she could cry alone.

With a guilty nod, Stu turned and let himself out.

Hilary hugged herself as the door closed behind him. She'd never been the type to demand that a boyfriend abandon his friends and devote himself exclusively to her. Besides military men were especially close-knit, sharing a bond that rivaled matrimony for its intimacy. She would not begrudge Stu that.

But if he told Tristan what he'd sworn to keep secret, she would know she'd never be his first priority. And that would break her heart.

"Please keep your promise," Hilary whispered.

Juliet tapped out the old combination at her door only to recall that she had changed it the morning after her return from California. Regret pierced her. So much for the hope that Tristan was sitting in her apartment with his feet propped up on her coffee table, waiting to demand that she take him back.

At this point, sleep deprived and lonely beyond words, Juliet probably *would* take him back. Luckily, since he didn't know the new code, there would be nothing to test her resolve.

Tapping out the new number sequence, she shoved her door open. Silence filled the dark rooms beyond the foyer. Her blinds had remained closed all day because she hadn't had the desire or the energy to open them before heading to the office.

Rolling her eyes at her pathetic moping, Juliet flicked on the lights as she shut and locked the door behind her. She hadn't realized when she'd walked away from Tristan how much she'd come to rely on his sunny disposition to brighten her day.

Work was her only refuge from loneliness. In fact, she might have stayed at the office all night if Hilary hadn't informed Juliet—rather huffily—that Stu had gone to fetch Tristan from the airport, so she needed a ride home. Hearing that Tristan was in the vicinity and planned to swing by her building to pick up his bike had made Juliet's heart beat erratically all evening.

What if Tristan stopped by to see her? Then, again, why would he? He had made it clear at the aquarium that he would never come crawling to her. This was what she had wanted, to be left alone.

Stepping out of her pumps, she plodded barefoot to the kitchen, dumped her purse on the counter, and opened the refrigerator. Why was she now hoping Tristan had changed his mind?

"I'm not," Juliet insisted while she glared at the paltry

contents of her refrigerator. Breaking off their affair was the best possible thing for Tristan. Juliet was moody, inflexible, and secretly insecure. Tristan deserved better than her. If he had any sense of self-preservation, he would grab his motorcycle and ride away.

Still, she hoped he wouldn't.

Juliet grabbed a Dr. Pepper from the fridge before flopping down on the sofa in her living room, where she recalled the thrill of a stubborn Tristan tossing her upon it.

That day, he'd gotten what he wanted—to spend some of his vacation with Juliet. Look how that had turned out. She couldn't be his other half. It didn't matter that they looked good together. That they *were* good together. Juliet lacked the faith it took to believe that nothing bad would happen to him.

Her fear went beyond the thought of what an aging KGB agent could do to him. Life had a way of throwing curve balls, and Tristan's career was dangerous enough as it was. Fear that he would be snatched away from her as violently and unexpectedly as her parents dwelled deep within her psyche, and it would never go away.

"God, I have issues," she sighed, taking a swig of her soda.

A rap at her door put an end to her lamentations. Only Tristan would have knocked that hard.

With a cry of hope, Juliet set the drink can on the coffee table and raced for the door. Emotions collided in Juliet—relief, anxiety, contrition, joy.

Maybe Tristan would give her one more chance. Maybe she could get counseling for her issues. Afraid he might change his mind if she took too long, she flipped the lock without glancing through the peephole and hauled the door open. "Tris—" Her smile of welcome fled.

Standing before her, holding a large, flat, rectangular object wrapped in brown paper, was Renata Blumenthal. The woman looked far less welcoming wearing a pair of black slacks and a black knit top. Renata's pale eyes noted Juliet's response as she reached for the door jamb to counteract her shock.

"Ms. Blumenthal," Juliet exclaimed.

"You missed our appointment this morning," the woman stated with a tight smile. "So I came to you, instead." Producing a silenced 22-caliber pistol from behind the package, Renata aimed it at Juliet's pounding heart. "The least you can do is invite me in, dear."

19

"So, Hack, what have you and Hilary been up to?"

Tristan's question, accompanied by a lascivious grin, intensified Stu's guilt, prompting him to snatch his beer off their pub table—only to recall he was the designated driver. His one beer needed to last all evening.

Tristan's grin intensified as he waited for an answer. Stu glanced at Jeremiah, who seemed more interested in Stu's reticence.

"Well, we've been keeping busy, doing research." Stu winced since his answer suggested that they were still after Coenen, which he wasn't supposed to admit. Instead of catching Stu's gaffe, Tristan clapped him on the shoulder.

"Atta boy," he praised the team's computer guru in a loud voice. "I knew you'd hit it off with her. Glad you're keeping busy."

Stu's ears heated at the implication that he and Hilary were busy in bed. Luckily, the dim lighting of the crowded Irish pub concealed his embarrassment, except to Jeremiah who saw what everyone else missed.

Tristan smothered a burp. "Did she talk to the task force guy yet? Isaac Calhoun—I knew I recognized the name." Tristan included Jeremiah in the conversation. "'Cept we called him Ike. Dude was my squad leader the first time I played in the Sandbox. Toughest SOB I've ever met." He turned back to Stu. "Has Juliet called him yet?"

Considering Tristan had warned them only moments earlier *not* to mention Juliet's name in his presence, the question caught Stu off-guard.

"Yeah." Stu pretended fascination with the bubbles in his beer. He nodded. "She met with him at the NCTC today."

"And?"

Stu swallowed hard. Withholding information from a teammate went against every tenet drilled into him by the instructors at BUDs. "They decided that Renata Blumenthal is really Bergit Coenen, Hans's sister."

"What?" Tristan nearly elbowed his mug right off their small table as he leaned closer to Stu. "Holy shit, are you kidding me?"

Stu shook his head. Tristan rarely cursed except when he was drunk, and Stu had counted five swear words already. Keeping the rest of what he knew to himself, he watched Tristan fold his arms across his chest and brood over the latest development. The Golden Boy's broad shoulders slumped.

"I don't know what that woman said to her," Tristan groused. "One minute everything was fine between us. Juliet gets a phone call from Renata and, next thing I know, she's telling me she's folding her investigation and flying back to Virginia without me."

Watching the animation fade from Tristan's face, Stu realized his buddy's boisterousness up to that point had been a façade, the same way Juliet's surliness concealed her hurting heart.

Blinking furiously, Tristan picked up his mug and drained the contents.

Stu and Jeremiah shared an unspoken thought over the tabletop. They would do whatever was required to get their friend through the evening. Stu theorized that would first entail talking Tristan off a ledge. Once they managed to hustle their rip-roaringly drunk friend out of this establishment, they would have to find him somewhere safe to sleep. It would probably be closer to dawn than to midnight by the time he set foot in Hilary's apartment. Damn it.

An alternate plan occurred to Stu. Regret skewered his heart because he had given Hilary his word not to say anything. A man's word was his bond. Once broken, that bond could never be mended.

In effect, she had given him an ultimatum: Choose him or choose his teammate. In Stu's mind it was one thing or the other. There were no shades of gray, no loopholes, no shortcuts.

He and Tristan, Jeremiah and all of his other brothers in Echo Platoon were fully committed to each other's well-being. Tristan was miserable. Knowing he could alleviate Tristan's pain by sharing a few vital pieces of information obviated Stu's quandary. Loyalty dissolved the guilt clogging his throat. Ignoring his disappointment over the loss of a relationship with Hilary, Stu accepted what he had to do—break a promise.

"Tristan," he started quietly.

His friend's empty mug struck the table top as he lowered it and searched Stu's face through bleary eyes. "What?"

"I know what happened at the aquarium."

"What d'you mean?" Tristan's words ran together.

"You weren't the only ones there. Hans Coenen was there, along with Irena Kapova. He spoke to Juliet while you weren't looking. He threatened her."

The lenses of inebriation seemed to drop from Tristan's eyes. He looked suddenly, starkly, sober. "What the fuck?"

"Kapova was standing right behind you holding a stiletto. Coenen told Juliet his girlfriend would slit your throat, or hunt you down and shoot you, if she didn't leave the past alone."

Tristan's mouth fell open. His eyes were on Stu, but he was visibly filling in memories with the details he'd just received. "Why the hell didn't she tell me that?" His irate question drew looks from the other tables.

Jeremiah put a restraining hand on Tristan's shoulder. "It's obvious, bro. She was trying to protect you."

"From a ballet dancer?" Tristan's incredulous query carried over the general din.

Stu leaned toward him and stated quietly, "According to Coenen, Kapova used to be KGB."

Tristan rolled his eyes. "Give me a break. I can't believe Juliet withheld this from me. What the fuck?" he repeated, visibly irate.

"They were probably still watching her," Jeremiah suggested.

Tristan didn't hear him. "She made up some bullshit excuse about how Goebel was dead so there was no point of holding his minions accountable. And then she kicked me to the curb."

Jeremiah sat forward to reason with him. "Listen, Tristan. You need to look at this from Juliet's perspective. Coenen showed up where he was least expected. He threatened your life if Juliet didn't back off. What would you have done, if your roles were reversed?"

Tristan's eyebrows met over his nose as he pondered the question. Several beats of silence followed. "I would have protected Juliet," he admitted. His frown abruptly cleared.

"Right. And if protecting Juliet translated into staying away from her, you'd have pushed her away for her own good." Jeremiah sat back, clasped his hands on the tabletop, and closed his eyes. Stu and Tristan, who were used to him slipping into semi-meditative states at random times, ignored him.

"Jesus." Tristan clapped a hand to his forehead. "How could I have missed Coenen? How did I not see him? And Kapova standing right next to me, without me noticing?"

"Stingrays," Stu explained with a magnanimous shrug.

A sudden thought had Tristan cursing under his breath. "Coenen knows Juliet's address," he told his teammates.

Jeremiah lurched in his seat, his eyes flying open. "We need to check on Juliet," he said, reaching for his cell phone. "I'll have Emma call her."

Tristan shot him a wary look. "Why?" he demanded, and then his eyes widened. "Wait, was that an intuitive hit?"

Jeremiah's gift for reading the intentions of foes and friends alike was an enhanced form of intuition. Stu didn't begin to understand it, but Jeremiah's insight had saved Echo Platoon from loss of life on multiple occasions. And ever since their cruise-ship vacation had gone awry the year before, Tristan put great stock in Jeremiah's premonitions and had told the whole Team they should be do the same.

"We should check on her," Jeremiah answered as he thumbed a message to his wife.

"Hell with that." Tristan reached for his wallet. "We'll check on her in person."

Stu glanced regretfully at his full mug of beer.

"That works." Jeremiah put his phone away, lending urgency to Tristan's decision.

As Tristan tossed two twenties on the table, Stu considered what he'd just forfeited by choosing his teammate over Hilary. Considering her generous disposition, she might forgive him for breaking his promise, but he would refuse her forgiveness. He had chosen Tristan over her, and knowing himself, he would always choose the Team over any woman. Certainly Hilary deserved better than that.

He had broken the Unbreakable Vow, and he would reap the consequences.

"Sit." Renata made it sound like an invitation—as if it were her house. She waved her deadly Glock to signify that Juliet should park herself on the sofa.

Juliet didn't want to sit. She wanted to dive for her purse and retrieve her Ruger to even the odds a bit. Unfortunately, her purse was perched on the breakfast bar in her kitchen—about three steps too far to keep from taking a bullet in the back. The fact that Renata carried a silenced pistol, albeit a small one, easy to conceal, could mean only one thing—she was planning to use it and didn't want anyone hearing the shot.

Panic threatened Juliet's control. Well, of course Renata was going to use her gun. The woman hadn't chased Juliet all the way from the West Coast to converse about her lover's art.

"Would you like a drink?" Juliet offered, praying for an excuse to head to the kitchen.

"Thank you, no. Sit," the woman repeated.

Renata's aim, centered over Juliet's heart, motivated her to drop swiftly onto the sofa.

"For you, dear." Renata's smile was a parody of graciousness as she offered Juliet the wrapped package. "I thought you might like to see one of Peter's best paintings. You'll recognize the subject, I'm sure. Unwrap it," she ordered coldly.

Masking tape held the brown paper securely in place. Juliet proceeded to remove it while weighing her odds of tackling Renata without getting shot. The woman had planted herself on the other side of the coffee table, just beyond grabbing distance. The safety on her 22-caliber was already off, her index finger curled in readiness around the trigger. One false move on Juliet's part and Renata—Bergit—would finish her. There was no more doubt that the two women were one and the same.

Conscious of the tremor in her fingers, Juliet drew a measured breath. Since Bergit wished to witness her reaction to the artwork, Juliet would take her time while seeking a way out of this predicament.

"Did your brother send you here?" she asked by way of distraction.

"My brother?" The question clearly startled Bergit, though she was swift to summon a mocking smile. "Oh, did you just figure that out? I wondered when you would make the connection. Actually, Hans ordered me to stay away from you. He wants to let bygones be bygones." Bergit waved a hand in the air to signify how insignificant his wishes were. "Hans had a thing for Anya—always did," she added, on a note of disgust. "Can't you do that any faster?"

Juliet pulled the tape from the wrapping to keep Bergit from snapping at her again, yet still slowly enough to buy more time. In light of the woman's statement, it occurred to Juliet that Coenen might have been sincere in his warning.

What if he hadn't been trying to scare Juliet so much as trying to protect her from his sister? Was that why he had thrown her cell phone off the patio—so Bergit would have difficulty finding her again?

"Your brother killed my parents," Juliet protested. "I saw him after the accident. He looked into the car to make sure they were dead."

"You think that accident was his doing?" Bergit crowed with laughter. "Please." Her laughter abated suddenly. "I'm the one who punished Anya for her betrayal. Hans begged to look into the car to make sure Anya wasn't suffering. Such a weak stomach he has." Her lips curled with disdain. "Peter used him strictly to recruit young people. My brother has a gift for that," she relented. "Anya was no impressionable idealist, and yet Hans persuaded her to advance Dieter's vision, at least for a while."

Juliet took note of the woman's reversion to Dieter Goebel's original name. "Is that what you've been doing with the mural center—advancing Dieter's vision?"

"Of course. America's youth despise the corruption born out of capitalism. They will rise up in protest and herald a new era."

"Did Hans recruit them the way he did my mother?" Juliet already knew the answer. In hindsight, Hans seemed almost noble compared to his sister, who was holding Juliet at gunpoint, forcing her to play this awful game.

"Some he recruited. Others he sent my way through the penal system."

The brown paper slipped abruptly to the floor exposing a portrait of a pretty blonde. Vaguely impressionistic and not the best likeness, there was still no mistaking the subject for anyone but Juliet's mother. Herein lay the motivation for Bergit's revenge, Juliet guessed.

"Dieter painted that one year before his death." Bergit's voice shook with disdain and jealousy so palpable that Juliet lifted wary eyes at her.

"Do you know what it felt like, knowing he was still

obsessed with her after all these years?" Bergit's voice roughened with loathing. "I was loyal to him from the day we met. Anya *betrayed* him. I found a way to empower Dieter, to lift him out of the ashes of the Cold War. What did Anya do? She married herself to the West. *I* loved that man for decades and tended him in sickness. Did he paint a portrait of *me* at the end of his life?"

Her face grew taut with rage. "No." A muscle ticked in her still-smooth check. "He painted Anya, the bitch who brought about his downfall. Why? Because he loved her still, that's why—in spite of everything. He loved *her* best, not me!"

Bergit's breath came in harsh pants that mirrored the wild beat of Juliet's pounding heart.

"At least she warned you first." Sensing the end was near, Juliet defended her mother.

Bergit's eyes flashed with outrage. "There is nothing you can say that will redeem your mother," she spat, raising the snout of the silenced gun to aim it at Juliet's head. "You act just like her."

"Is love no excuse?" Juliet demanded, desperate to keep the woman talking. "Love will make you do anything. My mother did what she did for my father. Look at you. You built your life around the man you loved." Her own thoughts went to Tristan, who—if Bergit had her way—would never know that Juliet wanted to build her life around him if she could only find the courage.

"No more talking." Bergit reached for the portrait, wrenched it from Juliet's grasp, and propped it on the recliner opposite the sofa.

With her heart racing, Juliet waited to see what the woman would do next. Bergit backed several steps from the portrait, raised her pistol, and fired it at Anya's likeness.

Juliet screamed involuntarily. "No!"

The gaping hole between the painted image of her mother's eyes suggested the bullet would have drilled straight through Anya's brain to blow out the other side had she been a living presence.

Bergit rounded on Juliet, who felt the blood drain from her cheeks. She was next. To her surprise, Bergit thumbed the safety on the Glock and laid it carefully on the arm of the recliner.

Cautious hope beat back Juliet's shock. What was this? The answer came swiftly as, without warning, Bergit hurdled the coffee table, sending Juliet's can of soda flying, as she attacked with her bare hands.

Stunned by the woman's brute strength, Juliet found herself pinned against the back of the couch, Bergit's hands encircling her neck. The strength in the woman's fingers brought to mind the ferocity of her handshake the day they'd first met. Juliet counterattacked, gouging her opponent's eyes. Within seconds, she thought she had secured her freedom, only to suffer a stinging blow to her cheek as she tried to slip under the woman's arm.

Springing up, Bergit seized Juliet by the hair, dragged her off the couch, and threw her face-down across the coffee table. The audible crack of a rib as it struck the table's edge preceded an explosion of pain in Juliet's right side. Ignoring it, she tried to scramble up.

Bergit grabbed her hair again. Yanking Juliet's head up and back, the crazed ex-spy seized her throat and applied a crushing grip to the delicate cartilage of her windpipe.

Juliet attempted to mule kick her attacker, but the jarring movement engendered so much agony in her ribs that the effort proved feeble. She seized the older woman's hands and tried to peel Bergit's powerful fingers from her larynx. Spots swam before her eyes. How could this be happening? How could a woman twice her age have beaten her so quickly? Bergit must have spent a lifetime honing her deadly skills.

The pulse hammering in Juliet's eardrums nearly disguised the knock at her door. Bergit froze, her grip slackening just enough that Juliet could sip in a life-saving breath.

"Juliet!"

Tristan! His voice, so beautiful, so dear, confirmed her

greatest hope and imparted a burst of strength to her oxygen-deprived muscles. Grinding her teeth against the pain, Juliet wrenched from Bergit's hold and managed to gain her freedom. She lunged for the woman's Glock, scrambling over the coffee table to reach it. Before she could reach it, Bergit seized the back of Juliet's blouse, jerking her backward. Then, with unerring accuracy, Bergit kneed Juliet hard in the ribs she'd just broken.

With a cry of agony, Juliet collapsed inward. Bergit flung her down again. Finding herself splayed across the carpet, Juliet tried to voice a warning. "Tristan!" But his name emerged as scarcely more than a whisper.

Retrieving her weapon, Bergit swung around and flipped the safety off as she aimed it at Juliet. "Not the way I wanted to kill you," she admitted, breathing heavily from her exertions, "but it will do."

"It's not working," Tristan snarled. The code he'd used the previous week resulted in nothing but a flashing red light.

Given the sounds coming from Juliet's apartment, the visions Jeremiah claimed he was picking up on their way from the pub were probably accurate. The intuitive SEAL had envisioned a stranger in his sister-in-law in her apartment—someone whose intentions were foul. From the other side of the door, came a chilling scream. "No!"

Picturing Coenen as he throttled Juliet, Tristan slammed his hand against the door in frustration and fear. "Juliet changed the code," he raged. Of course she would have, knowing Coenen had her address.

Jeremiah ran a hand over the solid steel surface. "We can't kick this in," he said. "The hinges are reinforced."

"We can shoot them," Stu offered, brandishing the high-tech pistol he'd pulled from his trunk.

Sweat breached Tristan's pores. "Good idea. Do it."

"Wait." Jeremiah stared at the keypad. "The last

combination was Emma's birthday, 0106. Try Sammy's, May fifth—0505," he translated quickly.

Tristan punched in the numbers, and a green light flashed. "That's it!" Signaling for Stu to cover him, he lowered the lever carefully, opening the door just far enough to peer inside.

A vision of Renata Blumenthal's pale bun drew Tristan up short. He'd expected to see Coenen, not his sister, terrorizing Juliet. She clutched a small silenced pistol in one hand, aiming it at something just beyond Tristan's view. Long legs stretching out from behind the recliner confirmed the worst. Juliet!

In a split second, even without consciously thinking of his plan, Tristan threw his weight into the door, relying on Hack to cover him as he exploded into the room, first at a run, then into a diving roll.

Renata's head swung around.

On her face, he read the same expression of fanatical resolve he'd seen from terrorists about to be apprehended. Her silenced weapon discharged. *Thoop.* Juliet's legs jerked at the bullet's impact, but it was the lack of a scream that chilled his blood while making it boil at the same time.

"Nooo!" Tristan's roar of denial sounded like the cry of a wounded animal. He tackled Renata—hard. Tangled together, they flew over the coffee table and onto the sofa where he wrested the weapon from her grasp and flipped the safety. It was all he could do not to knock her teeth out with it, but concern for Juliet had him tossing the pistol to Jeremiah and leaving Renata to Hack.

"Juliet!" Tristan fell to his knees next to her. Blood smeared the left side of her head, flowing from her temple and pooling before his eyes on the area rug beneath her. "Oh, God. No. No. No. Please. Wake up. Wake up!"

Except she wouldn't. Renata had shot her at point-blank range in the head. Juliet was dying or already dead. What an idiot he'd been to ever let her out of his sight! How the hell could he ever forgive himself?

20

With his heart in his throat, Tristan watched as Jeremiah sought a pulse on Juliet's bruised neck. He had seen his platoon medic attend dozens of injured SEALs over the years, and even a handful of civilians, but seeing Juliet in need of his teammate's ministrations distressed him like nothing ever had.

"Don't let her die," Tristan demanded. How could Juliet have believed he was the one in need of protection when she'd been the one in danger the whole time—not of Coenen but, rather, his crazy sister? If Juliet died now, they would never have the chance to reconcile. His life would cease to have meaning.

"Pulse is strong. She's breathing on her own." Jeremiah moved to examine her head wound.

A drop of hope fell onto the barren soil of dread. With the blood flowing from her wound so quickly, though, it seemed impossible to believe she could survive.

"Call for help!" Tristan shouted at Hack, only to realize he was already talking quietly into his phone. Renata lay face down on the floor at the cyber warrior's feet, fingers interlaced behind her head, his foot planted on the small of her back.

Jeremiah clamped a calming hand on Tristan's shoulder.

"The bullet seems to have only grazed her temple. I can't find an entry point. Go find me a clean towel, *now*."

Inspired by Jeremiah's calm, Tristan rose unsteadily to his feet and hastened to the bathroom in search of a towel. A glance at the tub brought to mind the memory of Juliet lounging in a sea of bubbles with a look of ecstasy on her gorgeous face.

The thought of her dying made him stagger against the cabinet, suddenly faint. He chased it from his mind. She was going to live. She had to live. Anything else was simply too unbearable to accept.

Hours later, Tristan glanced up at the sound of footsteps hastening toward the trauma center's waiting area. Guilt needled him as Hilary's flaming red hair came into view. Emma must have called her sister's assistant to let her know what had happened. He'd been too consumed with torment to think of notifying anyone.

It was Jeremiah who had called Emma as the trio of SEALs followed the ambulance to Inova Fairfax Hospital.

At Hilary's approach, Emma stood to greet her. Hack also took a step toward the petite woman, stopped, and sat back down.

"How is she?"

Tristan took in Hilary's wide eyes, her pink nose. Emma had obviously told her what happened.

He didn't want to hear Emma's response at that moment. Burying his face in his hands, he resisted the childish urge to cover his ears. If only he could be more like Jeremiah, who sat with his back to the wall, eyes closed, appearing perfectly relaxed.

"She was code yellow when the ambulance got here," Emma reported quietly, "which means her vitals are strong, but there's potential for complications. The bullet grazed the side of her skull. They're doing a CT scan right now to see if there's a brain bleed."

Brain bleed. The horrifying phrase made Tristan nauseated. Even if Juliet pulled through, there was the prospect of neurological damage, impaired speech, and a host of other complications. He couldn't envision his proud PI giving up her career because she had to learn to talk again.

"Dear Lord," Hilary breathed, articulating Tristan's dismay.

"She's going to be fine," Emma stated firmly.

"Right. Of course."

With an audible sniffle, Hilary lowered herself into the chair next to Hack, who sat as straight as a flagpole, his gaze averted. Touching his arm, she spoke to him quietly.

Emma resumed her spot next to Jeremiah, and silence fell among the five of them, broken occasionally by the murmurings of the other couple in the room, the sound of someone using a keyboard in an adjacent office. Everyone's ears remained tuned to the urgent stir behind the closed doors leading to the trauma center.

Hushed voices pulled Tristan's attention back to Hilary and Hack. He couldn't hear what they were saying, but Hack's tense jaw and Hilary's baffled and teary expression made it evident that Hack was refusing to listen to her. He jackknifed suddenly out of his seat to cross to the water fountain. Hilary stared after him, looking utterly bereft.

Tristan watched them, too distraught to be curious.

When Hack doubled back, he stopped by Tristan's chair. "Listen, I'm going to take off," he said, looking as uncomfortable as a worm in hot ashes.

Tristan eyed him with surprise then darted a look at Hilary, who stared at Hack like she couldn't believe what she was seeing.

"Right now?" Tristan asked. His world had ceased to spin and one of his buddies was leaving?

"To talk to the Taskforce lead," Hack clarified. "He's still waiting for a statement."

After calling 911, Hack had put a call through to Ike

Calhoun. Within ten minutes, the inter-agency task force lead had swept into Juliet's apartment accompanied by two burly men who'd read Renata Blumenthal, aka Bergit Coenen, her rights, slapped her in cuffs, and escorted her off the premises. With the paramedics preparing to transport Juliet, Calhoun must have instructed Hack to touch base with him later.

"Yeah, yeah, go ahead." Tristan was relieved to let Hack handle the details.

"I'll call Jeremiah to get updates on Juliet." Putting an awkward hand on Tristan's shoulder, Hack gave his teammate a pat, glanced one last time in Hilary's direction, and walked away.

Tristan watched Hilary grip the arms of her chair as if wrestling the impulse to chase after Hack. When a turn in the hall took him out of her sight, she bowed her head in private misery.

It was apparent to Tristan that the two techno-geeks had hit an impasse in their relationship. Right now, however, memories of Juliet's blood-smeared head kept him from pondering what their problem might be.

The door leading into the trauma center yawned open, ejecting a doctor, still wearing a surgery mask pulled down to hang round his neck, and a trauma nurse.

Juliet's family and friends looked up expectantly. Tristan shot to his feet.

The doctor cast an eye over the room. "Where's the family of Juliet Rhodes?"

"Here." Emma jumped up and crossed to him. Tristan followed right behind her.

"I'm her sister," she said.

"And I'm her fiancé," Tristan asserted.

Emma shot him a wide-eyed look but didn't call his bluff. "How is she?" she inquired, letting Tristan's lie go.

"All things considered, not bad," the doctor said on a cautious note.

Hope hit Tristan's bloodstream like a mainlined drug.

"Her vitals are stable. She has a fractured rib and

contusions, bruising on her neck, which looks bad but will resolve without treatment. The CT scan shows an intracerebral hemorrhage in the temporal lobe. She has a skull fracture that is not displaced, meaning she does not need surgery."

"Thank God!" Emma breathed. Tristan grabbed her arm as she started to sway.

"The small bleed in the temporal lobe could lead to complications later. We won't know the extent of those until Juliet regains consciousness. Anyway, she's holding her own, and her prognosis is good."

"When can we see her?" Tristan demanded. If he could touch Juliet, talk to her, he would feel he had some semblance of control over the situation.

The doctor glanced at the others in the waiting room. "We're settling her into ICU so it may be a while. Visitation is limited to five minutes every hour until she's well enough to move into a general-care room. And only family members are allowed while Juliet's in ICU." He winked at Tristan. "I think we can accommodate future spouses, as well."

"Thank you." It was all Tristan could do not to kiss the man's feet.

"Thank you, doctor," Emma echoed as both he and the nurse turned away.

When the door had closed behind the medical team, Emma leaned into Tristan and said out of the side of her mouth. "Getting in kind of deep, aren't you?"

He was glad not to hear any recrimination in her comment. "She needs me," was his simple answer.

Emma sighed and nodded. "That's true," she said. "Now more than ever."

Juliet floated in a space that defied dimension. Colors she had never seen, let alone imagined, danced around her. She knew she wasn't in her body, but she wasn't scared. Nor was she alone. A being resembling a pulsating globe of light greeted her lovingly, introducing itself as Juliet's guide. Juliet sensed feminine energy as the being invited her to reflect on her worldly experience. They began with her childhood and happy memories of a summer vacation in Cape May, her parents walking hand-in-hand at the water's edge.

"See how much they loved each other," her guide invited.

Juliet saw it. The radiance in her mother's face, the softness in her father's eyes. Her parents had chosen each other over everything else. There might have been moments of boredom but never of regret.

Her life fast-forwarded through a series of vignettes, right past the accident, to her second year in college. Juliet was nineteen and getting an apartment of her own because Emma, desperate to recreate what their parents had shared, had married her first steady boyfriend. Juliet threw herself into her studies. She'd decided to become a private investigator. Her drive was relentless. She studied on weekends when everyone else her age was going out.

"You knew what you wanted to do," her guide commented.

All too quickly, Juliet was twenty-five. The owner of the investigative agency had retired and left his practice entirely in her capable hands. She exhausted herself working sixty hours a week, sometimes more. Dragging herself home to her sterile apartment, where there was no one to greet her, not even a pet. With no love interests outside of work, she fell asleep each night only to wake each morning and do it all over again.

"Looks like fun." Her guide's insincerity was amusing.

"It wasn't," Juliet admitted. Yet she hadn't known what else to do.

A vision of her cruise-ship vacation offered a reprieve from grinding routine. Suddenly, there was Tristan, holding out his hand to her, his smile like a ray of sunshine. Memories of the two of them racing ATVs through the jungle in Belize panned past filling Juliet with sudden exhilaration.

"That's living!" said her guide.

"Yes," she agreed. Juliet's happiness faded as she recalled

that she was not in her body anymore "Am I dead?" The thought sobered her.

"It's up to you," answered the gentle spirit. "Perhaps you'd like to see what happens if you stay here."

Juliet balked at first, however curiosity got the better of her. "Show me," she requested.

It took a moment to understand what she saw next. Her sister Emma sat unmoving in a chair on a sunny porch. Her gaze was fixed and lusterless. She didn't see her daughter, Sammy, hiding around the corner of the house rolling what looked like a cigarette.

"Is that marijuana?" Juliet reeled. "What is Sammy doing with pot?"

"Ask your sister," the guide suggested.

"Emma?" Juliet tried to rouse her sister from her self-absorption, but she wouldn't stop staring. "Why is she holding her hand like that?" Emma's long fingers lay across her abdomen.

"She lost her baby."

"What baby?"

"The one she is carrying now."

"She's pregnant?" Joy effervesced in Juliet. She imagined Jeremiah's thrilled reaction, followed by the devastation of loss. "Why'd she lose the baby?"

"The doctors said it was emotional stress," her guide explained. "When Emma loses you, it throws her into a deep depression. She ignores her husband, her own daughter. Poor Sammy loses both an aunt and a mother."

"Stop. Please," Juliet begged, relieved when the vision vanished, leaving her in the warmth of her luminous guide. "I don't want to see anymore."

"I understand. Come, there's someone here who'd like to see you."

They turned toward a beam of pink light that streaked toward them, transforming into a familiar figure as it drew nearer.

"Mama!"

Anya's spiritual energy enveloped her with unconditional love. "My girl," she soothed as Juliet wept with mingled joy and sorrow. "Hush, now. You did well, just as you have always done."

Juliet peered around, suddenly afraid. "Where's Daddy?"

"He's here," Anya assured her. "He sends his love, but only one of us can visit you. This is not your time, Juliet. You must go back."

Having seen what Emma's and Sammy's lives would be like without her, Juliet had already determined that much. "I know."

"It's going to be difficult," her mother warned. "You will find that you can't immediately do the things you did before."

"What do you mean?" Uncertainty oppressed her.

"Owning your own practice, working out the way you do, even driving a car. It will take time and dedication to get those things back."

Fear loomed over Juliet.

"Don't be afraid," Anya counseled. "You will realize, even as you work to get back what you lost, that you have everything you need to be happy."

"What things?" Juliet asked.

Her mother's smile was radiant. "You'll see. Have faith. Go now, my love. He's waiting for you."

Kissing her daughter's cheek, Anya encouraged Juliet toward a whirlpool that swirled out of clouds of color. Something far away from her pulled Juliet down through the star-spangled tunnel she had floated up earlier. All at once, she fell through a brilliant veil into a harsh place where pain stabbed her temple, and something pinched the back of her hand.

Drawing a deep breath, Juliet inhaled the scents of bleached sheets and flower petals. Slitting gritty eyes, she blinked until a hospital room came into focus. Vases of bouquets splashed color against the sterile backdrop. Turning her head to take in the bright display, her gaze landed on the man snoozing in a recliner by a window.

Soft morning light slanted through the vertical blinds and gilded his golden mane. Tristan slept in an upright position with a pillow propped against the winged side of the chair. A growth of beard obscured his jawline, suggesting he hadn't shaved in days. His usually tan face looked sallow. Even in his sleep, he appeared stressed. At the sight of him, her heart expanded to the point of pain.

Memories came rushing back. She'd been fighting for her life against the same adversary who had killed her mother a decade before. Somehow, some way, Tristan had saved her life.

Juliet tried to say his name, to tell him she'd awakened, but her lips and tongue felt glued together. She strained to lever herself onto her elbows only to realize how appallingly weak she'd become. Falling back against her pillow, she jarred her head, causing it to throb.

The squeak of her bed brought Tristan out of his chair and to her side in a flash, as the pillow tumbled to the floor behind him. He stared down at her with a disbelieving gaze.

"Oh, my God, you're awake!" He seized her hand in a gentle grasp while frantically depressing the call button with his other.

"How…long?" To her relief, she found her voice.

If he noticed her difficulty in speaking, he didn't show it. Tears of joy crested his lower lashes. "Five days," he answered hoarsely. "You were in ICU for three. Then they moved you in here." A single tear slid down the lean plane of his cheek as he bent over her.

"S-s-sorry." Juliet had to concentrate to spit the word out.

"Don't say that." Love brimmed in his eyes as he stroked her jaw and smiled tenderly. "You're back," he marveled. "You came back to me."

To Juliet's dismay, Tristan bowed his head, apparently attempting to hide his emotions from her.

Her mind slipped briefly to the spiritual plane she'd visited. Juliet longed to share her experience, but her thoughts were as clear as muddied water, and the words wouldn't come. This must be what her mother had meant when she said, *You will realize, even as you work to get back what you lost, that you have everything you need to be happy.*

Concern flooded Juliet. What if Bergit's attack left her permanently impaired?

"The bullet...?" she managed.

"Hit your hard head and bounced off." Tristan's smile became a grin. "Thank God you're so thick-headed, honey." With his unkempt beard, he resembled a savage Viking.

Juliet's heart expanded with love for him. How did she, who had rebuffed this incredible man not once but repeatedly, deserve the level of devotion he had demonstrated staying with her all this time?

And where was her family? "Emma? S-sammy?" she asked, remembering with delight the baby growing in her sister's womb.

"Emma had to teach this week, but she's coming back tomorrow." Tristan's grin faded abruptly.

She could tell he knew something about her condition, something he didn't want to share with her yet. She already knew what it was. *Owning your own practice, working out, even driving a car. It will take time and dedication to get those things back.*

"I'm...," she fought to articulate the assurance her mother had shared with her.

Tristan nodded encouragingly, but his eyebrows pulled together as if it pained him to witness her difficulties.

"I'm going to be OK," Juliet stated.

A fresh wave of tears rose in his ocean-colored eyes. He cleared his throat. "Of course you are. You've got me, don't you?"

Miraculously, despite all she'd done to sabotage their growing love for each other, Juliet did have him. That was exactly what her mother had told her—that she had everything she needed for a life filled with happiness.

Gazing up at Tristan's beloved face, it was suddenly clear what that was.

"Hey," she said, managing to reach up and caress the side of his face.

"What?"

"I f-forgot to tell you something."

"What's that, honey?" He searched her gaze, clearly having no idea what she was going to say.

Getting her lips and tongue to form the words took more time than she wanted. She could hear someone, most likely the on-duty nurse, outside the door, getting ready to push her way inside.

"I love you, too," she managed, finally replying to the words he'd spoken in their hotel room in San Francisco, the afternoon she'd nearly been struck by the double-decker bus.

Tristan's expression told Juliet she'd said everything he needed to hear.

INSIDER THREAT
THE ECHO PLATOON SERIES, BOOK FIVE

Thunk!

Chuck wheeled behind the tall sculpture before his brain even registered, *That was a bullet!* In disbelief, he peeked around his scant protection at the man bearing down on him, and his heart dropped to his feet.

No, no, no. Not this. Not now.

It was Lee, dressed in black leather and wearing sunglasses, no helmet. The grim set of the man's mouth communicated his intent. Chuck cast about for better cover, but the hotel exit required a keycard. The entrance to the parking garage was too far away.

Heart pounding, Chuck assessed his nemesis. Was it too much to hope Lee's first shot had been a warning? Not with that hand hidden under his jacket.

Chuck wasn't entirely defenseless. From the ankle wrap he wore ever since his trip to Spain, he retrieved his three throwing stars, or *shuriken*.

He hurled the first one immediately. It struck Lee's leather jacket and bounced right off as if the jacket was lined with Kevlar.

Lee smirked, then fired in retaliation. The bullet sang past Chuck's ear, a near miss.

The ocean's roar drowned Lee's footsteps as he came closer.

Chuck flung his second star, aiming lower this time. It imbedded in the man's thigh.

With a grunt of agony, Lee halted. Gritting his teeth, he tore the razor-edged weapon from his flesh. Blood gushed through the slit in his leather pants. Chuck's confidence rose. He readied himself to hurl his last *shuriken* directly at Lee's face.

"Hey!"

Chuck glanced over at a woman's cry. Lee did not. He took off, firing at Chuck as he ran past him.

The impact of the bullet knocked Chuck off his feet. He sprawled onto the sandy brick plaza, dropping his last *shuriken* as pain seared his chest. *This can't be happening.* He clapped a hand to the source of pain, felt blood well between his fingers, warm and slippery.

Lee had disappeared into the parking garage. With a groan of defeat, Chuck gave his attention to the woman skidding onto her knees next to him. Her expression was nothing short of stricken.

"Oh, my God. That man just shot you!" She produced a cellphone from her zippered pocket.

"Wh-what are you doing?" Chuck didn't want to explain to *anyone* what had just happened.

"You need an ambulance." Her voice quavered but it brooked no argument.

In the distance, Chuck heard the little engine of a moped roar to life. He craned his neck, just in time to see Lee zip out of the garage, headed for Atlantic Avenue. Damn it all. He should have heeded his foreboding.

"Yes." Katy's words recaptured his attention. "I need an ambulance, stat, at the 18th Street Plaza near the boardwalk. A man's been shot. The assailant just drove off on his moped."

The horror on Katy's face suggested Chuck might not make it. The pain corkscrewing into his chest confirmed it.

"Just let me die," he pleaded. If the police managed to catch his handler, Lee would drag Chuck down with him.

Katy ignored him, crying into the phone. "Yes, the plaza.

Hurry!" She put her phone down. "The hell I am going to let you die," she added.

Her ferocity was beautiful. Chuck stared into her moist, determined gaze and realized he had only one regret—not getting to know her better.

"You're spectacular," he whispered. Why not tell the truth? He wasn't going to survive the shooting anyway. He could feel the bullet tracking toward his heart.

"Stop talking," she pleaded, while covering his hand with both of hers.

Chuck's gaze went up the columns of the sculpture to the three sea birds frozen in flight. Their golden patina caught and held the feeble sunlight. He wished he could take a photo of them. He wished he could start over with Katy and live a normal life. But he wasn't going to make it. Lee had seen to that.

Available in Paperback and eBook from Your Favorite Bookstore or Online Retailer

ALSO BY MARLISS MELTON

The Echo Platoon Series

Danger Close

Hard Landing

Friendly Fire

Hot Target

Insider Threat

The Taskforce Series

The Protector

The Guardian

The Enforcer

ABOUT MARLISS MELTON

Marliss Melton is the author of over fifteen counterterrorist/romantic suspense stories. She relies on her experience as a former military spouse and on her many contacts in the Spec Ops and Intelligence communities to pen realistic and heartfelt stories about America's elite warriors and fearless agency heroes. Daughter of a U.S. foreign officer, Melton grew up in various countries overseas. Exposure to other languages led to teaching high-school Spanish as well as linguistics at her alma mater, the College of William and Mary. She resides in Williamsburg, Virginia, with her youngest child and two dogs, one hour from the east coast SEAL Teams who have inspired so many of her stories.

www.MARLISSMELTON.com

facebook.com/marlissmeltonbooks
twitter.com/marlissm
pinterest.com/marlissm